Diary
of a
SUPER GIRL

Book 3

The Power of Teamwork!

John Zakour & Katrina Kahler

Table of Contents

Ape in the Morning...

I leaped through the air. I spotted the huge ape bounding down the street carrying a big bag of jewels in one arm and a bunch of bananas in the other. Yeppers, this was not the way I envisioned starting my first morning of summer break. I wanted to be sleeping in a bit, at least until 10. Not chasing down a crazy gorilla that the police couldn't stop. But this was my life now that I was super. I really shouldn't complain; after all, I probably am the strongest person on Earth. Like Mom tells me, with power comes responsibility. I just wish I could be responsible, especially after a nice breakfast.

"Stop, Ape!" I shouted. Not really expecting him (or her) to listen. After all, he (or she) was an ape.

The ape stopped and turned to me. "Actually I'm a gorilla," she said in a female voice.

I landed near the ape, ah gorilla. "Okay, fine," I said. Had to admit to being surprised the big gorilla had responded.

The gorilla pointed to me. "You know, being a superhero, I think you should know these things!"

I shrugged. "Sorry, it's summer break, my mind is on vacation. Plus, it's not even 8 am!"

The gorilla looked at a watch on her arm. "So it isn't," she laughed. "Like they say, the early gorilla robs the jewelry store and the grocery store and gets away!"

I shook my head. "Ah, nobody says that...."

The gorilla grinned and hopped up and down, itching her armpits. "Well, they will now!"

Looking over this strange gorilla I noticed she had a bandage around her head that seemed to be anchored to her temples by metallic disks. I guessed that these were what made this big gorilla not your average gorilla."

I dropped my hands to my hips trying to look relaxed. By now the police had caught up with us and had positioned themselves all around. "Look, you can't win this," I said to her, as I pointed to the police.

Channel 13's Oscar Oranga was also there filming with his crew. I was still not used to seeing myself in the news.

"They can't shoot me because I'm an endangered species," the gorilla laughed. "And I'm way too strong to be stopped by tranq guns!" The gorilla laughed louder. She pounded her chest. "I feel so powerful; I don't even think bullets could stop me!" she bragged. She put the jewels and bananas down. Something told me this wasn't because she wanted to surrender. She took a Kung Fu stance. Oh, there are times when it's a pain to be right. She motioned to me with her lead paw. "Come, little human, let's see what you got...."

"Fine, two can play that game," I told her. I also took a Kung Fu stance, one arm high, one arm low, legs bent

5

ready to pounce. Yep, this is what my life had become, Kung Fu fighting with a 600-pound bionic gorilla. I took a deep breath. I exhaled. "HIYA!"

My breath shot across the road and hit the big gorilla. Her nostrils flared. "Oh my…." She whimpered. Her eyes rolled to the back of her head. Her arms locked to her side. Her legs buckled. She fell to the ground stiff as a board. My super hearing could still hear her heart beating. Lucky for the big gorilla my breath hit from six feet away.

I pointed at her. "See, this is what happens when you make me fight crime first thing in the morning before I get a chance to brush my teeth!"

I covered my mouth, turned to the police and said. "Take her away!"

Leaping up into the air, I headed home. I didn't want to accidentally knock out the entire police force with my breath. That never goes over well.

Dear Diary: Yeah, I just clobbered a big strong gorilla with a whiff of my breath. It's a feeling of empowerment and embarrassment at the same time. I suppose I should worry a bit about who is turning gorillas into super strong, intelligent thieves. But something tells me I'm going to find out soon enough!

Breakfast of Champions...

A couple of leaps and bounds brought me home. After a quick shower and a good tooth brushing, I met Mom downstairs at the breakfast table. She had the TV on and was watching my battle. The headline read: 'Super Teen drops 700-pound Super Gorilla with Super Morning Breath.' I still didn't know if I should be proud or ashamed or both.

"Busy morning," Mom said sipping on a cup of great smelling coffee.

I sat down and gulped some orange juice. "You know, same old, same old…" I smiled. "I don't think that gorilla was much more than 600 pounds," I added. "Plus, they all kind of got excited by the fact that my breath knocked the thing out, rather than the fact that it was an extremely intelligent gorilla robbing banks and stores!"

Mom pointed to my pancakes. "Eat! You know as well as anybody we can't control what the press says," She shrugged. "Some people will love you, some people will be jealous; others might be scared of you. Your job is to do your best to make the world a better place. The more you do that the more people you will have on your side. No matter how many of them you KO with morning breath."

"Or BO or foot odor or farts," I added, chomping down on a blueberry pancake.

"Yeah, just more of who you are," Mom laughed. "And don't talk with your mouth full!"

I nodded, "You're right."

I knew I wasn't supposed to have my phone at the table but I couldn't resist a quick glance at my social media. Of course, Wendi and some of her crew think I'm a menace and should never leave the house, especially in such an outfit. Do you believe they still don't like my outfit?"

"Honey, you could wear the exact same clothes that

Wendi wears and she wouldn't think they looked good on you at all."

"Yeah, you're probably right!"

"Jason texted me earlier. Of course, he's worried about an intelligent gorilla popping up. Thinks this might be the start of a trend."

Mom bit on a piece of bacon. "You should ask your dad if he knows anything about this. This is the type of stuff BM Science loves to tinker and toy with."

I took a big bite of bacon. Man, I love bacon. "Yeah, Dad said he wanted to do lunch with me today."

Mom rolled her eyes. "That may not be a coincidence."

"Plus, he wants me to meet him in his lab," I added.

Mom steadied her gaze on me. "Yeah, definitely not a coincidence."

"Should I cancel?" I asked her.

She smiled and shook her head. "No, the man is your father. Sure he has flaws, lots and lots and lots and lots…"

"I get it, Mom."

"…of flaws. But he would never do anything to intentionally harm you." Mom finished.

"He built robots to test me!" I said.

She grinned. "Yeah, but he knew you could handle those." She paused and took a sip of coffee. "Besides, your dad knows if you went missing, your grandmas and I would rip that BM Science building to the ground!"

I grinned. "Yeah, Grandma Betsy says she'd love to knock the place down with one of her farts."

Mom nodded. "She would and she could. Your dad knows that."

I took a sip of hot cocoa. Sure it was a hot day but any day is a good day for hot cocoa.

"Yep, this is what my life has become, fighting super robots and super cyborg gorillas. Plus, having a grandma who can fart down a building. Not to mention having a couple of half-vampires living in my street and a witch in town. All the while juggling the same problems other kids do: school, social media, and boy-girl crushes."

Mom got up and hugged me. "Poor baby, the strongest person on Earth."

I hugged her back and although I knew she was being a bit cynical, it was still a lot to accept. "Don't get me wrong. I love my life and most parts of being super. But ya gotta admit, vampires and witches are weird!"

Mom shook her head. "Not weird, just different. I'm sure they simply have family mutations that allow them to do things most people can't do."

I liked Mom's way of looking at it. I had to admit that

Jess, Felipe, and Tomas did seem mostly normal. I still preferred them way more to 'Miss Perfect Wendi.' That girl had been driving me crazy since third grade, always putting me down and it seemed that would never change.

Mom started gathering the dishes. "I have a busy day at the hospital today. I'm scrubbing in with one of our newer doctors, Donna Dangerfield. She's brilliant and her research is cutting edge. We've been recruiting her for years, trying to get her to come on board. She finally said yes a month ago. She's now working for us, the university and BM Science as well."

"Wait I've heard that name…before…." I said.

Mom nodded as she headed to the sink. "Yep, back in the day, she was an MMA fighter. The woman is strong and smart."

"Impressive!" I said. "Can you get her autograph?"

"Nah, that wouldn't be professional, but you can ask her when you start volunteering at the hospital. You haven't forgotten have you?"

I finished off my cocoa. "Nope, it will be fun. That and my LAX coaching are my normal kid activities for the summer. They keep me grounded!"

Dear Diary: I am so glad my mom is so grounded. She's been through what I am going through and came through it just great. Man, I wrote "through" a lot. Back on topic, I love the fact that my mom may be super but she is still so normal and sane!

Sweet Dreams?...

After Mom left for work I had a few hours of free time before I had to meet my dad for lunch. Being the first day of my break after a long year of school, I figured the best course of action would be to head upstairs and get some much-needed sleep. So, I did.

I fought back the urge to check my Instagram and Facebook accounts just to see what people were saying. I've been Super Teen long enough now to know I had some fans and some haters and some people in between. No matter what I did, some people were going to like me. Other people just weren't going to like me.

Whatever, I couldn't bend them to my will and make them like me. Well, I could maybe do that, but then I wouldn't like me. I knew that was the important thing, I needed to like me. And I did. Yeah sure, I wasn't perfect. In fact, far from it. But I was making my part of the world a better place not only by being Super Teen but also by being Lia Strong. Sure, Super Teen could do amazing things. But Super Teen was only a small part of me. Lia Strong was who I was. And Lia Strong did a lot of good. I worked with kids. I was going to start working at the hospital. I'm true to my friends. And I don't turn people I dislike into dust with my heat vision. That last one made me giggle.

I set the timer on my phone for two hours and laid down on my bed for a much deserved "nap".

My head hit the pillow. Next thing I knew I found myself standing on a pavilion in a park. The sun shined brightly above in a clear blue sky. The birds sang sweetly. I noticed I was wearing a long white dress. It felt like silk. Oh wow, this was a wedding gown, a long flowing beautiful wedding gown. I felt something pull on my hair. Christa and Marie stood behind me adding the final touches. The strange

11

thing was, Marie had an electronic device on her temple, much like the gorilla I fought today.

Christa walked in front of me. "Oh you make such a beautiful bride!" she gushed. She had a makeup brush in her hand. She shook her head. "Girl, woman, your complexion is perfect as always!"

The wedding march started to play. "They're playing your song!" Marie told me with a smile.

Dad walked up to me, he had a white tuxedo on. By the way, he walked, he looked like a robot that needed oiling I knew he felt awkward so dressed up. He held out an arm for me. "You ready, honey?"

I took his arm. We began walking down the aisle. Man, it looked like the entire town was there. Wait! Was that the president? What! Is that Liam Hemsworth here too! Ah, he looks sad I'm getting married. Then I noticed the band had Taylor Swift singing for them.

I walked past my mom and all my grandmas. They smiled and blew me kisses. Wendi sat in the second row. But it looked like she was alone. No Brandon! Hey, wow, maybe I was marrying Brandon? Or could it possibly be Jason? Jason has been my BFF for as long as I can remember. I always thought it could turn into more… Maybe somebody else? Whoever my groom was, they had their back turned to me. Not very traditional, but part of me realized this was a dream: a very wonderful, strange dream.

Suddenly my stomach began to rumble. I put my hand on top of the rumble to ease it. No, no, I thought. This is not the time to fart! Okay, I guess there's never a good time to fart, but certainly not when you're at your own wedding. 'Hold it in, hold it in,' I thought to myself. But you know, sometimes these things have a mind of their own. A tiny silent fart snuck out. I smiled when it didn't make a noise. Phew, that was a close one. But I heard a bunch of gasps behind me. Looking over my shoulder I saw the entire crowd had fallen over holding their throats. A flock of birds dropped from the sky. I think I saw a plane crashing off in the distance. Woe, talk about silent but deadly...

OMG, I just wiped out my wedding! I just dropped my entire family, all my friends, Liam Hemsworth, the President, Taylor Swift and my husband.

I woke up in a cold sweat and looked around me. "I hoped that dream wasn't prophetic!"

Trying to calm my racing pulse, I sat up in bed and stretched, the dream still racing through my head.

Whoa, smelled like I needed another quick shower before I went to lunch with Jason and Dad. I believed this was a record; two showers before midday! Part of the price I paid for being super.

Dear Diary: It's amazing how fast a dream can turn into a nightmare. Does it work the other way around? Can you turn a nightmare into a dream? Truthfully, I'm not sure. I think about silly things. Well, at least my wedding gown was way awesome!

Lunch with Dad...

I was glad Dad invited Jason to our lunch at BM Science. Dad likes Jason because he says Jason reminds him of a young him. Not sure if that's good or bad. I am sure that Jason is my BFF and helps to keep me grounded. I love hanging out with him. I always feel more secure when he's around. I know without any doubt, Jason has my back and my best interests in mind.

"I'm glad your Dad invited me!" Jason said as we biked towards the BM Science complex.

One of the great things about Star Light City is the city has everything a kid or adult would want and it's all very well laid out. Everything is easy to get to. They have a great public transportation system and the Uber service is the best! On days like this though, nothing beats getting around on our bikes. (Well, besides leaping and running at super speed.)

"Me too," I told Jason.

"Not only does BMS have the best and latest high tech gadgets, they have a great cafeteria!" Jason smiled.

"Plus, you get to hang out with me!" I told him.

He beamed at me. "That's a given, Lia!"

There are times when Jason really knew the right thing to say.

He rubbed his stomach. "Plus, I swear their cafeteria has the best French fries in the world!"

Of course, other times he thought more with his stomach.

"Plus, the servers are robots!" he added.

Then there was the geek side of Jason. I did like the way that no matter what the situation, Jason was always Jason. I found that refreshing and comforting. When your life is changing fast, some constants are needed.

Jason, my family, and my friends were those constants. Yeah, sure they would grow and change just like me, but they were always there to support me. Even superheroes need the support of others.

We biked up to the security gate of BM Science. Three guards in green uniforms were there to greet us. The guards smiled when they noticed who we were. The lead guard, a tall man with a big jaw, gave me a salute, "Ms. Strong, its an honor to see you and your friend again."

He pointed to a bike rack (with two spaces) on the other side of the fence. "You and Mr. Michaels may park your transportation there. A shuttle is on the way to accompany you to your father's office area."

"Thank you," I said, though it felt weird being saluted.

As we parked our bikes, Jason whispered to me, "Do these guys know that you're Super Teen?"

I shrugged my shoulders. "I have no idea."

A driverless red golf cart rolled up to us and a computerized voice said, "Greetings, Lia and Jason. I am the Machine Automatic Communication System, MACS for short."

"Hi, MACS," I said.

"Nice to meet you," Jason said.

"Your father is quite anxious to see you both!" MACS continued. He beeped happily. "Now please enjoy the ride."

We sat down in the back seat. MACS pulled out. Both of the back seats had a little information screen in front of them.

"We are ten minutes away from your father's office space. Do you wish to watch anything? Would you like me to play some music? I am also capable of telling jokes...."

Two glasses of water popped out from under the back seat. "I have estimated you must be thirsty after your bike ride."

Jason and I both took our waters. "Thanks!" Jason grinned.

He sat back in his seat. "I could get used to this!"

"I have a massage setting for both the seats if you wish," MACS said.

"Sure," Jason laughed. "And tell us a joke....please..."

"My pleasure, Jason. Why is seven the scariest number?"

"No idea," Jason replied.

"Ms. Strong?" MACS prompted me.

"I don't know either," I grinned.

"Because seven eight nine," MACS responded in his robotic voice. He added a ba bump, bump drum sound.

"Funny!" I said, with a smile towards Jason.

"Now what type of music choices do you have?" Jason asked, clearly getting into this.

"I have all the music from Bach, as that music has been known to stimulate the brain," MACS answered.

"Fine, hit us," Jason said.

"Mr. Jason when you are in control of a car, hitting things is not an option," MACS replied.

"Just play the music…"

Music started to play. It sounded better than I thought. I couldn't help but be impressed, not only by MACS but by how the BM Science facility had grown in just a few months. There were even taller, shinier buildings than before and each of the building had more floors than I remembered. The grounds were perfectly manicured. Of course, the most interesting part was that robots of all sizes wandered around interacting with the human workers. The humans acted like this was perfectly normal. I guess for them it was. Could this be the future?

We drove through the large compound until we reached a tall round shiny glass building. MACS pulled up to the double doors of the building. "Your father is on the 20th floor…."

Looking up at the shimmering tower Jason gulped, "Wow!"

What MACS didn't tell us was that my dad's office took up the ENTIRE 20th floor of the building. The room was large enough for us to have a LAX game and maybe even two, side by side. As I exited the high-speed elevator, I could barely see my dad's desk across the room.

17

"Wow," Jason gulped again as we walked in. "I really want to be a scientist when I get older!"

Another red cart zoomed up. "Hello again," MACS voice said from the cart. "Would you like a ride to your father's thinking area?"

I shook my head. "No thanks, we'll walk."

"Yes, soak it all in!" MACS said.

After a bit of walking, we got close enough to dad's desk to see him clearly without using super-vision. He had been sitting there talking to a person I can only describe as the best looking woman or person I had ever seen. The woman had long blond hair that danced down her shoulders, big blue eyes, and a perfect porcelain complexion. She had the tall slim build of a master ballerina.

"Wow, your dad's assistant is beautiful!" Jason said, far louder than he should have.

The sound of Jason's voice was heard by Dad and his stunning assistant and they both looked at us.

"Thank you, Jason," the beautiful woman said.

Dad smiled. He pointed to the woman, "Lia, Jason I'd like you to meet Hana."

We reached Dad's large desk. Hana held out a hand to each of us. "Lia, Jason, I've heard and read so much about you two."

We each shook her hand. Her grip felt much more powerful than I would have guessed. Yeah, she had to be some kind of athlete.

"The pleasure is mine," Jason said unable to take his eyes off Hana.

"Nice to meet you, Hana," I said. I raised an eyebrow. "I've heard nothing about you."

Hana smiled and released our hands. "Your father is a man of many secrets. He doesn't believe in revealing them until the right moment. And then he likes to be dramatic!"

"You seem to know him well. How long have you

been working with my dad?" I prompted.

Hana smiled. "Oh, for as long as I can remember."

I shot Dad a look. Not sure why. He and Mom hadn't been together for a LONG time but I still felt weird that he hadn't told us his assistant happened to be the most beautiful woman in the world.

Hana noticed my look. Dad either didn't notice or didn't care.

"I'll go prepare the meal!" Hana said walking away.

Dad pointed to a couple of chairs across from his desk. "Come and sit!" he smiled. "I'm so glad you are here!"

"The place is amazing!" Jason said. "And so is Hana!"

"Thanks!" Dad smiled. "Now that I am mega senior VP of science and research I have some perks!"

"So I noticed," I said, a bit of contempt in my voice.

Dad looked at me, his eyes wide open. "Honey, why the attitude?"

If he didn't know, I wasn't going to tell him. "Nothing," I sighed.

The force of my breath knocked him over in his chair.

I shot up from my seat. "Dad sorry," I said leaning over his desk. "Sometimes I still forget how strong I am!"

He laughed as he stood back up. "No problem honey! I know it can't be easy being super. That's why I want to help."

"Help?" I looked over my shoulder. "Oh no, you're not going to attack me with another robot. Are you?" I looked back at him. "Really dad, that gets old fast!"

Dad laughed again. "No, you've passed all those tests with flying colors."

"Is this about aliens?" I asked. "You mentioned aliens before."

Dad's face became serious. "Yes, honey, I believe we are not alone in this wide universe. Heck, there may be many universes. The odds of us being the only intelligent beings is…." Dad raised his eyes to the ceiling as he did some calculations in his head.

"Very small," Jason said.

"Exactly!" Dad smiled. "I think I can safely say, we are not alone. In fact, aliens may be watching us. I'd be shocked if they weren't interested in Super Teen. You and other super beings may be the next evolution of man."

"Wow!" Jason said.

Now, that was a lot to take in.

Dad shrugged. "Then again, you might not be. You just might be genetic freak accidents that mean nothing to the course of human evolution."

"Gee thanks, Dad!"

Dad grinned. "Just stating a possibility. The thing is, no matter what, you are important to the here and now. That's why I am here to help."

"How so?"

Dad stood up. "Honey, I've built you a new uniform!"

Dear Diary: My dad may be a bit crazy, but he's still my dad and I love him. Could I be the next step in evolution? Nah! He just said that to toss me off guard so I wouldn't question him having such a beautiful assistant.

Uniform 2.0…

"Dad you don't build a uniform!" I told him.

"I do!" he said proudly, probably more proudly than he should have. Especially coming from a guy who seemed only comfortable in a lab coat or sweatpants.

Dad pushed a button on his desk. A table popped up next to the desk. On that table, I saw a white bodysuit, a pair of plain looking shoes, two clip-on earrings and a watch. The watch looked cool. But definitely nothing else.

"Tada!" Dad said, once again sounding much more proud than I thought he should.

"So mega cool!" Jason was clearly impressed.

I got up and walked towards the table. I picked up the plain white body suit. It seemed to be made of many little balls. The shoes also appeared to be made of the same substance. I showed them to Dad. "You gotta be kidding! I can't wear this in public!"

Dad's eyes popped open again. In fact, one of them began to twitch. "You don't understand. This is the latest in NACT: Nano Adaptive Clothing Technology."

I looked at it again. "It looks weird and high tech. I'll give you that. But I can't wear this under my clothing or out in public!"

Dad shook his head. "Yes, this can be worn under your outfit if you wish, but it's also perfectly capable of being the only outfit you need. It has self-cleaning nano-bots so you can wear it continuously for at least 24 hours without having to worry about pit stains or odor…"

"Oh, gross Dad!"

Dad nodded. "A normal human could wear it for weeks without the nano-bots needing to recharge. But in your case, thanks to your powerful sweat…24 hours should be the max. Then take it off so it can recharge."

"Gee, thanks, Dad!"

"Honey, I'm just stating facts."

I showed him the suit. "But this thing is ugly as anything!"

Dad turned to Jason. "Do you want to tell her? After all, this was your idea."

"What?" I asked, turning to Jason.

"Jase has been emailing me his ideas. They're great!" Dad smiled.

Nice to know my dad talked more with my BFF than he did with me. But I let that go for now. If Jason had thought of this, there had to be more to it. I showed the outfit to Jason. "What am I missing here?"

Dad pushed another button on his desk. A screen started lowering itself from the ceiling.

"What the?"

"Just put it on!" Dad said.

The screen landed between myself and dad and Jason,

giving me some privacy. I looked at the white outfit made of balls. I stuck out my tongue. Since Dad and Jason couldn't see me I made a loud "Blah" sound.

"Just put it on!" Jason shouted.

I kicked my shoes off. I kind of hoped my feet stank just to teach them a lesson. Sadly, for once they didn't. I sighed and put on the suit and the shoes.

"Don't forget the watch and the earrings!" Dad shouted over the screen.

"Watches are so 1990s!" I called back.

"Retro is cool!" Jason yelled.

I slipped the watch on over my wrist. It sealed itself automatically. A smile appeared on the watch face. "Hello again!" MACS voice said from the watch.

"MACS?"

"Yes, Ms. Lia, I am the interface for this suit and earrings. Please put on the earrings. Accessories are so important!"

I popped on the earrings. They were little studs that sat on my earlobes. I finally had an idea where this was going.

"Okay, raise the screen!" I called to Dad.

The screen started back up towards the ceiling. Did Dad have the screen installed on his ceiling just for this? Okay, Lia, think big picture here, I thought to myself. I turned my attention to Dad and Jason, who were smiling at me like I was the coolest Christmas present in the world. "You guys going to tell me how this works?" I asked.

"This will allow you to switch instantly from your regular clothes to your choice of uniform and back to your normal clothes again," Dad said.

"No need to carry your disguise around!" Jason added.

"I can't go around in public in this, and with no mask!"

Dad and Jason just smiled at each other. "MACS

uniform style one."

My suit of white balls instantly turned into a pretty pink top that buttoned down the front, and a fitted black skirt. The earrings projected a black mask over my eyes. "Okay, wow!" I said, jumping up and down in excitement. "What else can it do?"

"Touch the screen or ask MACS?" Dad replied. "He'll tell you anything you want to know. He makes Siri look like sad…" Dad smiled.

"Good one, Doc!" Jason told Dad.

I groaned. Dad jokes are the worst, especially when they come from your own dad.

"MACS show Lia her options…."

"Please look at my screen," MACS instructed me. "I can scroll through outfits on a timer or you can flick left or right. To select an outfit just tap it."

A really cool red outfit appeared on the screen. "I can also modify any colors choices you want," MACS explained.

I flipped through one, then another, then another. A super adorable yellow dress with little shoulder straps popped up on the screen. I smiled. I tapped the screen. Next thing I knew I had that outfit on.

"This would be perfect in light blue," I said.

The outfit instantly changed to a light blue color. "I'd like the shoes to be dark blue," I said.

My shoes became the exact shade I wanted. "How about some heels?" I asked.

"Sorry, don't do heels," MACS said.

Dad laughed. "Yeah, your mom would clobber me!"

I looked at dad and Jason. "You guys did good!"

"Oh great! She likes the NACT!" Hana said, walking back into the room, pushing a cart. The cart had BBQ chicken, hamburgers and hot dogs on it. Plus, there was fresh corn on the cob, a huge bowl of French fries and a platter of salad. To drink, we had lemonade.

"I have prepared the lunch!" Hana said proudly.

A picnic table popped up from the floor. Jason raced over to the table. "I'm famished!" Jason said.

"What a surprise!" I laughed.

Dad walked over and joined us as Hana began to prepare plates. Hana handed me a plate loaded with chicken, corn, and salad.

"Thanks!" I said.

"My pleasure!" Hana told me.

Suddenly it hit me. I sniffed Hana. "You don't have a scent!" I told her.

Hana smiled. "I will take that as a compliment!"

"Here's the thing. Every person I know has a scent!" I exclaimed.

Hana shrugged. "Perhaps they need to shower more?"

"I'm not saying they smell. Well some of them do. But my super smelling power can smell the differences from person to person..."

"Good for you!" Hana said, patting me on the shoulder.

I sniffed her. "You're a robot!" I said.

Hana grinned. "Actually the proper term is android..."

Dear Diary: So...instead of hiring the most beautiful woman in the world to be his assistant, dad built her. I'm not sure that's better! But at least she isn't beautiful and human. Wow, my dad is so smart...and weird...

A Bit of Business...

I shot Dad a look. "You built an android that looks like the perfect woman!"

Dad munched on a chicken leg. He looked at me. "Yes, yes I did," he smirked.

Jason stood up and walked towards Hana. "You look so amazingly lifelike."

Hana nodded. "I am alive. Just in a different way than you are."

Dad popped a French fry into his mouth. "We at BM Science, are very proud of Hana. After all, she was a team project. In fact, she helped us build her."

"Ah, come again?" I asked.

"They built my brain and interface system first. That enabled me to consult on the rest of my specs!" Hana said proudly.

"Best billion dollars this company has ever spent!" Dad said, drinking some lemonade. He spilled some on his lab coat but didn't seem to mind. Yes, even in Dad's big fancy office, he still wore his lab coat. I could see why now.

Hana looked at my dad. "You were right about Lia. It's amazing how quickly she deduced I was not human."

"That's my daughter!" Dad said trying to clean the spill off his lab coat. Of course, he just made it worse.

Hana looked me in the eyes. Her eyes seemed incredibly human at first glance, but when I peered deeper, something was missing. I just couldn't be sure what. Maybe it was my brain playing tricks with me now.

"I'd love to spar with you sometime," Hana told me.

"Ah, sure," I said slowly, not quite sure how to respond.

"Man, I'd pay to see that!" Jason said.

I shot Jason an unimpressed look. He turned back to

his seat, sat down and started to eat. "Great chicken!" he told my dad, a little awkwardly.

I turned my focus back to Hana. "Sure, some other time. Today I have LAX coaching with my team."

Hana nodded, "Yes I know. I put it on your father's calendar." She paused. "I look forward to a stimulating sparring session with you."

I looked at Dad. "Any other surprises for me today?"

Dad popped some lettuce into his mouth. "Actually there is one more...."

Of course, there was. It wouldn't be Dad if he didn't keep popping out surprises.

He took another bite of lettuce. "Yum, I love this dressing!"

"Dad, what's the other surprise?" I shouted.

The force of my voice knocked both dad and Jason backward. A few strands of Hana's hair flew out of place. She shook her head and the hairs dropped back into place.

"Remember that gorilla you fought?" Dad asked.

"You mean the one I fought a few hours ago?" I

asked.

Dad nodded. "Yep."

"Hard to forget a super strong, intelligent bionic gorilla," I noted. "Especially when the fight was like I said, literally this morning!"

"Actually it's not bionic it's cybernetic," Dad corrected.

"I knew that," I said. "Bionic just seemed more dramatic."

Dad laughed. "Do you really need more drama in your life?"

"Good point," I sighed. "Dad, where are you going with this?"

He sat back in his chair and put his hands behind his head. The chair started to tip. He sat forward. "We have the gorilla now."

"What?" I asked.

"Josh's dad knew the gorilla was too much for the Star Light City Police to handle. I mean come on, they just aren't equipped for a cybernetic super gorilla."

"Ah, my name is Jason," Jason told Dad.

"Right, I knew that!" Dad said.

"So you have the gorilla now?" I asked my dad.

"Of course we do! Your father just told you that!" Hana answered for Dad. "We are the most advanced facility on Earth."

Dad nodded as he chewed on another French fry. "We have her locked up nice and safe in one of the basement facilities."

I got quickly to my feet. "I want to see her!"

Dad smiled. "I knew you would. Let's just finish eating and Hana and I will escort you down to the subbasement!"

"Subbasement? So cool!" Jason said.

I looked at Dad. His smile didn't waver. "Trust me, honey, the gorilla is fine. Better than fine!"

28

I decided to trust him. After all, he was my dad.

Dear Diary: Seems like the more I get to know my dad the more I realize there's a lot I don't know about him. The man is brilliant. He built me a great uniform that will save time and help keep my identity safe. (And it keeps me smell free for a day!) But he also built a perfect android that wants to spar with me. Plus, he's holding the gorilla I fought with this morning. Man, parents are complicated!

Going Ape...

We finished lunch and then ate a dessert of fried ice cream made by Hanna. After that, Hanna and Dad escorted Jason and me down to the subbasement. I wasn't sure how far underground the subbasement was buried, but it seemed to take forever for the secure elevator to make its way down there.

The elevator opened up into a brightly lit hallway that spanned as far as the eye could see. Hana walked out and pointed down the hall.

"This way please," she instructed us.

"Is the gorilla alright?" I asked nervously. "She got a good whiff of my morning breath. That could drop a herd of elephants from a hundred yards away."

Dad smiled. "She was a little out of it when our team picked her up. Your breath does pack quite the punch. But my team tells me she is fine now."

We continued to walk for what seemed like forever. I don't know what I found to be weirder, me knocking out gorillas with my breath or Dad having a team. Never really thought of dad as an in charge kind of guy.

"How's she doing now?" I asked.

Dad hesitated.

"Dad, tell me!" I ordered. Not sure if I fired off some of my pheromones or not. I still had no control of that power.

"We removed her cybernetic attachments," he said slowly.

"And?" I prompted.

We came to a door. Hana put her hand on the door. It popped open. "See for yourself!"

I walked into a room that had a big cage in it. Still, as far as cages go, this was a nice one. There was a lot of green grass in the cage, a tree and a little stream of water. A couple of keepers in orange suits were feeding the gorilla some greens.

"She seems happy," Jason said.

"She does," I agreed.

Hana looked at me. "Before we removed her attachments she told us her name was Jodi with an i...." She motioned towards Jodi. "You can go visit with her. She's fine."

I walked forwards slowly. "Hiya, Jodi," I said with a smile.

Jodi tilted her head. She farted. Then she started laughing and clapping!

Dad laughed too. "Since we removed the attachments, she's become a normal gorilla, a normal gorilla with a sense of humor..."

I stuck my hand into the cage.

One of the attendants warned me. "I wouldn't do that ma'am. Even in this state, she's very strong!"

I ignored the attendant. I didn't like being called 'ma'am' but I knew they were trying to be polite and helpful. "I'll be fine," I said. "She'll be gentle with me."

Jodi took my hand. Her hand engulfed mine. I wasn't sure if she recognized me without my costume and without her super intelligence, but the look in her eyes seemed to suggest that she did. She shook my hand lightly. She smiled at me. I returned the smile.

"Good girl, Jodi!" I said.

"Hoo, Hoo!" She responded.

"See, she's fine," Dad said. "Sadly, the enhancement cybernetics disintegrated the moment they were separated from her. But Jodi shows no ill effects. We do know the implants must have been put on her recently since she had that wrap around her head."

"What's going to happen to her?" I asked still keeping my eyes on her.

"She will go to a nice gorilla sanctuary down south," Hana told me. "There are five others of her kind there. She will be comfortable."

"Do you know where she came from?" Jason asked, always looking for clues.

Dad shook his head. "Nope. There have been no reports of missing gorillas and I'll tell you a missing gorilla is hard to miss."

"Do you know who did this to her?" I asked.

Dad hesitated again.

"Dad tell me, please!"

He took a step back. He looked at the ground. I knew he didn't want to say anything. "We have no proof yet," he said.

"Dad..."

Hana spoke up. "The work has a resemblance to the groundbreaking work of Doctor Donna Dangerfield. She has done a lot of study on enhancing people through cybernetics."

"She just moved here like a month ago! That can't be a coincidence!" I said.

Dad shook his head. "Actually it can be. A lot of people now are working on cybernetics including us. It's a hot field. The number of older people in the world is growing rapidly. It would be great if we found ways to make growing old, easier. Cybernetics offers a lot of promise."

"But why pick on a harmless gorilla?" I asked.

"Cause gorillas are a lot like people," Jason said.

"Exactly," Dad said. He pointed to Jason. "I like this Joey guy!"

"Jason!" Jason, Hana and I all told dad.

"Right, Jackson," Dad said. He smiled. "I know it's Jason." Dad's smile straightened out. He put his arms on my shoulder. "Listen, honey, don't go accusing Doctor Dangerfield yet because..."

I lowered my head. "…she may be innocent?"

Dad shrugged. "Yeah she may be, but if she isn't, we don't want to scare her off by thinking we are on to her. So if you meet her just act normally!"

"I'll try dad, I'll try."

Jason pulled out his phone. "Speaking of normal, we've got to coach a LAX game in less than an hour."

Dear Diary: I was so happy to see Jodi safe and content. I'm not thrilled that somebody would experiment on her like that. When I find out who did, they are in trouble. PS: Dad really has to get Jason's name right!

LAX...

Peddling as fast as we could (without me actually using my superpowers), we got to the LAX field five minutes before the "game" was scheduled to start. Luckily our other coaches, Marie and Christa had the kids lined up and doing drills. Well, as much as you can with kids their age. When they are seven and eight years old, it's pretty much like herding cats.

Today, our green team was playing the red team. Normally, who they played was no big deal. After all, these games were supposed to be about having fun and learning the basics of LAX, so score didn't matter. But since we were playing the red team coached by Wendi (and Brandon and Lori and an older girl named Tanya Cone), today's game meant something.

Yeah, I know it probably shouldn't have. After all, Brandon is always nice and certainly has a great smile. Lori, for all her roughness, is actually a nice person too. She is a faithful teammate. During our season she made a great pass to me as I made the winning goal of the last game of the year. That felt good. Oh, and Tanya is a very cool kid. She must be fifteen or sixteen and only coaches this level because her little sister, Kayla plays on the team. Kayla's a cute kid too with dark hair and dimples. Like a miniature version of Tanya. Heck, the entire red team and their coaches are fine. They are all nice normal kids. Sure they can be high strung and annoying and at times, it's tempting to pop my shoes off and put them all to sleep with super foot odor. But I know they're just kids being kids. They aren't the problem.

The problem is Ms. Perfect Wendi. I knew if her kids beat my kids I would never hear the end of it. Sure, we weren't supposed to keep score but the kids do, and so do the coaches. I guess its human nature. Being superhuman doesn't change that with me. I wanted to make sure her kids didn't beat my kids. I had a secret weapon and his name was Felipe.

When Felipe saw me, he came running over and hugged me. "Yeah, Lia you're here!"

Felipe's cousin Tomas and Jess were also there to cheer on Felipe.

"Hey, Lia," Tomas said.

"Beautiful day for a game," I told them.

Jess smiled. "I wouldn't have it any other way."

Tomas used to have a crush on me, but I didn't return his feelings. He's nice and all but I don't think I'd want to date a half-vampire. (Even though vampires aren't really vampires like in the movies, just humans with slightly different genes...) Still, I didn't like him that way. And I was happy that he and Jess, the witch, had hooked up.

Felipe motioned to me to bend down to him. I did. He whispered in my ear, "Now I'm not supposed to use my powers of speed and strength here. Right?"

"Actually, Felipe, today we'll make an exception. Do you know what that means?"

His face lit up. "That I can have lots of fun!"

I nodded. "Yes, but we want to keep the game close."

"Got it!" Felipe said, running towards the other players on the field.

The referee, who happened to be Janitor Jan from school, blew her whistle for the two teams to meet in the middle of the field.

My coaches and I walked out to meet Wendi and the other coaches. Wendi shot me a look. I shot her a look. I really had to concentrate to NOT use heat vision on her.

"Remember, coaches, these games are for fun and learning," Ref Jan warned us all.

"Of course," Brandon said with a beautiful smile. "It's all about sportsmanship and a good game!"

"And having fun!" Jason added.

"And learning the rules," Lori added.

"And staying safe," Marie added.

"And sportsmanship," Christa said looking at me and Wendi.

I held a hand out to Wendi. "To a good game!"

Wendi took my hand without looking at me. "Good game."

We returned to the sidelines. Jan blew the whistle and the game began. Both teams just pretty much ran up and down the field chasing each other and occasionally making a pass. Most of the kids simply enjoyed the running.

The coaches would yell things like:

"Pass pass…."

"Fall back on defense…."

"Watch your man…."

"Keep those sticks high!"

"Stop chasing butterflies!"

"Guys, you're running off the field…"

"Guys, stop having a burping contest in the middle of the field!"

You know that kind of stuff. Like I said, it would mostly be easier to herd cats. The one exception on our team was Felipe. He darted up the field, dodged other kids and tossed the ball into the net. Wendi's team also had their own star player, Kayla Cane. For every goal Felipe scored, Kayla would fly up the field and score right back. I thought, wow, this kids amazing, as Kayla ran up the field with the ball in her stick.

She approached the goal.   Suddenly everything froze in place. Everything except Kayla, her sister Tanya, and me. But I still stood motionless, just to see what was going on. Tanya walked out to Kayla on the field.

"Kayla, you know this is a no, no!" Tanya scolded, her finger wagging.

Kayla sighed. "I know you told me not to slow time

this much but I was tired from all this running, and I needed a little break. This time control stuff is hard!"

Tanya crossed her arms and glared at her little sister. "Yes, yes it is. That's why we're not supposed to do it. Only in extreme emergencies. Playing a lacrosse game isn't an emergency."

"But I need juice now!" Kayla pouted. She pointed to our side. "We can take some of the other team's juice!"

Tanya shook her head. "No, that would be wrong."

Kayla pointed at me. "Hey, that girl is moving."

"What do you mean, Kayla?"

"Tanya, I saw her blink. When we time slow, people can't blink!"

Tanya and Kayla locked their eyes on me. I stood there trying not to blink. The thing is...when you try not blink it really makes you want to blink. I blinked. I sighed. I walked towards them.

"Yeah I'm not frozen," I admitted. "Actually everything seems heavier than normal but I can move through it all. It's weird."

Tanya nodded. "Yep, that's the time displacement you're feeling."

"How can she move?" Kayla asked. "Only you, mommy and I are supposed to be able to move." She looked at her sister questioningly.

Tanya held out a hand to me. "Lia Strong, nice to formally meet. Oh, should I call you Super Teen?"

I grinned and shook her hand. "Let's stick with Lia, please. So how did you guys get your powers?"

Tanya looked at me. "Wow, not big on small talk are you?"

I dropped my head. "Sorry, but your powers are just so cool."

Tanya smiled. "Our grandma was pregnant during the Chernobyl accident in Russia. Our mom, Meesha, was born with the ability to slow time. And now, so can we."

She shrugged. "No idea why or how. What about you?"

"I come from a long line of superwomen. When we turn 12, we've absorbed enough energy to activate our powers." I explained.

It felt good to talk to another who had powers and seemed normal. I mean, I like Jess and Tomas, but he's a little creepy and she's a little aloof.

"So we're going to keep each other's secrets?" Tanya asked.

"Of course!" I said.

"Good! Now let's get back to the sidelines and get this game over with, I mean going again." She looked Kayla in the eyes. "And no more stopping time!"

Kayla groaned. "OK!"

Dear Diary: Well Mom and Dad have always thought that there would be other super people out there. And now that I was super I would most likely notice them. This is something I don't often say, but wow my parents were so right. Actually, I'm hoping I can be friends with Tanya as it would be so cool to have another super kid I can chat with about being super. Somebody who can relate to the ups and downs. Plus,
having a friend who can slow time could come in handy!

Post-Game Meet and Greet…

The game ended in a 10-10 tie. We gathered up our kids and our gear. The kids lined up in the middle of the field and shook hands, giving each other high fives. I liked teaching the kids the importance of being good sports, even against Wendi's team.

Speaking of Wendi, I saw her heading towards me. A tall red-headed woman accompanied Wendi.

"Good game, Strong," Wendi said, a little begrudgingly.

"Thanks, Wendi," I said with as much sincerity as I could fake.

Wendi pointed to the somehow familiar woman. "My aunt wanted to meet you. She's kind of new in town, but also famous and a great doctor. Your mom works for her."

The woman stepped forward and offered her hand to me. Her arm was ripped with muscles. "Lia, I'm Doctor Donna Dangerfield. And I work *alongside* your wonderful mother." Doctor Dangerfield said with a smile.

I shook her hand. "Nice to meet you, Doctor."

She released my hand. "Please call me Donna."

By now Jason, Christa, and Marie had noticed Donna. Jason and Marie rushed over.

"Doctor Dangerfield, I've been a fan of yours for a long time!" Jason gushed. "I've followed your research in cybernetics and your fighting career!" he babbled on, turning a slight shade of red.

Donna turned to him and smiled. "Wow, I don't find many people who follow both my careers."

Jason turned even redder. He took a step back. He tried to talk but failed.

Marie stepped forward and grinned. "Doctor Donna, so nice to meet you, it's an honor to be volunteering in your lab!"

Donna smiled. "Ah, so you're one of my student lab rats, as Doctor Stone calls them."

Everybody else laughed thinking it to be a joke. But after the events of today, I wasn't so sure.

Marie grinned. "Yes, my friend Lori and I are hoping for careers in medicine and science!"

Lori joined the conversation. "Actually, I just loved your MMA work…how you systematically destroyed your opponents. I respect that!"

Donna nodded. "Thank you, I guess," Donna turned her attention back to me. "Well, I just wanted to introduce myself and to say you are always welcome in my lab at the hospital."

"Ah, thanks," I said.

Donna put her arms around Wendi and Lori. "Come on, I'll take you both out for ice cream, doctor's orders!" Donna turned to us. "Would you guys like to join us?"

"Sorry, we're taking our team to Mr. T's for food," I answered.

Wendi pulled on her aunt. "Come on, Aunt Donna, you'll see them at the hospital."

"Another time then," Donna said.

The three of them walked away.

"Wow, she's amazing!" Jason said, his mouth gaping open.

"Close your mouth," I told him.

Marie pointed to our equipment. "I'll go help Christa pick up our gear." Maybe Marie sensed I needed to talk to Jason.

I nudged Jason. "Remember, Doctor Donna may be an evil mad scientist!" I said softly.

"She doesn't seem evil to me!" Jason replied.

The thing was, she didn't seem evil to me either.

Dear Diary: Man, I don't know what's more annoying, the fact that Doctor Donna Dangerfield is Wendi's aunt or that she appears to be so nice. I mean I really should like this woman, she's smart and strong and everything I strive for. Yet I can't help thinking about what somebody did to that poor sweet gorilla, Jodi. If that was done by Doctor Donna, then she truly isn't a good person. I mean can you do something like that and still be good?

Senior Heist...

Not sure why but I always loved going to Mr. T's after the game with our kids and their parents. Sure, chaos reigned when we were there. Instead of herding cats, it became herding cats on sugar. But I loved it. Christa says it's because I love punishment. I enjoyed the bonding of team and family and food. Jason says it's because I'm a leader but also a team player. Not sure if he's right about the leader part.

Today as an extra treat, Tanya and Kayla joined us. Sure Kayla wasn't on our team but she knew every kid from school. That's one of the smallish town advantages, everybody knows everybody. Of course, that could also be a disadvantage at times. But like Grandma Betsy says, you take the good with not so good and the bad and the terrible. It all evens out.

We pretty much took over Mr. T's. But Mr. T and Mrs. T didn't seem to mind. In fact, they enjoyed this mixed crowd even more than I did. Of course, they were making money out of us, so obviously that helped.

We sat at a coach's table. The parents sat at a couple of parent's tables next to us. And the kids pretty much just ran around stopping by their parents' tables to snack now and then.

I sat and munched. I soaked in the atmosphere. Jason must have seen me smiling. He nudged me. "Wow, you seem happy."

I nodded. "I am. It's been a good day. "

Just as those words left my mouth, we heard police sirens. Lots and lots of police sirens. Darn, I shouldn't have mentioned the words, 'good day.'

Jason looked at his phone. He turned to me and whispered, "This might be a good time to test your new uniform."

I stood up. "I'm going to go check out those sirens."

Of course, the entire restaurant had already headed out the door to see what was going on. There's something about sirens and possible danger that gets people so excited.

Jason walked out with me. He showed me his phone. It read: Bank robbery in progress Star City National Bank.

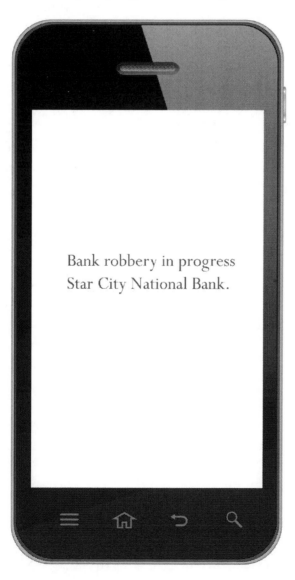

Since the bank was located right across from Mr. T's, we had a bird's eye view. Four police cars had pulled up in front of the bank. Four policemen took position behind their cars. Four other officers carefully approached the bank, their guns were drawn. The four officers, three men, and a woman entered the bank.

"Looks like the police have this under control!" I said.

The three policemen came flying out of the bank. They crashed to the ground – out cold.

"Okay, maybe not…" I groaned.

An old looking bald man in shorts and a white t-shirt walked out of the bank holding two big bags of money. His white shirt had an orange ink stain on it but he didn't seem to care.

"Ha! Nothing can stop me!" the man shouted.

The policewoman darted out of the bank. She aimed her gun. "Halt!"

The old man bent down and wiggled his butt in her general direction. The police lady dropped her gun, grabbed her throat and fell over, blue. The old man laughed. "Ha! Silent but deadly!"

The police all looked at Captain Michaels for direction. Captain Michaels aimed his weapon. "Last chance! Hands up or we shoot!"

The old man grinned. "You got me. Nobody ever says that Grandpa John is a dummy." He lifted his arms up. His smile grew.

The police in front of Grandpa John grabbed their throats and mumbled, "Oh the stench…" and fell over.

The cloud of old man underarm odor crept across the street. Everybody on the street dropped at once. I actually felt a little dizzy but fine, I fell over, pretending to be affected. I wanted to catch the old guy off guard.

Grandpa John sniffed his armpits, "You wimps! They don't smell THAT bad!" He started laughing and walking down the street.

I pushed the button on my watch to activate my new uniform and got to my feet. I had to admit that it was handy to have this uniform. "Excuse me, it's wrong to fart and use super BO without saying excuse me!" I shouted. Okay, not the best and wittiest comeback but I was still new to this.

I raced down the street at super speed. I moved in front of Grandpa John. I held out my hand. "You're lucky you didn't kill anybody. Give up the money now and I'm sure the courts will go easy on you." I noticed he had two electronic disks attached to the side of his forehead near his temples. The disks were pulsating.

Grandpa John looked at the bags of money. He looked at me. He shook his head. "I need this money. I might want to go to an old folk's home someday and those things are expensive. Actually, they are a rip off! Heck, I don't need an old folk's home. I need this money for a nice tropical vacation. Maybe I'll go with some beautiful swimsuit models. That Christy Brinkley is still very beautiful and only about 20 years younger than me. She'll come!"

I shook my head. "I really doubt you'll get her or any other model to go with you!"

"But I'm rich now!" he shrugged.

"It's not your money," I told him.

He shook his head. "Possession is 99 percent of the law."

Now I shook my head. "Nope, that's not how it works."

He dropped his bags of money and made a fist at me. "What do you know, you're just a kid!" He shouted like I had been standing on his lawn.

"His name is John Johnson," MACS said to me from my watch.

That caught me off guard.

"I am constantly monitoring your situation," MACS told me.

I put my watch close to my face. "How can you see

him?"

"I got his image from the bank's security camera," MACS informed me.

Grandpa John moved towards me. "You young kids, ya can't go three minutes without looking at your fancy dancy technology." He showed me his muscles. "Back in my day, our muscles were our technology."

"Okay, you know that makes no sense. Right, Grandpa?"

"It makes sense in its own way!" he insisted.

I shook my head. "Nope, it doesn't!"

He curled his hands into fists. "Young lady, I boxed in the army!"

He threw a punch at me. I caught his hand. I hit him with an open palm to his chest. He went flying backward and fell over.

"Okay, I never claimed I was a good boxer," he groaned from the ground.

He jumped back up to his feet. He turned and aimed his butt at me. "I hate to do this to such a pretty young thing but you asked for it!" He let out what had to be the loudest fart I've ever heard: PPRRRTTTTP!!!!!!!!!

"Oops that may have been a wet one!" he laughed.

I staggered back a step or two. "Is that all you got?"

He dropped his head. "Actually it is…those big ones take the wind out of me."

"Now are you going to give up nice and quietly?" I asked moving towards him.

He pulled out a pair of glasses from his shorts. He popped his glasses on his nose. "Look you can't hit a man with glasses!" he told me.

"Fine, have it your way!" I told him.

"You're letting me go?" He asked.

"Oh no, giving you a taste of your own bad medicine," I told him.

"Say what?" he said.

I turned and hit him with one of my own farts. A quiet ladylike pft…

I heard him drop to the ground before I even turned around. Yep, I had out-farted a pumped-up old man. But I still wasn't sure if I should be proud or ashamed.

"Your father would like pictures of the cybernetic disks he's wearing," MACS told me.

I bent down next to the out cold Grandpa John. The disks on his forehead melted away. "I so hope my fart didn't do that!" I said.

Dear Diary: First super gorillas, now super senior citizens. I need to get to the bottom of this and fast. Good news was, my new uniform worked great. Plus, having MACS as my contact "machine" would probably be useful. Maybe even get me closer to my dad! I'm glad Dad's back in my life.

Evening with Mom

Luckily the people on the street all recovered quickly. Since they were all out cold I didn't have to explain why Super Teen showed up while I was missing.

That night, Jason and I talked about the situation with my mom and grandma Betsy. Turns out Grandma knew this John Johnson guy.

"John Johnson is a good man," Grandma told us as we sat around the dining room table. "A bit on the crazy side, but I like that in a man."

On the TV we saw Oscar Oranga doing an exposé on whether super people were dangerous and what we could do to protect ourselves. Checking my social media, people seemed split as they pretty much always were. Some of the people pointed out that Super Teen showed up to save the day. Others, like Wendi, claimed that no super people popped up until Super Teen showed up. Others blamed BM Science. BM Science's online rep assured people they had nothing to do with this, or with Super Teen who was a treasure. I smiled at that.

"Lia, put your phone down and pay attention," Mom told me.

"Sorry," I groaned. "It's just good to know what people are saying. Lots of them are on my side which is good. I still think this is that Doctor Donna's fault. And I'm not just saying that because she's related to Wendi."

Grandma nodded. "Your dad did say the tech used on the gorilla and John seemed to resemble the tech that Dangerfield has experimented with!"

Mom shook her head. "The woman is brilliant, she has an M.D. and Ph.D. in physics and she's a Vet and I believe she's a lawyer as well. Her and her junior associate, Doctor Gem Stone even make house calls!"

"Doesn't mean she can't be evil," I said.

"She's also a world-class athlete and pretty good looking," Jason added.

I shot him a look.

Jason held his ground. "She is!"

"The boy's right honey, she is a hotty," Grandma told me.

I heard a knock at the door. "Who could that be?" I asked.

Mom pointed to the door. "I suggest you check!"

I opened the door to see Janitor Jan standing on my porch. "Ah, hi..." I said.

Jan walked past me. "I think you ladies need to hear what's going on...."

I staggered. "Wait? What?"

I grabbed Jan by the arm. "What are you talking about?"

Jan looked at me like I was a child, a very dim child. "Oh, so your mom hasn't told you yet?"

"Told me what?" I said with a tap of my foot.

Jan reached into her purse and pulled out a card. She showed it to me.

"Ah, Jan that's a coupon for odor eaters," I said.

Jan put a finger up. "Right, very important item." She put the coupon back and pulled out another card.

I read the card. "This is a gift certificate to MacDonalds," I sighed.

"So it seems!" Jan said holding up the card with far more pride than I thought she should have. She shook the card and shouted, "WAMMO: card be true!" The letters on the card started moving around and reforming until they read: Sorceress Supreme.

I looked at the card and wiggled my head. I blinked my eyes.

"You're seeing it right! I'm Sorceress Supreme!" she said proudly.

"But you clean our school!" I exclaimed.

Jan started towards the dining room table to join the group. "Who says a lady can't have two jobs? The school gives me health insurance and dental. Plus, I keep an eye on you!"

Jan looked at my mom. "I thought you told her Isabelle?"

"I was waiting for the proper time," Mom said.

Jason stood up, "Do you want me to get you a seat?"

Jan grinned. "Sorry kiddo, I like you, but this conversation is just for us ladies," She pointed at Jason, "WAMMO! You're a stool!"

In a flash of bright energy, Jason glowed. Shrank. And became a stool. Jan walked over and sat on him.

"Ah, I'd like to point out you just did that to my BFF!" I told Jan.

Jan laughed. "Don't worry it's not permanent, and I probably won't fart."

Mom leaned on the table. "Jan, what do you have to tell us?"

Jan crossed her arms and adjusted her butt on Jason. Now that was another phrase I never thought I'd say. "Yesterday, when I was cleaning the hospital, I saw that John Johnson guy visit Doctor Dangerfield's office."

"Wait, you work at the hospital now?"

"Big picture, honey," Mom told me.

"Right," I looked at Mom. "So Jan's at my school to keep watch on me?"

"And to clean," Jan said. "I love cleaning things!"

"It was her idea," Mom told me. "And when Jan gets an idea in her head, you don't get in her way, unless you want to spend a few days as her shoe insoles," Mom said, as if she had been talking from experience.

"Darn straight!" Jan said. "Can we get back to the business of who the bad guy or gal is before I turn you all into shoe insoles!"

"Right," I said. I set my gaze on Jan. "What did you learn at the hospital?"

Jan rolled her eyes. "I just told you! I saw that John Johnson talking to Doctor Dangerfield and her people. That can't be a coincidence."

"See Mom!" I said.

Mom put her head in her hand and leaned on the table. "I admit it looks bad. Let's just not focus on her though. It could be a setup."

"Well at least there will be three of us in the hospital, starting tomorrow," Jan stood up. "I gotta be at work early tomorrow, so I'd better get rolling."

Jan stood up and looked at the Jason stool. "He'll turn back in a bit."

"Hey, why'd you zap him? You didn't tell us anything he couldn't have heard?"

Jan walked by me and smiled. "I know. He just dropped some paper on the floor. He didn't mean to, but littering really makes me mad."

Jason popped back into himself. "Wait? What did I miss? Why does my back hurt? Why do I smell a butt smell?"

I patted him on the shoulder. "From now on be sure to keep the school as clean as possible!"

That night, getting ready for bed, I put on a pair of clean pink PJs. MACS sent me a text (which was weird BTW) saying that after the day I'd had, it would be good if I removed the suit so the nanobots had an easier time keeping it fresh. I would have taken it off anyhow. There are times when you want to wear your usual comfort clothing and tonight I wanted a bit of comfort sameness.

Out of curiosity, I sniffed the armpit area of the nano suit. It smelled a little but not THAT bad. I picked up one of my nano shoes and sniffed it. It had a little kick to it, but I was pretty sure they weren't lethal. I guessed the suit and even the shoes could keep up with me as long as I wasn't overstressed. The good news was…I could lift my arms up without having to worry about knocking everybody out. The not so good news was that I'd lost a potential weapon. But I figured if I got nervous or angry enough I could sweat through those nanobots. ☺

Shep popped into my room. He loved sleeping by my side and I loved having him with me. Shep, as always, just couldn't resist sniffing my shoes. I'm not sure why. I guess he wasn't as smart as he seemed. Shep walked over to the shoes beside my bed and took a whiff of them. He didn't drop over stiff, instead, he laid down and went to sleep. He started dog snoring and sounded so cute. So yeah, my shoes still had some punch, just not an instantly drop everything

52

in their tracks punch.

MACS sent me another text from the nightstand I had put him on.

MACS: Okay, even the latest tech can't quite keep up with your feet.

For some strange reason that made me feel good.

Dear Diary: Wow busy day today. I got a new uniform. I met an android. I met some siblings who can slow time, and I learned our school janitor is also a sorceress. Who would have thought that out-farting a super senior citizen wouldn't be the strangest thing that happened in my day?

Doctor Stone...

The next day, on the drive to the hospital, Jason and I went over our plan with Mom. "Now remember," Mom said from the driver's seat. "You have no actual proof Doctor Dangerfield is behind this!"

"True," Jason chimed in from the back. "My dad interviewed her and she seemed very honest. She admits that the technology used on the gorilla and the old guy, John, was very similar to hers, but not hers."

"She talked to John at the hospital!" I insisted. Yeah I know I was being a bit stubborn and pigheaded here, but this woman was related to Wendi.

"She showed my dad the video," Jason said. "They talked about John's poor health problems and his frequent farting and burping. Doctor Dangerfield told him her work wouldn't help him with any of those! At least not yet."

I looked across the seat at Jason. "I'm just glad you'll be working in her lab so you can keep an eye on her!"

Jason nodded. "Oh I plan to... she's so smart and strong and pretty," he sighed, a dreamy look on his face.

"Lia, just make sure you're not biased just because she's related to Wendi!" Mom warned me. "Our hospital administrator, Mr. Thom, spent a lot of time and money recruiting Doctor Dangerfield. Plus, she's working with the University and with your dad's company."

"I'll try," I said, shaking my head in frustration.

We pulled into the hospital parking lot. The hospital was an impressive brick building with large windows that looked out onto the well-groomed patio that led into the main building. The original building had to be one of the oldest structures in Star Light City but it had been updated many times. According to Mom, we now offered all the latest services and some cutting-edge technology that wasn't available anywhere else. Mom insisted we were lucky to add Donna Dangerfield to the list of talented staff who worked there. I still wasn't sure.

Walking into the reception area of the hospital, I was reminded of how big the place was. Mom had signed me up for volunteer work because she thought it would be good for me. I guess she didn't like my initial summer plan of sitting around all day just chilling and relaxing. I told her I needed my downtime to recharge and fight crime and stuff. She insisted that donating three hours of time each morning to the hospital would allow me plenty of time to recharge. Plus, she said it would make me feel better about myself. It would show me I can contribute to society as Lia. I knew she had a point. That's why I didn't put up too much of a fight. Of course, now that Doctor Dangerfield worked here, I figured I could keep an eye on her as well.

We found Marie and Lori standing in the lobby. They were talking to a short, pale-skinned, red-haired woman in a pink lab coat. Marie and Lori pointed at Jason. The pink lab coat lady nodded and started walking over to us.

"Who's the lady in pink?" I asked Mom.

"She's Doctor Gem Stone, junior associate to Doctor Dangerfield."

Doctor Stone nodded to my mother. "Doctor Strong, nice to see you as always."

Doctor Stone looked at Jason. "Jason, I'm here to introduce you to the Dangerfield lab. I'm sure you will find this to be a rewarding experience. Doctor Dangerfield may be fairly new to our town but she is a leader in many fields."

"Yes, I'm very excited!" Jason said.

Doctor Stone pointed to Marie and Lori. "Go join the girls. There is an introductory welcome speech being given by Mr. Thomas in the conference center. Doctor Dangerfield would like her interns, as she calls you, to sit together. Then I will escort you to the lab."

"Excellent!" Jason said. I could feel his excitement. I

even heard his heart rate speed up.

Doctor Stone turned her attention to me. "You must be Lia Strong," she said extending a hand to me.

I shook her hand. Her grip was surprisingly strong.

"Nice to meet you, Doctor Stone," I said.

"Your mother is part of our hospital family. Call me Doctor Gem…"

"Nice to meet you, Doctor Gem," I said.

Doctor Gem grinned. "We wanted you to be part of our group too, but your mother told us she'd prefer you to have more general duties. Of course, we honored your mother's wishes. After all, she is one of the finest doctors in the hospital." Doctor Gem paused. "Well, I'd better get back to my charges. I hope you have a great time here! I look forward to seeing you around!"

Once Doctor Gem was out of earshot I turned to Mom. "Wait, I could have been in Doctor Dangerfield's lab? I could have been watching her all the time?"

Mom sighed. "It's good you're not there. I don't want you obsessing."

"I don't obsess!" I insisted.

Mom put her hands on her hips. "You're obsessing now!" she insisted.

"I'm persistent," I admitted.

Mom pointed to a blue hallway. "Follow the blue hallway. You'll find the conference center."

I knew enough not to push my luck any further with Mom. I gave her a hug then started towards the conference center.

Dear Diary: I know I shouldn't jump to the conclusion that Doctor Dangerfield is guilty. But my gut says...don't trust her. I trust my gut.

The Talk...

Christa had saved a seat for me next to her in the conference room, which to me was actually more of a small auditorium. There were about 30 of us kids there. My friends and I were certainly the youngest. I recognized some of the older kids, Tanya and Michelle Lee. Tanya gave me a cool nod. Surprisingly, Jess also sat there on the other side of Christa.

"Jess, nice to see you here," I told her.

Jess nodded. "Thanks, it looks good on the resume."

"Never thought of you as the type of person who would worry about resumes," I said.

She smiled. "Hey, Witch College can be very competitive!"

On the stage on a podium, stood a big bearded man in a suit that seemed too tight. The man cleared his throat. We all turned our attention to him. "Greetings and salutations to our Lab Learners and Helping Hands, student volunteers," the man said. "I am Mr. Thomas lead administrator at this hospital. This program was my idea along with Doctor Strong and Doctor Dora. You won't meet Doctor Dora because she is exploring the Amazon. But our newest doctor, Doctor Donna Dangerfield has agreed to take her place in this program and accept Lab Learners. We are pleased to have you all here. I am sure you will help us as much as we will help you prepare for the future. I now pass you over to Nurse Payne.

Mr. Thomas sat down. A tall skinny woman in a white nurse's uniform took the podium. She adjusted her hair and it seemed to make her bun even tighter. "You will all be given uniforms to wear over your regular outfits. The Lab Learners will be given green lab coats. The helping hands will be given light blue smocks. Please note, these are only on loan to you all, we expect you to keep them clean."

Nurse Payne took a deep breath then continued on. "The rules for you all are very simple. Lab Learners, you are to watch and learn from your doctors. You may do anything they ask you to do. You may not do anything they don't ask you to do. It's very easy. Any questions?"

By the look that Nurse Payne gave the group of Lab Learners, it was obvious that she didn't want any questions. "Good." She turned her attention to us helping hands. "Now for you helping hands, your rules are a little more complicated. Your role here is to aid the patients. You must give them an extra human touch. So here is what you must always do: offer them something to read, talk with them, hold their hands, change the channel on the TV, help them with their computers and phones."

She paused to let that sink in, even though it wasn't that tricky.

"Now, here are the things you can do IF, and ONLY IF, a nurse or doctor says you may: Give them a snack or water, raise their bed, take them for a walk." She paused again. "I know these things sound simple and harmless, but for some patients, they could be disastrous. So do not perform any of those tasks without checking with a nurse or doctor."

We all nodded.

"Finally, if a nurse or doctor or technician asks you to do something, you do it. If they want coffee, you get it for them. If they need something taken from floor 1 to floor 10, you do that. Even if it's pee. If they have a spill that needs to be cleaned, you do that. By making the nurses happy, you also help make the patients happy. Any questions?"

Christa raised her hand.

"Yes, young lady?" Nurse Payne said.

"Will anybody vomit on us?" Christa asked.

Nurse Payne smiled. "Good question. And most likely, yes. If that happens though, we will issue you with a new gown."

Dear Diary: Oh yeah, I am volunteering to get vomited on! Man, being a superhero in real life isn't nearly as glamorous as in the comics and on TV. I'm not at all happy with my mom for signing me up for this, but at least I can keep an eye on Doctor Dangerfield.

Anthony...

First, I read a story to a cute little girl named Tiz. She needed to have her tonsils removed, and my mom was her doctor. I assured Tiz the operation would be over in a snap and she would be fine. Tiz seemed happy knowing that her doctor was a mom.

Next, I met with a young woman named Tess and her husband, Juan. Juan paced up and down the room nervously, as they were expecting their first child. He showed me his hand. It was red from Tess squeezing it so hard. I let Tess squeeze on my hand for a bit. All the while, I patted her head with a wet towel the nurse had given me. Both the nurse and Juan seemed grateful for my help.

After that, I checked in on an older man. The man sat up in his bed and smiled when I walked in. He put down the American Science magazine he'd been reading.

"Well hello there, young lady!" he told me.

"Hi, my name is Lia and I'm a helpful hands volunteer," I smiled.

The man put his hands behind his head. "I'm Anthony," he said with a slight grimace. "Sorry, sometimes my arthritis gets to me a bit."

"Anything I can do for you?" I asked.

"Can you make me 50 years younger?" he asked.

"Sorry, no," I said with a little shake of my head.

He patted a chair next to his bed. "Then come sit, talk for a bit..."

I did as he asked. After all, I liked talking and sitting.

"You don't mind talking to an old man?" he asked.

"Nah," I said with a little wave of my hand. "I know that older men know stuff!"

He laughed. "Only thing I know is, I wish I knew what I know now when I was younger. I could have done something about it then!"

"What are you in here for, Anthony?"

He pointed to his hip. "Getting a new hip. Went eighty years with the original. They tell me this one will last just as long."

"I hope it doesn't hurt too much," I said.

"Lia, I fought in two wars. This is nothing," He laughed. "Got shot in the buns in Korea!"

"Say what?" I said, trying not to snicker.

"You can laugh, honey, it was pretty dang funny, if you weren't me! Oh, I wasn't running away, a sniper hit me from behind in the behind."

"Good to know," I giggled.

"I got a purple heart for my butt!" he said proudly. "If I can handle being shot in the butt, I can handle a new hip. I was actually hoping for one of those fancy new cybernetic implants."

"Really?" I said.

He bobbed his head. "Yes, ma'am. I'm an engineer by trade so I love all the new technology. Sure, I can't figure out how to lock my phone and keep it from pocket dialing, but I still love it."

"So you met with Doctor Dangerfield?" I asked.

"Yeah, nice lady. She didn't think I qualified. She told me and the other guy there she would like to help, but her techniques are still too new to try on older patients."

"Oh…" I said. "Do you remember the other guy?"

"Nice guy, John something. He farted a lot but pretty much everybody does at our age." He looked at the ceiling then back at me. "Funny thing is, her assistant doctor came to us afterward. She gave us her card and told us she might be able to help us."

"But you didn't take her up on that offer?" I asked.

"Nah, I'm too old to want to be a lab rat!" Anthony said with a grin.

An announcement came over the hospital intercom.

"Doctor Sparks, please report to the basement level."

I knew there was no Doctor Sparks in this hospital. In fact, that happened to be the emergency code for security to show up. Something weird was going on in the basement. I needed to check it out. First of all as Lia, then if needed, as Super Teen.

I looked Anthony in the eyes and took his hand. "I'll be back to see you! I promise!"

He grinned at me. "I'll be counting on it!"

Dear Diary: I've actually found working in the hospital to be very rewarding. I don't say this often but maybe Mom was right! Anthony was such a nice old man. Not only that. But I learned something interesting… Doctor Dangerfield discouraged patients from working with her. And more interesting, Doctor Stone didn't agree with that.

Lab Rats?...

I slipped down to the basement at super speed so I wouldn't be spotted. When I arrived, my mouth dropped open. There, standing in the hallway stood the biggest gray rat I had ever seen. The rat stood so large he took up the entire width of the hall. Two security men stood in front of it, their guns were drawn.

A man in a lab coat stood between the rat and the security people. "Don't shoot Algernon!" the man pleaded. "He's just scared…."

"Okay now this is different," I mumbled.

The big lab rat started forward, pushing the doctor down. The security men opened fire.

"No!" I shouted.

Everything froze in place. "Did I do that?" I said out loud.

"Ah, no!" I heard from behind me. I turned to see Jess

and Tanya standing there. "I did," Tanya said.

"We thought you might need some help!" Jess told me.

"Thanks," I said. "We're like a teen or almost teen girl justice league!"

Tanya walked up to me. "You can pick team names and costumes afterward. First things first." She pointed at the bullets frozen in flight. "You grab the bullets, they're too hot for me. I'll disarm the guards."

"Nah, I got the guards' weapons," Jess said. She waved her hands and the guns vanished from the guard's hands. "I love vanishing things!" Jess said.

Meanwhile, I walked forward and grabbed both the bullets out of the air. I crushed them to dust in my fist. I pointed to the cameras. "What about those?"

Jess grinned. "I've been jamming them with magic."

I walked forward and picked up the giant rat. Its breath reeked of cheese. "I'll put it back in its cage," I carried the rat down the hall. I found a room that was a giant maze. I dropped the rat into the middle of the maze. I worked my way back out. "Now that was weird," I said. "I wonder why the hospital has a giant rat and maze?"

"I'll un-slow time and then Jess can interview the scientist," Tanya said.

"Want me to turn the guards into lab rats?" Jess suggested. "I don't like that they were going to shoot a poor defenseless giant rat!" She pondered what she had said. "I stand by my words."

"Just make the guards go away," I said.

Jess raised her arms. "You mean make them vanish?"

"No, just make them forget and go back to work."

"Right, I knew that," Jess said, flicking her red hair behind her shoulder.

Tanya snapped her fingers and time started moving at regular intervals again.

The guards and the scientist seemed confused. "What

the…" they all said.

Jess waved her hands in front of the guard's eyes. "Return to work. Nothing to see here! Nothing happened here," she ordered.

"Yes, master," they said, as they walked away.

The scientist stood up and straightened out his lab coat. "My gosh, what are you girls?"

"We're the cool teen girl league of super people!" I said. I turned to the other two. "Okay, yeah I'll work on that name."

Jess walked up to the scientist. "You won't remember any of this."

The scientist shrugged. "Of course not. I'm a brilliant but absent-minded kind of guy. Now, what do you wish to know?"

I had to admit that I was a bit envious of Jess's control of her mind control power. I wished I could control mine as well.

"Why the giant rat?" Jess asked the doctor.

"Well funding is always tight, so we're using the same rat to do a growth study while working on treating memory loss. We made an extra smart giant lab rat. He's a nice rat. We just accidentally left the door to his maze unlocked and he got out. Rats are curious creatures. He got scared when the guards showed up. He'd never hurt another creature. Except for a cat, he hates cats."

"So, you'll make sure this never happens again?" I told the doctor.

"I thought you'd erase my memory like the security people?" The doctor answered.

Jess grinned. "Oh I will, but I'll let you remember that."

"Sure," the doctor said.

Jess locked her eyes on the doctor's eyes. "Look into my eyes, you will do whatever I wish. You will forget about all this, except leaving the door unlocked."

"As you wish, master, your wish is my command," he said with a bow. He turned and walked back into the maze room.

I looked at Jess. Jess shrugged. "I might have hit him with too much power."

I put my arms around Jess and Tanya and walked them back towards the elevator.

"A girl could get used to this teamwork!" I told them.

"I'm only available in emergencies," Tanya said, "playing with time is not something that should be taken lightly!"

"I'm only available for things I find fun!" Jess said.

Dear Diary: Okay, I gotta say it was great having other super kids on my side. Not only does that give me people who are also different, but there are some things, heck, probably most things that are easy to solve with teamwork.

The talk...

I waited for Jason outside of Doctor Dangerfield's office and labs. As I sat there checking out social media on my phone, Doctor Gem Stone walked by. She stopped when she saw me.

"You're Lia Strong, correct?" she said.

I looked her in the eyes. "Yes, Doctor, I am." I didn't point out that she had just met me a few hours ago.

Doctor Stone smiled. "Lia, no need to be so formal. After all your mother is senior staff here. She's part of the reason Doctor Dangerfield wanted to come here. Please call me Doctor Gem."

"Thanks, Doctor Gem," I said. I paused for a moment, then asked. "How goes your research?"

Doctor Gem smiled and her face lit up. "You've heard of cutting edge? Well, our technology is laser cutting edge! It's the latest and greatest. We are helping the old and weak feel young and strong, very strong."

"Wow, that's great!" I told her.

Doctor Gem patted me on the shoulder. "My dear girl, we are helping to make the entire human race better. Soon we could have an entire planet of people who are as strong, if not stronger, than Super Teen!"

"So that's good, right?"

Doctor Gem's eyes shot open wide, almost taking up the top half of her head. "My gosh, yes! So so good! They will have the power, yet they'll also have control. They can remove their shoes without knocking out a mall!"

"Ah, I think Super Teen just knocked out a part of the mall," I said defensively, probably more so than I should have.

Doctor Gem looked at me with a tilted head. "Yes, knocking out part of a mall with super stink foot is SO much better!"

"Actually, many of the people that Super Teen put to sleep claimed it was a pleasant experience," I pointed out, unable to stop myself.

"Yes, well their heads were most likely spinning from whatever pheromones Super Teen zapped them with!" Doctor Gem retorted.

Before I could respond, Jason came popping out of the lab. He had an extra kick in his step. Jason must have heard our conversation as he seemed anxious to break it up.

"Ah, hi, Lia and Doctor Gem! It's been a great morning and now I'm ready to walk home." Jason grabbed me by the arm. "Come on Lia, let's get moving."

I didn't budge. Jason pulled back. He knew if I didn't want to move, he couldn't move me. Still, he knew he had to make me move. Jason gave me a friendly nudge. "Come on, ice cream is on me! I'm so anxious to tell you about all I saw in this amazing lab!"

Somehow that brought me back to my senses. I took a deep breath. I took another deep breath. I looked Doctor Gem in her green eyes. "I really look forward to learning more about your amazing technology!"

"I'd love to demo it for you any time!" Doctor Gem told me. She pulled an old pocket watch out of her lab coat pocket. "Look at the time, I have an appointment with a potential patient!"

Doctor Gem walked into her lab. Jason and I started walking home. Jason pretty much rushed me out of the hospital, just in case I was tempted to start up my conversation with Doctor Gem again.

"So, how was your morning?" Jason asked, giving me a little nudge.

"You know, same old, same old," I told him. "Met a few nice people, including this older gentleman named Anthony, who wanted to be a patient of Doctor Dangerfield's. Oh, and of course I had to carry a GIANT

HUMONGOUS lab rat back into his maze!"

"Oh man, you got to meet Algernon!" Jason sighed in a weird mix of sadness and jealousy and awe.

I stopped walking. "Wait, you know about this?"

He nodded. "Yes, of course. Doctor Dangerfield is very open about all her research with us. She says she wants to encourage great young minds like ours to go to college and do amazing things."

"So the good doctor does cyber implants and grows giant rats?" I asked.

"Well yes, she's more interested in the intelligence aspect of it though. She's all about helping people to improve. She's also into robotics," Jason spat his words with excitement. He was talking a million words a minute.

I wiped a bit of spit from my face.

"Oops, sorry," Jason said. "I do get excited sometimes." He paused. "Wait, you met one of our potential patients?"

"Yeah, a nice man named Anthony. He was cool. But Doctor Dangerfield didn't think he was a good fit."

"She said the same thing to the lady we met today," Jason told me.

"Okay, can you get her name and address?" I asked Jason.

"Sure, I think so, but why?" he asked.

"I want to talk to her, to see if Doctor Gem offered her anything," I said. "My gut tells me something is rotten. Now I'm not sure if it's Doctor Gem or Doctor Dangerfield!"

Jason looked at me. "So you've opened up your mind?"

"I'm willing to consider other options."

Jason smiled. "I'll see what I can find." He tapped me on the shoulder. "You know you can use google too!"

I nodded. "Yes, I am aware of that. I just don't have your flair for it. I believe your superpower is being a wiz with computers," I smiled.

"You're flattering me, Lia."

"With the truth, Jason."

He sighed. "I'll see what I can do."

We arrived at our home. "Okay Jason, thanks. When you find out that info, please let me know as soon as possible."

Jason nodded. "I think her last name was Gold... but I'll check."

As I headed into my house, I thought Gold? I wonder if she's related to Brandon.

Strange Visit...

I walked into my house and kicked off my shoes. Funny thing, Shep didn't rush up to meet me. I picked up my shoes and sniffed them. Could they have knocked Shep out from a distance? "No, they weren't THAT bad...."

I moved into the living room. I dropped down on the couch. Sure, I had only spent a half day at the hospital but it had been an eventful half a day. I saw Shep sleeping in the kitchen. Now that struck me as strange. Shep usually got up as soon as he saw me enter the house.

"Man, I didn't think my shoes smelled that bad?" I said out loud.

"Actually I don't believe they are near lethal to mammals," I heard a familiar voice say. "Your father's and my nano-technology is working just great."

I turned to see Hana coming in from the kitchen. I

jumped up. "What the heck are you doing here?"

Hana looked at me. "Your father wanted me to check in on you," Hana said innocently.

I pointed at Shep. "If you hurt my dog!"

Hana shook her head. She turned her head totally around to look at Shep. That creeped me out. She looked at me. "No, he seemed nervous about me being in your home so I used a sonic beam to put him to sleep."

"Why?" I asked.

Hana grinned. "I don't want him to interfere with our testing."

I tilted my head. "Wait, are you checking in or testing me?" I asked, sounding far more confused than I wanted to.

Hana walked towards me. "For me, checking in and testing is the same." Her arms expanded outwards. She grabbed me and lifted me up. "Remember, yesterday you said we could spar!"

"Put me down!" I ordered.

"If you insist!" Hana said. She flung me across the room. I crashed into a wall, leaving a big dent. I rolled down the wall and landed on my feet. Before I could say 'what the heck?' I saw two fists racing towards me. I ducked. The fists each left more dents in the wall.

I looked over my shoulder at the dents. "If I don't rip you to shreds my mom will."

Hana walked towards me slowly. "Don't worry, our construction people will make all repairs."

I rolled my sleeves up. "Let's hope they can put you back together again!" I said. I leaped at her, "Actually let's hope they can't!"

I hit Hana so hard her head popped off. The head flew up, crashed off the ceiling, then hit the floor. Her eyes looked up. Her hands on her now separated body pointed to the new cracks in the ceiling. "Now that is your fault!" she said. Her body walked over, reached down and picked up her head. The head molded itself back to the body.

Hana took a fighting position. "I hope you can do better!"

My initial reaction was to flatten her with a fart, but Shep was behind her and I didn't want to risk hurting (or killing) him. I dropped back into a fighting stance. I waved her forward with my front hand. "Come on, machine, let's see what you have!"

Actually, I felt kind of excited about the chance to be able to really test out my powers. Normally, I have to be extra cautious when dealing with people or animals. But here and now I could let it rip. And boy, did I!

I flashed forward at Hana. I pummeled her with at least a hundred punches in less than ten seconds. Each punch, I felt her body bending and contorting a bit. I pulled back. Hana looked like a beat up trashcan. But I had to give her credit, she stayed on her feet.

I blew on her. She fell to the ground. Just to make sure she stayed there, I thought cold thoughts: ice, ice cream, icebergs. I covered her with a blast of frozen super breath.

My watch beeped. I put it up to my face. Dad's face appeared on the watch face. He smiled. "Wow, that was amazing!"

"Dad, why did you send your Android assistant after me?"

Dad didn't stop grinning. "I wanted to test you and help you let your power out! I knew she couldn't hurt you."

I showed him the house. "Yeah, well our house isn't nearly as indestructible as I am!"

Dad still had that grin on his face. "Repair crew will be there in five. They will also return Hana to me."

"Yeah, I don't think all the king's horses and all the king's men will be able to put Hana together again...," I said. "She won't be rebooting!"

"Don't fret!" Dad said. "I've got Hana 2.0 here!" Behind Dad, I saw another Hana stick her head over his shoulder. She gave me a thumbs up. Gee whenever I think my life can't get any weirder it does.

Dear Diary: my dad sent a super Android out to test me, and by testing me I mean attempting to rip me apart. Luckily for both of us, I'm pretty darn strong and tough. Extra lucky for Dad that his crew was able to put our house back together before mom got home. They worked fast, I give them that. I must admit, I did enjoy cutting loose. I guess Dad knew I would. After all, this wasn't the first time I'd battled a super machine made by Dad's company. I wonder if I should worry about that?

TXT U...

That night after dinner, I sat on the couch. Mom rested next to me pretending to be reading a medical journal, but I knew she would sneak peaks at what I was watching. I planned to veg out and just watch some of my favorite TV shows. I wanted to turn my mind off and relax. That's when I got a text from Jason.

JASON>Got her name, it's Greta Gold

LIA>Great! Thks! Address?

JASON>She's unlisted

LIA>Think she's related to Brandon????

JASON>Want me to ask him?

I had to think about this reply for all of one second.

LIA>I'll txt him

JASON>U sure? U'll risk the wrath of Wendi!

LIA>I'll take my chances

JASON>Good luck.

Mom looked at me. "What's going on?" she asked.

I shrugged. "Just a text from Jason..."

I could tell Mom wanted to pry more. So I gave her just enough information to keep her happy. "Just work stuff!" I smiled.

"I hope you're not asking Jason to be your spy on Doctor Dangerfield!" Mom said. Yeah, Mom read me well.

"No, no," I assured her. "This isn't about Doctor Dangerfield!" I didn't lie.

Okay, I had to be careful with this text to Brandon. I mean, after all, Brandon was the best looking boy in the school. Yeah, he went out with Wendi, proving he wasn't perfect. But outside of that, he seemed pretty darn close. I found him to be smart, handsome and really nice. Plus, he seemed to enjoy being school president. And I know Jason says Brandon makes a great teammate in LAX. But still, he does go out with Wendi. Well, like Grandma Betsy says, "no accounting for taste…"

I wanted to word my text carefully. My phone gave me an alert.

JASON> Don't over think this. Just ask him about his grandma. Tell him it's 4 work

Man, Jason knew me well too.

LIA>I am not over thinking!

JASON> Have you sent it yet?

LIA>Been talking to my mom…

JASON>Sure…sure

Oh man, he really did know me

LIA>Sending it now

LIA>Just want to make sure it's perfect!

JASON> You know I like the guy, but he's not perfect. He farts like everybody else!

JASON>Okay, actually I've never heard him fart

JASON>Oh NM

JASON>C U 2morrow

My my, did I detect a bit of jealousy from Jason? Jason is so darn nice though. Even when he's jealous, he still can't put a guy down. I smiled. But I got off track.

I sent this text: LIA STRONG>Hey Brandon, this is Lia, just wondering if your grandma's name is Greta?

But I didn't expect an immediate reply. My eyes popped open when I received a sudden alert from my phone. From the sound, I knew it wasn't Jason. Looking down I saw…

BRANDON GOLD>Hey Lia, yes as a matter of fact Grams is named Greta. Why?

Oh how cute! He called his grandma, Grams. Could that Brandon get any more adorable?

LIA STRONG> She left her reading glasses at the hospital. I'd like to return them to her. After all, she is such a sweet woman.

BRANDON GOLD>Yeah, Grams is the best! But yes,

she's forgetful. I can pick up the glasses from u and bring them to her!

OMG, Brandon offered to come to my house! That would be great. I took a breath. Except of course for the fact that I didn't really have any glasses to return, and I needed to talk to Grandma Gold. I pressed back the urge to say, sure.

LIA STRONG> That's so nice of u but I better do this myself. It's my job

BRANDON GOLD>Ok that's great!

LIA STRONG>Can I have her address?

BRANDON GOLD>Doesn't the hospital have it?

Oh, that was a good point. Brandon wasn't just a handsome face. Think, Lia, think. Come on, brain.

LIA STRONG>Yes of course they do. But silly me, I was so excited about my first day, I misplaced it. I don't want to look bad. Sorry…. ☹

BRANDON GOLD>No, I get it. She lives at 72 Creek Street

LIA STRONG>Thanks Brandon, ur great. Please don't tell anybody

BRANDON GOLD>I think most people know I'm great

What the?

BRANDON GOLD>LOL ☺

So I had it.

I texted Jason.

LIA> I got it. 72 Creek Street

JASON> Great

LIA> We can visit her before work tomorrow…Creek Street is on the way 2 the hospital.

JASON>Sure

LIA>Oh by any chance do you have an extra pair of reading glasses?

JASON>I will c what I cn do!

Dear Diary: How did kids talk before texting? I mean yeah, they probably used the phone and talked in person but texting is so fast and fun.

Morning has broken...

I got up, grabbed a quick breakfast and left mom a note saying because it was such a nice day, Jason and I had decided to walk to the hospital. I knew she'd suspect something was up, but she wouldn't be able to ask me about it until after she got off her shift. By then, the deed would have been done. Nothing to be done about it after that, I don't think even Tanya can reverse time.

Heading out my door, I noticed none other than Wendi pacing up and down in front of my house. I swear I could see steam coming out of her ears. My first instinct was to super speed by her. But no, I couldn't do that. This was a real-world problem and I needed to deal with in a real way. My second instinct was to just knock her out. One fart in her general direction and she'd be toast for the day. But nope, as good as that might have felt and as tempting as it may have been, I needed to face Wendi. Heck, I had done nothing wrong.

I took a deep breath as I opened the door. Wendi shot across the yard towards me. Her face growing redder and her eyes growing smaller with each step. "Strong, what are you doing texting Brandon?" she shouted.

I walked towards her slowly, like I'd approach a very dangerous cobra.

"Ah, Wendi..." I said.

Wendy got in my face, so close that I could smell her breath. Of course, it smelled pleasant. "Don't oh hi me! I invented the innocent, oh hi!"

I put up a hand. "Wendi, I just texted Brandon about his Grandma Greta..."

"Wait. What? Who? Why?"

I took a step back. "Wendi, we had some contact with Grandma Greta at the hospital. She left her reading glasses there. Jason and I were going to return them to her in person. She seemed like such a sweet lady."

Wendi put a finger in my face. She really wanted me to get upset and lose my calm. "Of course she's sweet! She's related to Brandon. The guy is as sweet as they come."

I fought back the urge to say, "yeah what the heck does he see in you?" Wendi dropped back, slouched and sighed. "Sometimes I think he's even too sweet for me..." She took a breath. She looked up at me. "I mean I've never even seen him in a bad mood or complain. He got a 90 on a test once, and told me how it was his fault for not working harder."

"Yeah, I can see where that could be annoying," I said, stopping myself from rolling my eyes.

Wendi put a hand on my shoulder. She looked me in the eyes. "Good, I'm glad. Most people think it must be great having a perfect boyfriend. But I tell you, it's a lot of pressure. I guess that's why I get so defensive I'm always afraid he'll see I'm not good enough for him and leave me."

I'd never seen this vulnerable side to Wendi before. I kind of liked it. I put my hand on her shoulder. "I assure you, Wendi, the texts were purely business. His grandma seems like a nice lady who Jason and I want to help out. That's it. I'm sure Brandon won't break up with you." I took a step back and pointed at her. "Look at you, you're pretty, you're smart, you're a great LAX player! You're pretty perfect yourself." Okay, my stomach churned with nausea just a little, saying those last words.

Wendi looked at me. "I've got nothing to worry about?"

I shook my head. "Nope," I told her. Then added. "Well, except maybe global warming. I think we should all be worried about that."

Wendi laughed. "That's what I like about you Lia, you're funny in your own simple way!"

"Gee thanks…" I said.

She patted me on the shoulder. "I don't know WHAT I was thinking! No way Brandon would ever leave me for anybody. And certainly not you! Woah, sorry to bother you, girl. Thanks for returning Grandma's glasses."

Wendi turned and walked away. I fought back the huge urge I had to burn her in the butt with my heat ray vision. I gave myself a pat on the back. Not only for not burning Wendi's butt, instead, for solving a real-world problem without using any superpowers.

I saw Jason walking towards me. He had a pair of glasses in his hands. Yep, Jason always comes through. "What was that all about?"

"Ah, Wendi was jealous that I was texting Brandon. She thought he might leave her for me."

Jason laughed. "Yeah like that would happen!"

Okay, now I had to fight the temptation to burn Jason in the butt.

He straightened himself up. "Sorry, didn't mean to laugh. I mean you are way nice, but Wendi is just…" he sighed.

I gave him a nudge. "Come on, let's go see Grandma Greta!"

Dear Diary: I did see another side of Wendi. I guess even she has fears about not being good enough. Who would have thought that!. It still doesn't give her permission to brag about herself over the rest of us. But at least, now I sort of see where she's coming from.

Man, I still would have loved burning her in the butt with heat vision.

GGG...

We found Grandma Greta outside, pulling weeds from a garden in front of her home. The house even had a lovely white picket fence surrounding the yard. Jason and I unlatched the gate and walked up to Grandma Greta. She was focused so intently on her weeding; she didn't even notice us.

I gave a polite cough.

Grandma Greta looked up at us. "Oh, hello kids, are you selling cookies?"

"No ma'am, I'm Lia Strong and this is Jason Michaels! We volunteer at the hospital."

Greta smiled. "Oh right. Your mom is the doctor and your dad is the sheriff and your mom is a judge!"

"Actually my dad is police captain," Jason said.

Greta grinned. "Yes, sorry my memory is not what it was. That's why I went to see that nice Doctor Strange."

"Actually it's Doctor Dangerfield," Jason corrected.

Greta popped herself in the forehead. "Like I said, my mind isn't as sharp as it used to be…too bad Doctor Strange Dangerfield told me her treatment wasn't ready yet." She pointed to her brain and spun her finger around. "Oh well, at least I am happy. So why you kids here?"

I nudged Jason. He took the glasses out of his back pocket. "I believe you left your reading glasses at the hospital," He showed the glasses to her.

Greta leaned forward and squinted. She stood up. She walked towards us. Shaking her head, she said, "Silly me I didn't even remember I used reading glasses!" She took the glasses from Jason. She put them on her head. They fell off. "Silly me again!" she said.

I bent down and picked up the glasses. "You know, I bet silly Jason made a mistake and these weren't your glasses after all!" I said.

I handed the glasses to Jason. "Yes, silly me!" Jason said.

Greta chuckled. "Well, it was nice of you sweet kids anyhow!" She scratched her head. "Hey, do you young ones know my grandson, Brandon?"

"Yes, ma'am, he and I play LAX together," Jason said.

"I'm on the girl's LAX team so I know him too!" I said quickly.

"Oh, I didn't know Brandon played LAX I thought he only played Lacrosse, basketball, and football."

"LAX is what we call lacrosse ma'am," Jason said.

"You kids today with LAX and LOL and hashtag and inyourfacebook! I can't keep up!" She paused. "My grandson, Brandon is quite the handsome young man. Isn't he?" she beamed.

"I guess…" Jason shrugged.

"Oh, I hadn't noticed," I said shyly.

Her eyes popped open. "Oh really?"

"Yeah, oh really?" Jason said cynically.

Greta nodded. "Probably for the better, Brandon seems taken with that lovely Wendi girl!"

"Not to change the subject ma'am, but I was wondering if Doctor Stone talked to you after Doctor Dangerfield did?"

"You mean the lady with the pretty green eyes?" Greta asked.

"Yes ma'am…."

Greta's eyes lit up. "Actually yes, she did. She said she would like to talk to me about another project she was working on. She thought I'd be perfect for it. She wants to meet with me tomorrow."

"At the hospital?" Jason asked.

"Nope," Greta said. "She told me by doing it outside of the hospital she can do it much cheaper. I will get the details tomorrow."

"Ah, by any chance do have the address she wanted to meet you at?" I asked.

"Of course!" Greta said. "She wrote it down for me."

"Can I have it?" I asked, probably with more excitement than I needed to.

"Ah, why is that?" Grandma Greta asked.

"We just need it for official purposes," Jason said, using his most adult voice.

"I have her card inside on my stand by the door. I'll be right back!" Grandma turned and headed towards her door.

"Nice save there!" I told Jason.

"Hey, I may not be as good looking as that Brandon guy you 'never' notice, but I still have my uses," he grinned. "So what's the plan once we have the address?" he asked curiously.

"We go check out the place after work and see what we can find," I replied.

"I pretty much thought you were going to say that," He laughed.

"You know me well."

"Maybe too well," Jason added.

We waited a few minutes. Then finally Grandma Greta came out of the door, smiling and holding a card. She walked over and handed it to me. I read the card: 1 LOLIPOP LANE.

"Why does that name sound so familiar?" I thought out loud.

"It's the old animal hospital," Jason told me. Man, Jason did know everything.

"I also called that nice Doctor Gem and told her how great it was for her to send some students over to check up on me," Greta said with a smile.

I took a step back. "And what did she say?"

Greta shrugged. "I don't know. I just got her machine. You know doctors always too busy to talk to actual people."

All right, now this changed our schedule a bit. "Thanks, Grandma Greta," I said. "We'd better get to the hospital now!"

Once we got down the street, Jason turned to me. "We're not going to the hospital. Are we?"

"Nope..." I said. "I need to get to the bottom of this ASAP. Now that Doctor Stone has been warned, we have to act fast."

"We could lose our jobs at the hospital," Jason pointed out.

I increased my pace. "We're volunteers; we make our own hours."

"Good point!"

Dear Diary: I felt a little bad tricking Grandma Greta like that, but it had to be done to help get to the bottom of this. Plus, I did lie when I said I've never noticed Brandon. I notice him the minute he walks into a room. Sometimes I have to force myself to take my eyes off him. But I can't help the way I feel. He's so good looking!

Angry Birds...

"What are we going to do when we get to Lollipop Lane?" Jason asked me.

I hadn't really considered that very carefully. I pretty much just wanted to see what we could find, to help prove that Doctor Stone or maybe even Doctor Dangerfield was behind these recent crazy cybernetic people (and animals). Once I got there I'd figure out a way to stop it.

"We're going to see what we can see!" I said, making a fist.

"Oh, in other words, you don't really have a plan..." He sighed.

I couldn't argue with that statement.

We made it to Lollipop lane in record time. The lane was just a long road that led to one building, the old animal hospital. The place had to be 100 years old so they shut it down last year and opened a sparkling new facility on the other side of town. The new place has a lot of windows and green area, even Shep likes to go there. This old building, not so much. It was grey and dingy. It looked like the roof was made of tin foil.

"Okay, Jason be on the lookout for anything strange!"

Jason pointed up at a flock of birds coming towards us. "Like those pigeons..."

I looked up at them. "They look like normal birds."

Jason shook his head. "Nope, they aren't flying like normal pigeons!"

I have no idea how Jason knew this. But I knew enough to trust him. Using super-vision, I zoomed in on the birds carefully. They each had a small cybernetic disk on their heads. "Yep, you are right. This is strange."

The birds flew past us. They pooped over us.

"Incoming poop!" I shouted.

Jason and I dodged the gross poop. It splattered on the ground and burned holes wherever it landed.

"Acid poop!" Jason gasped.

"Man, that is so wrong and so nasty!" I said.

I realized this was just too dangerous for Jason. I may be super and able to take a lot of damage, but Jason is just a regular guy. He's smart and great and all that, but he's not built to take on poop acid. Actually, I wasn't sure I was either. But I didn't have much choice.

I pointed in the opposite direction. "Jason, run! Get to the hospital and tell Mom what I'm doing and what's going on!"

"You could text her…or dare I say it, call her…." Jason suggested.

"No, I don't want to give her a chance to tell me not to do this," I said.

"Yes, of course. Why bring common sense into this when we are facing ACID POOPING PIGEONS!!" He pointed up at the birds. "They're turning around and getting ready for another run at us…"

"So get out of here!" I yelled at him. "Go! I'll rush the building. They'll have to follow me!"

Jason stood there, his eyes locked eyes with mine.

"Please do what I ask…." I said.

Jason frowned, clearly worried about the situation, and for a moment he didn't budge.

Then he nodded and took off. "I'm bringing back help!"

Acid poop started raining down on me. Most of it missed, leaving sizzling holes in the ground. "Who thinks of this stuff!" I said. "MACS activate my uniform!" I shouted.

"No need to shout, Ms. Lia," MACS told me. "Do you wish me to alert your father to this situation? I am sure he would want to help."

"No…not yet…" I answered.

"Very well, ma'am."

"Don't call me ma'am!"

"Yes, Lia, ma'am!"

I leaped up into the air towards the ugly old animal hospital. As I jumped, a couple pieces of acid poop (man I never thought I'd say that) hit my shoulder. It sizzled my suit and then burned through to my skin. It hurt, but not nearly as much as I thought acid on me should hurt. Still, it bothered me enough to upset my leap.

I landed on my face, about halfway to the building.

"I am repairing your suit now!" MACS told me. 'The acid is extremely powerful, but I believe I can counteract it. After all, acid and pigeons are old school, and I am very new school!"

I pushed myself up off the ground. I turned and looked up to see another barrage of white poop acid falling towards me. Out of pure reflex, I inhaled quickly, then exhaled -- hard. My breath shot the acid back up at the pigeons who were pooping on me. Half of them began to caw and flap their wings wildly after being splattered by their own acid. A few dropped to the ground. I felt bad doing that to the birds, but I had no choice. The remaining birds regrouped. They dive-bombed towards me.

"Okay, I've made the angry birds even angrier..."

"Lia, this may be a good time to tell you that your dad designed your suit with a secret airtight pocket."

I looked at the birds closing in on me. "Thanks, MACS! Nice to know I have a pocket and all, but it's not that helpful just now!"

"Actually, your dad put a piece of condensed garlic in that pocket," MACS continued.

"Now that's something worth knowing about!" I told MACS. A pocket on my suit popped open. I reached in and grabbed a small piece of something that felt like a nut. I tossed it into my mouth. It tasted like garlic. Luckily for me, I like garlic. I looked up at the birds. I opened my mouth.

The flock of birds dropped from the sky.

"My, that packs a punch!" I said. "If I talk to anybody I'll drop them in their tracks!"

"Your father calculated the garlic dose so it would wear off in three minutes," MACS told me.

"Well let's hope that if I need extra super bad breath, it will be in the next three minutes!" I leaped towards the building.

Dear Diary: Jason really is a good friend. He always has the best ideas and my best interests at heart. That's why I couldn't risk him getting hurt in this fight. It was my battle. And as great as Jason is, he is just a normal guy. A super smart and loyal normal guy, but still just a guy. As for my dad, I love the way his strange brain works!

Not Monkeying Around...

I peered into one of the windows of the old animal hospital. I saw a bunch of big and small cages along the wall. A couple of large freezers sat in each corner. The middle of the room had a long lab table with all sorts of specialized looking instruments and needles on it. Looking closer, I saw the cages had bunnies and mice in them.

I raced around to the front. There, stood a big metal door with a red light above it. I figured the door must have had an alarm system. I fought back the urge to kick it down. Instead, I moved to the side of the door. I took a few steps back. I took a deep breath. I rushed at the wall smashing a 'me' sized hole in the wall. I turned and looked at the hole. It reminded me of something you'd see in a cartoon.

Three monkeys in lab coats came rushing in from a back room. They looked adorable. They pointed long rods at me. Okay, not so adorable. They squeezed the handles on the rods. Beams of electricity shot into me. I crackled and surged. I shook it off. I believe my behind started smoking a bit.

The three monkeys looked amazed that their shocks didn't stop me. Two of the monkeys started jumping up and down in fits. The third stayed calm. He or she turned to the other two. "The boss said she was strong…"

One of the other monkeys pointed at me. "But not this strong!"

The third nodded. "Yeah, man, we hit her with everything and all it seemed to do was tickle her!"

"It did kind of tickle a little," I told them.

The two monkeys tossed down their weapons. They threw off their lab coats. "Man, I don't need this kind of stress!" one of the monkeys said.

"Me neither," the other monkey said, rubbing his

stomach. "I think I have an ulcer now."

"But we have a job to do!" the lead monkey protested.

The other two shook their heads. "She literally pays us in peanuts and bananas."

"But she does pay us!"

The other two each rolled their eyes. I found it to be both adorable and strange.

"But we're cute monkeys, people would feed us anyhow!" one monkey objected.

"Yeah and without all this stress. Plus, I don't like injecting bunnies and thinking so much. I miss the days of just eating, sleeping, swinging and throwing poop at people!" the other monkey lamented.

"We can still do all those things!" the lead monkey said. He pointed to his brain. "Only with more intelligence. Maybe we can make our poop splatter off walls and hit more people?"

The other two looked at each other. "You make a compelling point!" one said. "But you still can't beat the fact that ignorance truly is bliss!"

"Yeah, plus then we wouldn't have to deal with over-powered teens who run through walls and clobber malls with foot odor."

I cleared my throat. "Guys, you know I can hear you, right?"

"Yeah, but you can't remove your own cyber implants!" the lead monkey said, arms crossed.

The two other monkeys looked at each other. They smiled. They each reached up and pulled the other monkey's implant off. They each howled for a moment. They stopped. They contently hopped away.

The lead monkey shook his head. "So hard to get good help these days..." He turned to me. "Girl, can you believe those two?"

I walked towards him and pounded my fist into my hand. The sound forced him to stagger back. "Looks like it's just you versus me now. I like those odds…."

The monkey looked at me. "Yes, I understand that you would." He rolled up his lab coat sleeve, exposing a watch. "So let me improve those odds!" He pushed a button on this watch. A cage in the middle of the room popped up. Out jumped two kangaroos.

"These guys aren't as smart as my fellow monkeys. Which means they will follow orders better!" He pointed at me. "Get her Skippy and Dundee!"

The two kangaroos who were charming BTW leap at me. They each kicked me in the head. Okay, that wasn't very charming. I didn't fall. But the two kangaroos landed on their feet and started pummeling me with rapid punches. Their punches didn't really hurt. But this had to stop as I couldn't concentrate on the lead lab monkey.

"Guys, I don't want to hurt you!" I told the kangaroos.

They continued to mindlessly pound me with punches and kicks. Since I didn't want to hit back, I just let them punch and kick me. I figured these animals may have been pumped up. But they were still flesh and blood and would punch themselves out.

After around two minutes, the punch speed slowed down. After about three minutes the punches were pretty much just weak attempts. By the fourth minute, the two kangaroos just stood there panting for air. I knocked them each over with a little puff of my breath. "Enjoy your sleep!" I told them as I walked by.

I concentrated on the lab monkey. "You ready to give up now?" I asked.

He nodded and held up his hands. "Yeah, I'm smart enough to know when I can't win!"

I walked forward. "Great! Glad to see you are a smart monkey."

He waited for me to come towards him. There was something about his grin I didn't like. Just as I got right in front of him, he pushed another button on his watch. A trap door underneath me opened up. I started to plummet downwards. I landed on my feet in a small metal room. I've been in bigger closets. Yeah, this monkey was really making me mad. The room went dark with a clank. I assumed that meant the trap door had closed over me. I bent down and leaped upward extending my arm. I crashed through the trap door.

I grabbed the surprised monkey and lifted him off the ground. "Okay, buddy! You asked for it!" I said, making a fist.

"Look please don't hit me. I'm just a poor defenseless little monkey!"

"One that has electrocuted me, sent kangaroos after me and tried to trap me in a metal cage!" I pointed out.

He shrugged. "You must give me credit for being persistent... I also sent the pooping birds..."

"Good point," I told him. I dropped him back to the ground.

"Phew thanks!" he grinned.

"MACS! Deactivate the under arm shielding in my uniform!" I ordered.

"But Miss Lia, without that... you're.... Oh right I get it!"

The monkey waved his arms frantically. "Wait, wait! Stop, stop! What's going on?"

I aimed my armpit at the chump monkey. "He just basically deactivated my deodorant," I told him.

The monkey fell over holding his throat. He was stiff as a board.

"I hope you have nightmares!" I told him.

Dear Diary: I learned I do have a bit of a nasty side when I get angry. But man, that monkey deserved that.

With Friends Like These...

With the monkeys and kangaroos out of the way or out cold on the ground, I started looking the place over. I now knew Doctor Stone was at least partially behind this. After all, she did give Greta this address. But had Doctor Stone acted alone or was she ordered to do this by Doctor Dangerfield? After all, Stone did work for Dangerfield.

Searching through one of the draws of the lab table, I found a notebook. I opened it and read the words. It was handwritten...

I can't believe those jerks at the hospital and at the University and everywhere else are so in love with Donna Dangerfield. Yeah, sure she was my mentor in med school, and the first person to give me a job, but she's never thought big enough. She's always taken the safe and cautious road. We could have been so much further ahead with our cybernetics. We could have had our devices all over the world by now. We could have made people and animals more intelligent and more powerful. But no, she couldn't see it. She thought we needed more fail-safes. More ways to protect our patients. She didn't see that by giving them more power, it would give us the power to control them. To make the world in our image. A place where science and justice could thrive.

So I did my own research on the side. Everything was progressing nicely but now my mentor comes to my hospital and takes over the lead on my program!! I can't let her slow me down!

Yikes! That seemed scary! I had to face facts. Wendi's aunt wasn't an evil scientist. The evil scientist was Doctor Stone.

"Girl, don't you know it's impolite to read somebody else's diary?" the now familiar voice of Doctor Stone said to me.

I turned to see Doctor Stone standing there, flanked

by Lori and Marie. Marie looked at me. "Sorry about this Super Teen, but Doctor Gem is making us do this!"

"Making you do what?" I asked.

Lori smiled. She stomped her foot on the ground, sending a shock through the floor. The floor actually shifted like a wave in the water coming at me. The force knocked me down. Lori leaped across the room on top of me. She drew back her fists. "I don't want to do this but it feels so great!"

Lori fired a punch at my head. I darted my head to the side. The punch left a huge hole in the floor.

"Careful!" Doctor Stone shouted. "You super brats are ruining my lab! I know it's not much, but it's all I could afford!"

Lori turned to look at her. "Ah, sorry…."

I lifted my leg up and flipped Lori off me.

I jumped back to my feet.

I heard Doctor Stone tell Marie. "Get into this fight!"

Marie lowered her head. "Super Teen, you have to stop." She pointed at the disks on her temple. "These things have enhanced my brain so much I can see sense and change the structure of things…."

"Which means?"

Marie touched an old lab table. The table turned to gold.

"What the?"

Marie shrugged. "When Doctor Stone did this to me, I was thinking man, I could use some money for college. Then poof. My touch turns things to gold…" She paused. "Please don't make me touch you. I'm not sure I can reverse it. Just give up."

"You know I'm pretty fast. I can be hard to touch," I told her.

"I don't have to touch, touch you," Marie said.

"Now what exactly does THAT mean?" I asked.

A couple of flies flew past Marie. She blew a little puff

of breath on them. The flies fell to the ground and turned to solid gold.

Lori stood up behind me and locked me in a bear hug. Lori's grip was hard but I knew I could break it. "Good, I hate flies!" Lori laughed.

Marie walked towards me slowly. I knew she didn't want to hurt me, but somehow Doctor Stone had control of her and Lori. I had to time this right or I could end up golden and not in a good way. I didn't know if Marie's power would work on me but I had to assume it would. I had no interest in being a gold statue.

I grabbed Lori's arm and threw her over my shoulder into Marie. When the two made contact, Lori turned into a solid gold statue that pinned Marie to the ground.

"Oh no!" Marie cried. "This is bad! Our team really needs Lori!"

I ran up to Marie. "Don't worry. If you can see the structure of things like you say, I know you can reverse this!" I bent down and touched her gently on the shoulder.

Marie smiled at me. She took my hand. Much to my relief, I didn't turn to gold. "Thanks, Super Teen! Sorry I tried to turn you into gold! It was like I was in a dream. Luckily I seem to be me again."

"Good!" I said. I took another chance. I lifted the golden Lori off Marie. I pointed at the statue. "You turn her back while I deal with her!" I stared angrily at Doctor Gem.

Gem screamed at Marie, "I made you! Now I want you to make her into gold!"

Marie shook her head. "Sorry lady, no can do...."

Gem grit her teeth. "Fine, I'll do this myself!"

Gem squeezed her fists together and grunted. It looked like she had a bad case of constipation. Suddenly Gem started to grow and grow and grow. She crashed through the ceiling of the building, sending roofing material spiraling to the ground. I leaped back and shielded Marie and Lori.

"Thanks," Marie said.

Doctor Gem Stone now towered over us. Oh man. This was bad.

I turned to Marie. "I know you can undo what you did to Lori!"

Marie trembled. "You sure?"

I put my hands on her shoulders, "Yes, I am. Look, you broke Doctor Crazy Ladies' control on you. Now you're touching me and I didn't turn to gold. You can turn Lori back!"

"How do you know that? You don't even know me!"

Oh right, I was still in my suit. "MACS blink off the mask...." I ordered.

"But Ms. Lia, then she will know who you are!" MACS said in my head.

"Exactly...." I said.

Maria looked at me and smiled. "I thought your voice was familiar! I told Lori you sounded like Lia and she said that I was crazy; either that or had been sniffing my socks for too long!" She gave me a quick hug. "I knew I was right!"

I looked at her. "And I know you can fix this!"

Marie nodded. "I can do it! I can do it!"

"Great! While you're doing that, I'll find a way to stop a super-powered cybernetic giant mad scientist!"

"Be careful! She put those cybernetic disks behind her neck and all the way down her back!"

Dear Diary: I was so glad I was able to snap Marie out of being mind controlled, by showing her I trusted her. I knew the power of kindness would come through. Yeah, it's corny but it's true.

101

The Not So Good Doctor...

Doctor Gem bent down, her hand engulfed me. She lifted me off the ground. She stomped over the building into the street. Man, it seems like I always end up fighting giants in the street. I guess it's my thing, my niche. Problem was, last time I fought something this big it was a non-living robot that I beat by throwing out into space. I couldn't do that to Doctor Gem. After all, she was a living breathing person.

"So you're Doctor Strong's little brat, Lia!" she cackled.

"I am her daughter, yes," I said.

"I'm activating your mask again!" MACS told me.

"Sweet outfit!" she said.

"Thanks!"

"Hey, how did your clothing grow with you?" I asked. Yeah, I probably should have been worrying about other things at that moment, but I was curious.

"I stole some of the technology from BM Science!" Doctor Gem said. She glared down at me. "Your mom helped bring Dangerfield here!"

Doctor Gem squeezed me harder. I pushed back with my arms, trying to squeeze out, but being a super cybernetic giant person she squeezed with an amazing amount of force. Since I'm also a living breathing person, I wasn't sure how long I could keep this up.

"Put the girl down or you are fired!" I heard from below.

Looking down, I saw Jason had led Mom, Jess, and Tanya here.

"I order you to put her down!" Jess said, in her commanding hypnotic voice.

Doctor Gem smiled. "Sorry kid, my many cybernetic

implants make my mind very strong!"

Tanya smirked. "You forced me to use my time powers on you!"

Doctor Gem laughed. She popped her foot out of her shoe. She waved her foot over my mom and friends.

Tanya's eyes rolled to the back of her head. "Man, I really have to learn not to tell the bad guys what I'm about to do…" Tanya gasped with her last breath.

They all fell to the ground.

"You're not the only one with a foot odor problem!"

"It's not a problem!" I said defensively. "My feet sweat. I'm human, just superhuman."

Doctor Gem looked down her now giant nose at me. "Okay, now can we get to our battle? Though so far, there hasn't been much of a fight."

I looked up at her. "Look Doctor Gem, I don't think you've actually really hurt anybody. If you give up now I'm sure they will go easy on you…."

Doctor Gem squeezed me. "So now you are a super lawyer?"

"No, I'm just saying, nothing you've done can't be undone. In fact, I think I stopped all the robberies your controlled people attempted."

She glared at me. "Thank you very much BTW. Do you have any idea how much this research costs? I was able to siphon budget money from the hospital as I'm also a computer genius. But I needed some quick cash and you got in the way."

I shrugged. "I'm a hero. It's what I do." I accented my words with action. I zapped her hand with heat vision.

She screamed and loosened her grip. I dropped slowly to the ground. I pointed up at her. "We can do this the easy way or the hard way!"

Doctor Stone lifted a foot and tried to stomp me. I caught her foot over my head. "Figures you'd pick the hard way!"

I leaped upwards forcing her foot to go flying backward. Doctor Stone crashed to the ground with a huge thud. In the background, I heard police sirens.

"Your father has alerted the police and also sent BMS security copters!" MACS texted me in my mind, which was kind of freaky. But when you're fighting a fifty-foot mad scientist, you get used to freaky really fast.

Doctor Stone rolled over on her stomach. She started to push herself up. I blasted her in the butt with heat vision. I got a kick out of that.

The not so good doctor pushed to her feet. She turned and started blowing on her now smoking buns.

"Nice to see you have hot buns!" I told her.

Doctor Stone pointed at me. "You really have to work on your banter!"

I put my hands on my hips. "Yeah, people keep telling me that. It's hard being witty under pressure."

"You want pressure! I'll show you pressure!"

Doctor Stone bent down then leaped at me. She landed on me with a decided thud! Now I found myself squished by those same giant buns I had just burned. She twisted her butt, trying to ground me into the ground. "Can you tell I do a lot of Pilates!" she laughed. She bounced up and down on me. "Man, I so wish I could fart now." She grinned. "Ah, here it comes…"

She let out the nastiest fart. PPPPPFFFFFFFFRRRRRAPPP!

She laughed. "Wow, all those years of grad school and med school and I still find a fart to be hilarious!"

It did stink like about a million skunks who had eaten stinking cheese and rolled in garbage for a week. Yet it didn't knock me out, though I kind of wish it did. Still, I went limp. My hope being, she'd get her big butt off me.

Doctor Stone stood up. She laughed. "Ha! Not so tough now are you?"

I jumped up into the air, spun around and gave her a

punch to the jaw! The punch sent her reeling backward. I dropped back to the ground.

"Listen, Doc, I don't want to hurt you!" I said.

The police sirens drew closer.

The doctor shook her head. "Fine. If I can't finish you off I'll deal with the police first."

I ran past her at super speed. I jumped up and hovered above her. "Doc, stop! You're a doctor, you heal people, not hurt people…" I told her.

She paused. "Yes, that's true, but sometimes you have to hurt a few people to help a world of people. I know some people will think I'm jealous of Doctor Dangerfield because she's so smart and so pretty and so good at sports…."

I nodded. "I can relate…"

Doctor Stone went on, "But that's not the case. My research was at least as good as hers if not better. But she was the big famous doctor, so she got all the big bucks and the top job. I should be her boss!"

"Ah, wasn't she your teacher?" I asked.

Doctor Stone smiled. "Yes, of course, but even a silly kid like you must have heard the saying, the student surpasses the teacher."

I nodded.

Doctor Stone rambled on. "So now I'm like way smarter. And she won't listen to me. She wants to go slow with our research. I wanted to go fast. Look what I've accomplished…."

"Yep, you turned yourself into a giant cybernetic mad scientist!"

She shook a finger at me. "No! No! No! Not a mad scientist, an angry one. She got the breaks just because she's prettier and better with people than I am!"

Doctor Stone swatted at me like a fly. I dodged it. She swatted me again and this time she hit me, knocking me to the ground. Now that hurt. I pushed myself up off the ground. I spit dirt out of my mouth. "Oh gross."

I heard a familiar voice behind me. "Hey, Doc, crazy lady!" Lori shouted. "Stop now, or else you'll force me to stop you!"

Doctor Stone did stop for a moment. She turned to Lori and laughed. "Ha, your cybernetics are good but not nearly enough to stop me."

Lori smiled. "Yeah, I was kind of hoping you'd say that." Lori turned to Marie. "You ready teammate."

Marie nodded. "I'm ready…."

Lori picked Marie up over her head. Lori flung Marie, arms extended out, at Doctor Stone. Marie flew through the air and touched Doctor Stone on her knee. Marie started to fall. I jumped over and caught Marie before she hit the ground.

Doctor Stone looked down at her knee. It had turned golden.

"How dare you!" she shouted. "I made you special!"

"I didn't ask for this," Marie told her. "You told Lori and I these were dummy test devices!"

"Yeah. I tested them on two dummies…." Stone smirked.

Marie pointed to Stone's knee. "Who's the dummy now?"

Doctor Stone watched in horror as the gold slowly started to creep up her leg. She lifted up her still non-golden leg. "I'm taking you down with me!"

I thought cold freezing thoughts: running outside in the winter without shoes and coat, eating ice, jumping in an ice bath. I exhaled super cold breath at Doctor Stone. Her leg froze above us. In fact, the upper half of her body froze and turned golden at the same time. The golden, frozen statue started to tip over towards Oscar Organa and his film crew, who must have just arrived on the spot.

I flew up behind the falling statue and caught it. I guided it down slowly to a safe open spot.

Chief Michaels and my father rushed up to me. "Are

106

you okay Super Teen?" my father asked.

"I'm fine sir..."

Chief Michaels looked at the frozen golden statue that was a scientist. "Man, I'm getting too old for this job!"

Mom, Jess, Tanya, and Jason had all snapped out of their foot odor-induced state. Dad and Mom, along with Chief Michaels, stood there trying to decide what to do with a giant golden statue.

Oscar Oranga walked up to me and flashed his mic in my face. "So, Super Teen, can you turn people into gold?"

I didn't know how to answer that. I certainly didn't want the world to know that Marie could do this and that she and Lori were cybernetic. But I didn't need the world extra scared of me either.

Doctor Dangerfield stepped forward and smiled. "Hi, I'm Doctor Donna Dangerfield I was one of Doctor Stones' bosses. Doctor Stone turned to gold as a side effect of using too many cybernetic improvement disks. These things are only in their early stages. I'm afraid this was an unfortunate side effect. We will find a way to cure her."

Jess walked up to Oscar and his crew. "*Now get out of here!*" Jess said in her command voice.

Oscar and his crew bowed, packed up their stuff and walked away.

"And cluck like chickens!" Jess ordered.

Oscar and his crew started clucking.

"Thanks, Jess," I said.

Jess gave me a nod. "I love doing that!"

I heard Mom, Dad, and the chief still pondering what to do. "We can't keep her like this? Can we?" Chief Michaels said. "I mean, she broke the law and has to pay for her crimes but this seems unfair..."

I huddled next to my super teen team of Jess, Tanya, Lori, Marie, and Jason. "Okay we need a way to turn her back to a regular human," I said.

Jason looked us all over. "Now let me get this straight, Jess can control minds and do some magic, Tanya can control time, Lori is cybernetic muscle and Marie cybernetic brain, which lets her change the structure of things."

They all nodded.

Jess looked at the statue. "I could just vanish her!" she suggested.

"Ah, let's go for something that doesn't involve vanishing," I said.

"I've always wanted to turn somebody into a toad," Jess offered.

"Still looking for other options," I laughed.

"I got it, Tanya rewinds her in time to the moment before she turned into a super cybernetic mad scientist. Jess makes everybody else believe that this was a natural occurrence," Jason said.

"Now that could work," I nodded thoughtfully.

"I've never reset somebody in time before," Tanya admitted, a little concerned.

I put my arm around her. "Well, my friend, there's a first time for everything!"

Tanya, Jess and I walked up to the golden doctor. They looked at each other. They knew the timing would have to be perfect to stop her from pounding away again.

Tanya locked her eyes on the golden doctor and lowered her head. Doctor Stone began to shimmer. She turned back to flesh and blood. She started to shrink. "How long do you have to set her back through time?" Tanya asked.

"She inserted all those things on herself today when she panicked," Lori replied. She stuck out her tongue. "She forced us to stick some of the ones on her lower back and her butt."

Tanya took a breath. "Good I can do that…I think…."

Doctor Stone stumbled to her feet. "What's going on?

108

What am I doing here?"

I nodded to Jess. "Okay, do your stuff!"

Jess walked forward. In her cool hypnotic voice, she uttered. *"You over-loaded yourself with those weird cybernetic enhancements. You turned into a giant mad scientist. Luckily Super Teen was able to stop you. You exerted so much energy, you burnt out the enhancements. And now the police are taking you to jail!"*

Chief Michaels stepped forward, "Yep, that's exactly what happened." He pointed to two of his officers. "Officers, take her away!"

"But, but…I only wanted to do good…" Doctor Stone whimpered. She glared at Doctor Dangerfield. "You are too cautious!"

Doctor Dangerfield pointed to all the damage Stone had done. "Look at the destruction you've created! Not to mention all the poor animals you experimented with!!"

The police took Doctor Stone away. I smiled. Things had worked out pretty well. My friends and I had teamed up to stop her.

Doctor Dangerfield walked over to me and offered me her hand. "Thanks for stopping her!"

"No problem, Doctor! I'm just glad I could help. I'm sorry you had to see your research abused like that," I told her. Yep, it looks like I misjudged Doctor Dangerfield.

Doctor Dangerfield looked around at the destruction caused by Stone. "Actually I do owe a thank you to poor Gem, she did show me what great potential my work has!" Doctor Dangerfield gave me a weird smile.

Okay, maybe I hadn't misjudged her. I guess time would tell!

For now, though, it had been an amazing start to my summer break. I kind of hoped the rest of my summer would be a bit calmer. Of course, if it wasn't, that would be cool too. After all, l am Super Teen and now I have super friends! So mega super cool!

Dear Diary: I love the idea of having friends that are super like me. After all, some things, actually most things, are easier when you use teamwork. Good thing, I knew I could count on my family and friends to help me, no matter what.

***

Find out what happens next in

Diary of a Super Girl: Book 4 – The Expanding World

AVAILABLE NOW!!

You can also read the next 3 books in the series as a combined set at a DISCOUNTED PRICE!

**Diary of a Super Girl – Books 4, 5, & 6
OUT NOW!**

We hope you enjoyed Diary of a Super Girl – Book 3!
If you did, can you please leave a review?
Reviews help us to make more sales and write more books.
We would be really grateful if you can spare some time.
Thanks so much!
Katrina and John ☺

Here are some more great books that you're sure to enjoy...

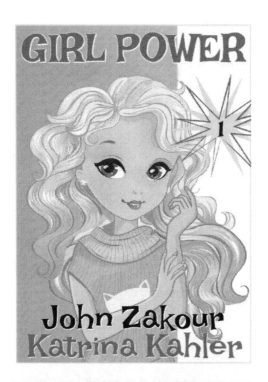

About the Authors

John Zakour is a humor / SF/ fantasy writer with a Master's degree in Human Behavior. He has written thousands of gags for syndicated comics, comedians and TV shows (including: Simpsons and Rugrats and, Joan River's old TV show.) John has written seven humorous SF novels for Daw books (the first The Plutonium Blonde was named the funniest SF book of 2001 by The Chronicle of Science Fiction). John has also written three YA books, four humorous self-help books and three books on HTML. John has also optioned two TV shows and three movies. His books may be found here:
http://www.amazon.com/John-Zakour/e/B000APS2F0

Katrina Kahler is the Best Selling Author of several series of books, including Julia Jones' Diary, Mind Reader, The Secret, Diary of a Horse Mad Girl, Twins, Angel, Slave to a Vampire and numerous Learn to Read Books for young children. Katrina lives in beautiful Noosa on the Australian coastline. You can find all of Katrina's books here:
Best Selling Books for Kids.com

Made in the USA
San Bernardino, CA
30 March 2020

THE 12 LEADERSHIP PRINCIPLES

OF

DEAN SMITH

David Chadwick

NEW YORK

For information about permission to reproduce selections from this book,
please write to:
Permissions
Total/SPORTS ILLUSTRATED
105 Abeel Street
Kingston, New York, 12401

Interior Designer: Elena Erber

ISBN: 1-892129-08-6
Library of Congress Catalog Card Number: 99-63226

Printed in United States of America by Quebecor Printing Inc.
10 9 8 7 6 5 4 3 2 1

To Marilynn

CONTENTS

Acknowledgements

D ean Smith's vision throughout the years has been that the team is more important than the individual. Without the team that helped me finish this project, it would have been impossible. Therefore, as Coach Smith always taught us to thank the teammate making an assist by pointing to him, I point a "thank you" to the following.

My close friend Rick Ray, who read the first draft of the first chapter and put more red marks on it than any teacher I've ever had! Suzanne Waddell, my administrative assistant, for her countless hours of typing, copying, and sending out manuscripts, and for listening to my frustrations. Lee Allison for helping to pull the original manuscript together with Suzanne. Gary Curtis and Ross Bennett, my traveling companions and advisors, for many hours of insight, help, and encouragement.

Connie Reece, my editor, and all the others who read the manuscript and made suggestions — Todd Hahn, Wanna Dayvault, Greg Keith, Ron Smith, Pat McCrory, and especially my Dad (who will always be my hero and greatest influence in life). My Mom contributions are, obviously, equally unmatchable in their way.

My staff, leaders, and friends at what seems to me to be the greatest, most unconditionally loving church in the world, Forest Hill, especially Charles Overstreet. Janet Thoma, Joni Evans, and Grey Coleman, for pats of encouragement along the way!

All the interviewees, whose lives have been touched by Coach Smith, especially Coach Guthridge, whose first year at UNC was my first year.

Coach Smith, who let me write the book despite his desire for privacy and his sincere humility, and for whom it was difficult, knowing people were talking to me about him. I hope this book allows many to learn from Coach Smith, as I have. And that it thanks him for his profound, principle-centered life and leadership. It's a wonderful gift to a leadership-starved world.

Finally, Marilynn, to whom this book is dedicated, my life partner and best friend. She was the first person with whom I shared this idea, and later, when I doubted I could do it, she insisted I go ahead. It was not an easy project, and I simply couldn't have finished it without her. Thanks for the incessant encouragement.

IT'S HOW YOU PLAY THE GAME

Let's see if you can complete this phrase: "It's not whether you win or lose…"

If you have a modicum of understanding of the American competitive sports scene, you undoubtedly are able to supply the ending: "…it's how you play the game." Reflecting on this thought, the great football coach Vince Lombardi purportedly said, "If that's true, then why keep score?" Lombardi is also credited with having said, "Winning isn't everything, it's the only thing."

Yet are these ideas — that the goal of sporting events is to win or that it is in the manner of playing — mutually exclusive? I don't think so. Perhaps it's because I played for Coach Dean Smith, college basketball's all-time winningest coach. His number-one priority was developing his players as people — teaching us how to play the game rightly on and off the court, showing us how to be persons of integrity. He doggedly believed it *is* how you play the game that counts the most. In fact, if any phrase encapsulates Coach Smith's leadership, it's this one: it's how you play the game.

What then, was the result of Coach Smith's placing the emphasis on how the game should be played?

One number says it all: 879!

That's how many games Coach Dean Smith won over the span of his career. He has won more games than any other coach in the history of college basketball — 879 wins. It's a remarkable feat that makes Dean Smith's name synonymous with winning.

However, in my opinion, it's not just *that* he wins, it's *how* he wins that should be pointed out. It's how he lives his life, how he distributes accolades and deflects praise, how he represents the university, how he cares for his players, staff, and the people with whom his life has intersected through the years that set him apart from others in the coaching profession and leaders in general.

Listen to some of the people whose lives have been touched by Coach Smith:

Donnie Walsh, president of the NBA's Indiana Pacers and a former Carolina player:
> *"I admire this guy more than any other coach because he's not just in it to win games. It's more important that his players come out of there with a well-rounded, well-balanced idea of themselves."*

Larry Brown, coach of the NBA's Philadelphia 76ers and former player and assistant coach under Smith:
> *"Whether you were a starter or a twelfth man, he made us all feel like we were the most important player who ever played for him."*

Rick Pitino, head coach of the Boston Celtics:
> *"It was one of the illustrious careers in all of coaching, and he did it with a great deal of dignity and class."*

Mike Krzyzewski, head coach of Duke University:
> *"He brought out the best in you, because you knew coaching against a Dean Smith team would mean playing at a very high level, a championship level."*

Roy Williams, a former assistant under Smith and now head coach at the University of Kansas:

> *"He has a basketball program, he doesn't have a team. And when you have a program, you're concerned about the kids' entire lives, even after they leave. That's his greatest strength. I've always felt he's the best there is on the court, but he's even better off the court in what he gives to those who come in contact with him."*

Christopher Fordham, former chancellor of the University of North Carolina:

> *"He was more than the best of coaches. He consistently exemplified strong values, respecting his student-athletes, giving academics a very high priority, and encouraging good sportsmanship and civility."*

Michael Jordan, former player and simply the best basketball player in the history of the sport:

> *"The camaraderie he has with his players goes a long way. He's taught a lot of us similar traits and we've moved on as people and as players. That's something we treasure maybe more than our basketball experiences — the things we learned away from the game."*

Bob Knight, head coach of the Indiana Hoosiers:

> *"The very best thing you can say about another person, and you can't say this about many people, is that the more you get to know him the better you like him. That's what I say when someone asks me about Dean Smith. We're good friends. And I have grown to genuinely like him more as I have become more acquainted with him over the years."*

The accolades for Coach Dean Smith could go on and on. Why? What has made this man such an amazingly successful leader? Let's think about what leadership is for a moment.

General George S. Patton defined leadership as the art of getting subordinates to do the impossible. Someone else has said that leadership is the expression of courage that compels people to do the right things.

In the business world, the difference between an effective or ineffective corporation is leadership. In the military, the difference between a good unit and a bad unit is leadership. In sports, the difference between a successful team and an unsuccessful team is leadership.

In his book *Managing for the Future*, Peter Drucker writes that there is no substitute for leadership, and he defines leadership simply as "getting things accomplished by acting through others." Warren Bennis, another who has studied leadership, writes, "Around the globe, we face three threats: the threat of annihilation as a result of nuclear accident or war, the worldwide plague of ecological catastrophe, and a deepening leadership crisis. In my mind, the leadership crisis is the most urgent and dangerous of the threats we face today."

In a world starving for effective leadership, Dean Smith has proven to be a very effective leader. Therefore, I believe there's enormous value in looking at his life and leadership style. As one of his former players, I have seen up close and personal the practical, transferable principles by which he lives. These principles, consistently practiced over almost four decades as a leader, have been the foundation for his outstanding success.

Dean Smith's goal in coaching was not to become college basketball's most winning coach. Indeed, many of us former players had to convince him to surpass former Kentucky coach Adolph Rupp's record. Over and over again Smith had threatened to retire when he was one game behind Rupp. We had to beg him to stay at it, to break the record for all of us who had played for him, if not for himself. Fortunately, he finally agreed.

But breaking the record and winning the most games was not his life's goal. I firmly believe his intent was simply to teach basketball to young men through systematic, disciplined life principles. He would have been happy doing this at any level. The wins followed naturally. Sure, he enjoyed winning. He's extremely competitive. But 879 wins were never the end goal. His players and those who worked for him were his real motivation.

What are these principles Dean Smith imparted to his players? That's the reason for this book. For 30 years I've known and observed him, originally as a player and now as a friend. I believe these principles encapsulate why he is extraordinarily successful as a leader and a man. They are not principles he thought up or invented. They are natural laws, inviolate principles of the human, relational dimension, as real as gravity is to the physical reality. These principles guide civilization. Every positive, meaningful human relationship throughout history observes them. When these laws are obeyed, harmony exists. When disobeyed, there is disharmony, disintegration, and destruction.

Indeed, I would suggest that when people see someone committed to living by these principles, an instinctive inward trust motivates them to follow. Again, I believe this is the real reason for Coach Smith's effectiveness as a leader. Those who know him well consistently see these principles in action. We instinctively sense he is a man of character and ability. We therefore trust him and desire to emulate and follow him.

This is not to imply that he is perfect. He has flaws, some of which I will point out in this book.

In fact, when I approached Coach Smith about his permission to write this book, he quickly granted it.

"David," he said, "it's a free country. You can do whatever you wish."

Then he paused for a moment. Silence engulfed his office. An uneasy look crossed his face. I sensed his discomfort. Finally, he spoke. "Please," he said. Then another moment of silence. "Please don't deify me!"

I won't, although you'll consistently witness my sincere admiration for him. I'm sure, like all of us, he has been forced to live in the fog of deep convictions that at times he doesn't necessarily practice. Surely, like most of us, he has disappointed friends, family, and followers. But when his life has been shrouded in uncertainty, these principles grounded him on a firm foundation and allowed him to persevere. When life has not made sense for him, or when he has made mistakes and been forced to face consequences, these principles continued to guide him.

When I asked Coach Smith about these principles, he said he's not overtly aware of them guiding his life. Yet they're there. They're obvious to anyone who examines his life. Ask any former player. Ask any of his assistants. We would all extend super-human effort for him. Why? We believed in him. We saw his life principles lived out.

Outside of my father, Dean Smith may have had the greatest impact on my life, especially in the area of leadership. That's the real legacy I think he should leave. Leaders in the twenty-first century need to know this man and the principles by which he has lived. Unless someone spends the time to put these insights on paper, future leaders will miss his wonderful example of leadership. That's the reason I have spent countless hours during the last two years writing this book.

As I traveled all over the country and interviewed people and players who have been profoundly impacted by Coach Smith's life, three different core values kept arising that seemed to define his leadership. These three core values are what James Collins and Jerry Porras, in their highly successful *Built to Last*, state are the kind of successful habits every visionary company possesses and drives deep into its corporate culture. First, he placed people above everything else — yes, including wins and losses. People are first in his life. Second, he believes the team is more important than the individual. The individual talents of the player, even if a superstar, must be submitted to the good of the team. Third, personal integrity and character are very important. The leader leads by conviction, care, and character. Then people will trust him and naturally follow.

From these three core values I have identified what I refer to as 12 secrets of successful leadership. If read and practiced, these principles will help anyone become a better and more effective leader.

That's the legacy I hope to leave about Coach Smith to a generation that has admired and venerated him, and to future generations that can learn and grow from his extraordinary life and leadership.

A record of 879 wins in collegiate basketball is impressive. It's a record that may never be broken. Who is the man behind those wins? What allowed him to be so successful? How did he last for so long in today's sports climate of cheating and scandal? How did 97 percent of his players graduate, almost half of whom later attained post-graduate degrees? How have many of these players become fine citizens, leaders in their communities? What are his secrets for successful leadership for the long haul?

It is my privilege to try and answer these questions for you. And in the process I believe we'll discover that it is, after all, how you play the game.

—David Chadwick

THE RECIPROCAL LAW OF LOYALTY

"If you ever need me, call!"

When Dean Smith says, "If you ever need me, call!" he genuinely means it. Every player has heard Coach Smith make this statement at one time or another, and many of them have discovered first-hand that it's true. While he might not think about it in such terms, when college basketball's winningest coach extends the offer to call him, he is expressing the reciprocal law of loyalty to his players.

It's an immutable law. Others have stated it differently through the ages. "You get what you give." Or, "You reap what you sow." Or, "If you want to be loved, be lovable." Or, as the Hebrew scripture says, "The generous soul will be made rich, and he who waters will himself be watered" (Proverbs 11:25). Or, as Jesus said, "How happy are the merciful, for they receive mercy in return" (Matthew 5:7).

It doesn't matter how you say it, the principle still operates the same way: *If you are loyal to people, they'll be loyal to you.* If you put others first, they'll work and play very hard for you. Dean Smith understood and practiced this reciprocal law of loyalty, and every player returned his loyalty. It's not blind loyalty that allows people to take advantage of him. It is a genuine caring for others that fosters mutual care.

When I asked Coach Smith about this principle, he shared with me what led him to reach the conclusion that loyalty to others mattered more than success. "I loved to win and hated to lose," he said. "Yet for years I struggled with something internally. We would play poorly and win, and I'd feel great. We'd play well and lose, and I'd feel terrible. That didn't make sense to me.

"If two of your children were playing tennis against each other, would you really care who won? Is winning all that important in the scheme of things? No. That's why I have ultimately placed compassion above competition. I want to win, but caring for people is much more important to me. I finally concluded that success is not defined by winning or losing, but in doing the best you can, where you are, with what you have."

Putting People First

Why is Coach Smith such a successful leader? I believe it is because he cares first about people. They are his most important products. He knows that everything meaningful in life flows out of relationships, and he steadfastly refuses to manage people as things. Before considering the product, or profit, or goals, or objectives, or action plans — or, especially in his case, wins and losses — he is most concerned about the players who play for him and the people who work with him. He pours his life first and foremost into them. His greatest desire is that they succeed, as players and people, even above his own success.

One of the ways he has demonstrated this desire is by counseling gifted players such as Jerry Stackhouse, Rasheed Wallace, Antawn Jamison, Vince Carter, and, yes, even Michael Jordan, to forfeit remaining years of eligibility for their own financial security. If they had stayed at UNC, Coach Smith's chances for more victories and the golden national championship would have been greatly increased. But he was more concerned about the individual players and their future careers.

After Antawn Jamison and Vince Carter announced their decisions to forego their senior seasons and enter the NBA draft, Ademola Okulaja, another member of that team's starting five, was asked about coaches Smith and Guthridge encouraging both players to leave early. Okulaja said, "It's different here than anywhere else. The coaches really do put us number-one. Many programs squeeze the players out like an orange and then throw them away. But there is respect and honor here — the players have it for the coaches, and the coaches have it for the players. Therefore, there is a certain obligation not to let each other down."

Bobby Jones also knows the value Coach Smith places on caring for people. When Jones was playing for the Denver Nuggets, he began to suffer from epilepsy. The team doctors couldn't figure out what was wrong with him, and the managers just wanted him to play. He was really feeling the pressure. "Then I got a call from Coach Smith," Jones said. "Coach wanted me to come see this doctor in North Carolina that he knew. I did, and he's the one who helped me the most. In fact, he is still my doctor today. When Coach Smith does things like that for people — and he does it a lot — it communicates that he cares for you as a person far beyond an NBA player. That meant a lot to me."

For John Swofford, Coach Smith's practice of putting his players first often meant going to the end of the line himself. Swofford, former UNC athletic director and now commissioner of the Atlantic Coast Conference, was Smith's boss for 17 years. Swofford told me, "Sometimes I think the Carolina basketball program was wrongly caricatured as IBM. It suggested the program was structured like a corporation. A very cold image. It was intended as a compliment because of its wonderful organization. But what got lost was the way Dean always made sure the players came first, before the athletic director, the chancellor, anyone! There were times I would call him about something and he would politely say, 'John, I'm in with a player right now, so we'll need to talk later.' I always understood. He's loyal to his players. They come first. It sent a tremendous message to the players, and it's why they're so loyal to him."

Evidently this reciprocal law of loyalty worked with his assistants too. Bill Guthridge would do anything to protect Coach Smith. For example, when former Maryland coach Lefty Driesell lost to Carolina in a heated game in Carmichael Auditorium, he refused to shake Coach Smith's hand after the game. That was a huge mistake in Coach Guthridge's eyes. He chased Driesell down and chewed him out for his lack of courtesy and respect. Driesell later said, "I really respect Bill. He's a good man, and if he ever got mad at me, well, I must have deserved it."

That's the reciprocal law of loyalty: if you are loyal to people, they will be loyal to you.

Accepting Others Unconditionally

Not only did Coach Smith always put his players first, he also demonstrated that he accepted them unconditionally.

Dave Hanners, who played for Coach Smith in the early 1970s and then became one of his assistants in the late 1980s, says that Smith's loyalty knows no bounds. "Most loyalty tends to float to people who can help you the most. This was not so with Coach Smith. He was loyal to us all, superstar or sub alike."

In 1982 Hanners called Smith and announced he had quit his job because he just didn't want to work where he was any longer. Sensing that Hanners needed to talk about it, Coach Smith had his secretary set up an appointment as soon as possible.

"We talked about what made me quit my job," Hanners said, "and what I planned to do. He was very understanding, but also very tough with me. Frankly, he told me I was fairly stupid to quit my job without having another one lined up. He then evaluated my strengths and weaknesses, not as a player, but as a person. He knew them intimately!

"But when I left his office, I felt great. I didn't have a job. I didn't know where I was headed. But he helped me believe in me. He didn't offer me a job as one of his assistant coaches. That didn't happen until seven years later. I just knew that Coach Smith believed in me, and I would be all right."

What struck me most about my interview with Hanners is what happened while he was talking. It was so powerful it's almost impossible to capture with words. While describing that time in 1982 when he went to Coach Smith for counseling, tears formed in his eyes. He was so overcome with deep emotion that he had to stop a moment and compose himself.

I couldn't help wondering, "Would any of my staff break down and cry when talking about my leadership and loyalty to them? What a supreme compliment!"

That's an important question for every leader to ask. How would those working under you feel when describing their relationship with you? Would they be overcome with deep emotion when describing how you have loved and treated them? Would they unabashedly know your absolute loyalty to them as people first, then as employees? Would they cry when talking about you? If not, why not?

When I asked Hanners why he teared up, he said, "It's this sense of unconditional love from him toward us. The world doesn't understand it. Everything is performance-based. But that's not the case with Coach Smith's loyalty. It's not bologna. I go to the staff meetings. He doesn't say we'll treat the twelfth man one way and the superstar another way. He makes sure every player is treated the same way. It is unconditional loyalty. I think that is what separates him from all the other coaches."

Caring for a Lifetime

Scores of players have found that Coach Smith's unconditional acceptance is not a one-time event. It lasts for a lifetime.

John Kilgo, longtime host of the Dean Smith Show, calls this player–coach loyalty "mesmerizing." The loyalty is so strong, according to Kilgo, that people "want to repay him double. They just don't want to disappoint him. That even goes on long after they leave the university. Along with practically all his former players, I still call him to seek counsel for difficult life decisions. How many people, after they have left a company, would call their former boss and ask for counsel, twenty, thirty years later?"

That's the kind of impact Dean Smith's loyalty has. He influences people for a lifetime.

Richard Vinroot, former mayor of Charlotte, North Carolina, played for Coach Smith in the 1960s. "I feel incredible loyalty to him," Vinroot told me. "But that's because I know how much he cares for me, how loyal he is to me. When I was in Vietnam, he regularly wrote me and checked on my parents. I teasingly say that Michael Jordan and I are the two bookends of the Carolina basketball program. That's how little I played. Yet Coach Smith still treated me like a superstar."

I have experienced this kind of loyalty in my own relationship with Coach Smith. When I talk about his putting people first, about his unconditional acceptance, about his caring for a lifetime, I am describing leadership traits that are personally well-known to me.

I first met Coach Smith in December 1966. He had come to Orlando, Florida, to observe my basketball talent. He was extremely business-like, dressed as if he had just stepped out of *Gentleman's Quarterly*. His dark black hair was slicked back from his forehead. A decided midwestern twang was evident in his voice. I can't remember being that impressed with Coach Smith. He seemed nice enough. A bit stuffy, perhaps even distant. But in the recruiting deluge going on during my senior year, I was not particularly impressed with any coach. I had averaged 22 points and 18 rebounds and been selected first team all-state for the second consecutive year. Some 130 schools wanted my services, and I was absolutely convinced that any school would be lucky to have me.

Was Dean Smith a good coach? At this point, no one really knew. He had recruited some good players in his five years at UNC, but he had yet to win an Atlantic Coast Conference title, much less make it to the Final Four. I was most concerned with his coaching and recruiting ability; I wanted to win, and winning took good recruiting and good coaching. After narrowing my final three choices to Florida, Vanderbilt, and North Carolina, I eventually decided that everything felt right about North Carolina.

So I signed a letter of intent in the spring of 1967. I was so brash about my basketball ability that when I called Coach Smith to announce proudly that I had decided to come to UNC, I also informed him that I wanted to play in the NBA.

Looking back, I realize he must have been laughing on the other end of the line. He had seen me play. He most certainly saw the athletic gifts …as well as the limitations! But he politely said, "Well, David, we want to help all our scholar-athletes to achieve their life's ambitions." That is vintage Dean Smith. He wanted me to be successful, and he did not want to squash my dreams. But he undoubtedly knew my potential. So he gave me a political answer. Every reporter who has ever asked him a pointed question knew what I was feeling. He is a master at refusing to overstate!

In 1967 freshmen were ineligible to play on the varsity team in all Division I athletics. Our freshman team played a 16-game schedule, designed to allow 18-year-olds the opportunity to concentrate on academics without the pressure of big-time collegiate athletics.

I thought I had an outstanding freshman year. We were 12–4, capturing the mythical "Big Four" championship among Duke, Wake Forest, North Carolina State, and UNC. I was the team's leading scorer, averaging 19 points per game, and the second leading rebounder, averaging almost 11 per game. My dream of playing in the NBA kept appearing before my eyes. I couldn't wait for my sophomore year, when I would join a returning team of veterans who the year before had gone to the Final Four. "Why," I thought to myself, "with me and these returning veterans, we could win the national championship!"

Being Honest with Everyone

During the first day of practice of the 1968–69 season, I learned another aspect of Coach Smith's loyalty: he is honest with everyone.

In the first scrimmage, the ball was thrown to me. I wanted to show what I had to offer. I drove to the basket. Jumping as high as I could, I stretched my arm toward the basket, nerves tingling as the ball slipped off my fingertips. I envisioned it nestling softly into the basket to the sound of oohs and aahs from my team members and, especially, from Coach Smith.

You can therefore imagine my stark surprise when the ball ricocheted off my face, spiked downward by Bill Bunting, the team's six-foot, nine-inch all-ACC forward. My face turned red from the ball, but also from embarrassment. I recall a few chuckles. Coach Smith's face hardly changed as he looked at me. "That's not a good shot," he said. "We can do better than that."

The season went downhill from there for me. The team was quite successful. Once again we won the ACC Tournament and the Eastern Regional, and we went to the Final Four for the third straight year. However, I hardly played. I was a seldom-used reserve who was best known around campus as the one who scored the hundredth point in several of our blowout wins.

I was so frustrated that I amassed a list of my concerns; there were about 12. Then I made an appointment to see Coach Smith. I needed to find out how he felt about me. I said to myself, "If he can't convince me that these concerns are invalid, I'm outta here!"

As always, he was very cordial when I arrived at his office. I immediately launched into my diatribe. Months of frustration spewed forth as I ticked off point after point with lightning precision. Each item raised my voice a decibel or two. After about five points, he tried to offer a response. I arrogantly snapped back and said, "Coach, would you mind letting me finish my list. Then we can talk!"

He politely nodded as if to say, "That's okay. I understand."

I finished my list, threatened to transfer, then folded my arms in picturesque exasperation, waiting for some plausible explanation.

To this moment my face flushes in embarrassment when I think about my adolescent outburst. I was an impatient child. Life had not gone as I'd wanted; therefore, I threw a temper tantrum. At the time, however, I felt totally justified.

Coach Smith patiently waited for me to finish. A few moments passed as he looked me over. He had undoubtedly never seen this side of me before. But with a quiet confidence, he said, "David, you are an important part of this program. I think you possess many fine gifts as a basketball player. You have some weaknesses you need to work on. But every player does. If you'll continue to work on those areas, and continue to strengthen the positive parts of your game, I don't see any reason why you can't be a contributor to the success of this program over the next two years. I don't want you to transfer. I hope you'll stay. But if you do transfer, please know I'll always want the best for you."

He waited for me to respond. I didn't know what to say. Then he got up and ushered me to the door. He told me if we needed to talk further, he would be willing. I left confused. My concerns were not fully answered. But he had given me a fair hearing and an honest answer.

For the first time I began to wonder if maybe I wasn't the problem. Perhaps my lack of maturity as a basketball player and as a person was what was holding me back. I wrestled with the possibility of transferring for about a month. Finally, I simply felt this overwhelming conviction that I was supposed to return to Chapel Hill for my final two years. I had made a commitment and needed to honor it.

Between my sophomore and junior years, I worked hard and felt some steady improvement. My junior year was more successful. I moved up to the seventh man on the team. I actually started four games and had some moments when I knew I was a big part of helping the team win a game.

That success my junior year spurred me to work even harder for my senior campaign. In the summer of 1970, I ran and lifted weights every day. I went down to the inner city and played against the best players in Orlando, Florida. I told them they could do anything they wanted to me and I would never complain, never call a foul, even if blood were spilled! I knew I needed to become quicker, stronger, and more aggressive.

I put on 15 pounds. I got tougher. I came back and ran the pre-season mile in five minutes and 26 seconds, the second fastest time on the team and well ahead of any other big man. In the first preseason practice, Coach Smith always allows the seniors to be on the White team, the first team. They stay there until an underclassman beats them out. I stayed there the entire preseason. I played so well they couldn't get me out.

It was a terrific season. We finished 26–6 and won the National Invitational Tournament post-season championship in Madison Square Garden when the NIT was still a very prestigious tournament. We blew by Massachusetts and Julius Erving in the opening round. Then we proceeded to eliminate Providence, Duke, and Georgia Tech for the championship.

I averaged almost nine points per game, was able to start 11 games, and was the first forward substitute off the bench. As I cut down my part of the net after beating Georgia Tech in the NIT championship game, I felt great pride — for playing for UNC and this man named Dean Smith.

What he had told me was true. I worked on my game, became better, and he gave me every chance to show my talents.

But the NBA didn't draft me. I had played very well in the NIT tournament, and a couple of free-agent offers appeared. But my high school dream no longer looked like a reality. It was hard to admit, but I knew I did not possess the physical skills necessary to play in the NBA.

As I began to explore other vocational opportunities, a team from Europe contacted me. They had seen me play in the NIT and were impressed. They flew me over. I tried out. They offered me a contract. I returned home and, naturally, counseled with my dad and Coach Smith. Both thought it would be a tremendous opportunity and adventure. So I seized it. I played in Europe for three years without any regret, three of the most enjoyable years of my life. One was spent in Ostend, Belgium, the other two in Nice, France. I know it's difficult to think about a young man living for two years on the French Riviera, but someone had to do it!

Right before I flew overseas for my first year, I went by the basketball office to say good-bye to all the coaches. As I shook Coach Smith's hand, I'll never forget his final words to me: "If you ever need me, call." At the time I thought these to be perfunctory, hackneyed words from a former coach. I didn't really think he meant them. But I thanked him and went on my way.

That was nearly 30 years ago. At different junctures of my life, I've had to make crucial decisions. Whom do I call? My dad and Coach Smith are the first people. "If you ever need me, call" were not worn-out words from a polite well-wisher, but sincere thoughts from one who has moved from being my coach to my friend. Countless other former lettermen share the same experience. He has said the same thing to them, and backed it up when they called.

In my opinion, it's the primary principle by which he tries to live. Loyalty is foundational to him. When we hurt, he hurts. When we're struggling, he's struggling. Because of this unconditional loyalty, we are very loyal to him. While at Carolina, we play very hard. We adopt his concepts. Then, after we leave, we would do anything to help him and the program. That's why I've called it "reciprocal loyalty."

Empathy for All

Amazingly, those he recruited who went on to sign with rival schools have also experienced this loyalty. For example, Adam Keefe signed with Stanford after being recruited by Carolina. He's a wonderfully gifted athlete, now playing in the NBA. To this day, Coach Smith stays in touch with him.

Mitch Kupchak, former All-American and now the assistant general manager of the Los Angeles Lakers, told me that players from other schools on the 1976 Smith-coached Olympic team also feel like they are a part of the Carolina family and regularly call Coach Smith for counsel. One former ACC player, who spurned Carolina to go to a rival school told me, "The biggest mistake I ever made in life was not to go to Carolina. Yet, recently, I called Coach Smith and asked him to help me obtain a job — and he did! He interceded on my behalf."

Can you imagine a CEO of a major corporation recruiting a young man out of college only to have him commit to a rival corporation, and then continuing to send Christmas cards to him and his parents? Moreover, can you imagine him helping this person years later obtain his dream job? Would the CEO say to these people, "If you ever need me, call"?

Yet Coach Smith does just that. He puts people first. His primary concern is their success, not his. His first priority is to serve, not to be served. He lives by this law: if you are loyal to people, they will be loyal to you.

This principle of reciprocal loyalty helped build IBM in the 1950s. Part of founder Thomas J. Watson's business genius was changing people's perception of salesmen. When the term *salesman* was used in those days, people thought of a shady character trying to do a con job. Watson created an image exactly the opposite of this caricature: a smile, a slap on the back, and a shoeshine. John P. Imlay Jr., a longtime IBM competitor and chairman of Dun and Bradstreet Software said, "He brought real credibility to the sales force."

Watson's values focused on developing closeness among the workers. He hosted family dinners annually for all employees and sponsored intramural team sports, for example. One of his founding principles was "respect for the individual." Many friends who presently work for IBM moan to me about their concern that the bottom line has become the highest corporate value. This may work for the short-term, but I can't help but wonder about being able to sustain long-term morale when reciprocal loyalty is not as important as it once was.

Let me give you a final example of Coach Smith's reciprocal loyalty and his great empathy for others.

When the desire to write this book hit me, I knew I had to have Coach Smith's permission. I therefore made an appointment to see him. Yet as I thought about visiting him, a strange uneasiness overtook me. It grew larger and larger, to the point where I contemplated not going. I searched my soul. What was going on? Finally, I was able to discern what was bothering me. My mind flashed back to 1969 and the time I entered Coach Smith's office with my notorious list of grievances. Did he remember that horrid encounter? Might he possibly hold it against me and not permit me to write this book?

It was a cool, spring day when I arrived at his office. He graciously received me, as always. For the first 15 minutes of our time together, we talked about family. He expressed concern for my aging parents, sharing with me in great pain the agony of watching his mother struggle with Alzheimer's Disease and eventually lose the battle. He had also recently lost his father. He shared how no one is ever prepared for this and exhorted me to enjoy my parents while they were living. Then we talked theology, our similarities and differences. It was a deep, delightful conversation.

Yet I continued to have a gnawing discomfort. I could not believe I was still bothered by my adolescent outburst in his office 30 years earlier! I knew I had to have some peace. I waited for the right opportunity. Finally, a pause in the conversation occurred. I sighed deeply, garnering courage, before I spoke. "Coach, one of my most embarrassing moments was at the end of my sophomore year when I came to you thinking about transferring." I then retold the story in vivid detail, graphically remembering every painful minute.

When I finished, I felt a burden lift off my shoulders. I peered into his eyes. Did he remember? I couldn't tell.

He finally spoke. "David, look behind you."

On the wall behind me hung the composite pictures of all the players who had ever played for him. He continued, "There's hardly one player up there who, at one time or another, hasn't thought about transferring from this program. And most, if not all, have been really mad at me because they didn't think they got enough playing time. We all learn from past experiences. What you did was just part of growing up."

Did Michael Jordan or James Worthy ever complain about playing time? Did George Karl, Mitch Kupchak, Bobby Jones, or Eric Montross ever become angry with Coach Smith? Probably.

In his empathy, Coach Smith tried to put me at ease. I was one of his former players, a part of the Carolina basketball family. Mostly, however, I was his friend. To him, my angry outburst was in the past and did not really matter. He simply reaffirmed his loyalty to me.

Putting the Principles to Work

I have personally learned how to use this principle of reciprocal loyalty in my own leadership. I pastor a large, growing church in the suburbs of Charlotte, North Carolina. The entire budget is around five million dollars, and I oversee a constantly growing staff of more than 40 people and a lay ministry of 2000 people.

In my early leadership, when the church was just entering its growing stage, I did not practice this principle very well and it cost me dearly. For example, a member of the church once approached me with concerns about a particular staff person and his division's effectiveness. I was a bit surprised, for I had heard from others who thought this staffer was doing a credible job. I pondered the problem. Finally, I told the church member to gather more information for me behind the scenes. I thought this would give me all the facts I would need to address the situation.

That was a huge mistake, and it began a disastrous scenario for me.

My staff member somehow heard through the grapevine that I had appointed a behind-the-scenes mole to study the effectiveness of his work. He angrily entered my office and confronted my apparent lack of loyalty to him. He rightly asked why I had not approached him personally about the accusations. In my youthful naiveté, I became extraordinarily defensive. He continued his protest, raising his voice. I got even more defensive and raised my anger level to match. He reciprocated.

I was guilty of first desiring to be understood instead of understanding. It's one of the cardinal sins of a leader.

Our relationship, from that point forward, slowly but surely deteriorated and eventually fractured. Mistrust grew. His job performance began to dissolve, and it became inevitable that he would have to leave. Moreover, he shared his frustration with friends on the staff. His disgruntlement began to spread throughout the entire group. Others thought, "Well, if David would do it to him, why wouldn't he do it to me?" There was a malignancy of mistrust everywhere!

What is most depressing to me about this story is that most of the rumors proved to be unfounded and wrong. Now not only did I have a fractured friendship (which, fortunately, later was healed), not only did an important part of our work become paralyzed for several months, not only did mistrust proliferate among other staff, but a potentially valuable and gifted person was irrevocably lost to this organization.

It was a terribly painful time for everyone involved. In the months that followed, I seriously evaluated what had happened. I chewed on the problem over and over. I read management books by the dozen. Yet none of them gave me the kind of answer I wanted.

From where did the solution ultimately come? It came when I simply asked, "What would Coach Smith have done in this situation?" When I asked myself this question, I remembered his leadership principle of reciprocal loyalty. Why did we play so hard for him? Why did we mostly experience unity on his teams? It was because we felt his unyielding loyalty to us, and we reciprocated with extraordinary effort.

In light of this principle, I began to ask myself, "How should I have handled this? What did I do wrong? Second, what can I initiate for now and future staff members, based on this leadership principle, to help insure this never happens again in my own leadership?"

Looking back, I realized I should never have asked the critic to find out whether the rumors were true or not. I should have immediately called the staff member into my office, affirmed my loyalty to him, told him what I had heard, and lovingly asked for his response. If anyone should have gathered information for me, he should have been the person. Then I could have easily managed him, the process, the information, and his division's output. The relationship would have remained solid. His job could have been saved. His potential would not have been threatened. And the rest of the staff would not have experienced a creeping paralysis that took months to overcome.

At that point I had to perform damage control. But I also wanted to formulate some preventive medicine. So I gathered the rest of the staff together, honestly shared my mistake, asked for their forgiveness, and then tackled with them how we could prevent this disaster from ever happening again.

We decided as a staff to live by the core value of reciprocal loyalty. We covenanted together to live by a principle outlined by Jesus in Matthew 18:15 on handling conflict. It simply says that if you have something against someone else, go to that person, face to face, immediately, before the sore has a chance to fester, and try to reconcile the problem. If that doesn't work, go again with two others who sense the same problem. If that doesn't work, then it's time to get the entire board involved. But that's the absolute last resort.

Moreover, we communicated this commitment to the members of the congregation (who would be similar to the customers in another organization). We said we were committed to exemplifying for them how to handle conflict. We also said that if anyone ever came to one of us and complained about another staff person, we would tell the complainer he had 24 hours to go to that person or we would tell him what was said. We wanted all our members to learn and practice reciprocal loyalty. We believed it to be very important as a principle, and we still do to this day.

It has been 11 years since my disloyal faux pas. But I did learn from my mistake. Every new staff person who has come on board since then must agree to this covenant of loyalty. Together, as a staff, we carefully go over this principle during the interview process with each prospective staff member. We ask if they totally understand it, if they have any questions about it. If they balk in any way, we know they won't fit on our staff.

Not once since we initiated this covenant principle has anyone ever rejected the idea of reciprocal loyalty. In fact, they have been extraordinarily thankful for this process to be in place. I think good staff people instinctively know the importance of such loyalty and yearn to live by it.

Over the ensuing years, relational bumps have naturally occurred. A few have even been strangely similar to the one experienced 11 years ago. However, not once has it caused any relational or organizational damage. In fact, when a staff person once said something that seemed to suggest disloyalty, two other staff people went to him and confronted him before the problem ever got to me. He immediately recognized his potential disloyalty and went to the other staff person and asked for forgiveness. The issue was never discussed again.

Since initiating this principle, staff morale has been extremely high. Our commitment to teamwork and one another has never been better. The congregation takes this principle very seriously. Gossip has abated. Unity is incredibly high between staff and church members. Moreover, during the last 11 years our membership has doubled and the budget tripled. We're now in the middle of a huge expansion program that will build an auditorium to seat 2,000 people.

What's the result? Charlotte and the whole area have benefited from our ministry, largely because we have learned and are practicing the leadership secret of reciprocal loyalty.

My youth pastor and close friend, Robbi Fischer, shared a story about this principle of reciprocal loyalty. Several years ago the church was going through a transition time, refocusing our vision. We decided to reach out to those who would normally not attend any church.

Fischer began to attract a large number of "fringe kids," as we call them. Some had green hair. Others had tattoos. They were not your normal church kids. Fischer received a lot of criticism from parents who worried about the effect these fringe kids might have on their own.

"During a parent's committee meeting," Fischer said, "David walked in the room. He knew it was tense and emotional, and he knew that if he said something it might open himself up to more criticism, which he was also receiving for this transition. But he walked up to me, put his arm around me, and said before the group, 'You've got to know that I am one hundred percent behind the youth ministry and the desire to show God's unconditional love to today's teenagers.'

"That meant more to me than a thousand words of affirmation behind the scenes. It not only began to calm the storm in my ministry, but it gave me a clear picture of what David had been talking about in our covenant of reciprocal loyalty."

It's amazing that when the congregation senses this commitment to loyalty among the leadership in the church, they tend to relax and quit their complaining. It's the same way when a child senses that Mom and Dad are on the same page; they feel secure and quit complaining. But if they sense tension between their parents, they start acting out.

From where did I learn this easy and practical leadership principle? From Coach Smith. Peter Drucker, the contemporary management guru, once said, "Efficiency is doing the thing right, but effectiveness is doing the right thing." Dean Smith is very effective as a leader. Why? Because he does the right thing. He cares for his players above all else. People are his most important assets, his most valuable product, even ahead of wins and losses.

Profits or People?

What would happen in companies and organizations across America and the world if leaders would see their people as their primary product? What would happen if every leader desired above all to see his underlings succeed and be happy in life? What would happen if reciprocal loyalty became a core value of all managers and their organizations?

Here is a good example of the potential of this principle to affect a corporation. Slumping sales of athletic shoes and the sullied reputation of sports figures have forced Nike and its competitors to examine whether they want to continue signing athletes to multi-million dollar promotional deals. Expense cuts, even layoffs, loom on the horizon. What should be done?

At Nike's quarterly international sports marketing meeting in January 1998, managers discussed the relative merits of signing the two most promising players in the NFL draft: Ryan Leaf versus Peyton Manning. Someone finally suggested the company save money and not sign either one. Sources at the meeting told the *Oregonian* newspaper that Nike CEO Phil Knight said he would rather cut athletes than lay off a single employee.

I personally think Phil Knight is thinking rightly. If he did this, would Nike's profits shrink or diminish? I dare imagine that a company's profit margin and success would exponentially increase when others are placed first. Right principles, especially being loyal to people and caring for them above all else, will only foster closeness and a greater desire to succeed.

All other life and leadership secrets outlined in this book are rooted in this one principle of reciprocal loyalty. If this one falls, like dominoes, all the other ones do too. If the leader is not loyal to his underlings, teammates, and associates, success, especially over a long period of time, simply will not follow.

I certainly understand that sometimes, albeit painfully, leaders are forced to prune people for a variety of different reasons, from deregulation to new technologies to international trade, to mention a few. No one can argue that leaders have a duty to their shareholders. But is profit the entire ethos of business? Is "shareholder value" our only concern? Aren't there other expressions of value, especially our people?

Or, as Collins and Porras suggest in *Built to Last*, successful visionary companies never fall prey to the "tyranny of the OR." They believe you can pursue caring for people and profits, both, at the same time, all the time. As Don Peterson, former CEO at Ford, said in 1994, "Putting profits after people and products was magical at Ford." Yet Ford was still very profitable!

Is profit the leader's primary duty? Isn't there also an especially high calling to the workers? Aren't they our most valuable asset? In a different time, the chairman of Standard Oil said in a 1951 address: "The job of management is to maintain an equitable and working balance among the claims of the various directly interested groups: stockholders, employees, customers, and the public at large."

More and more leaders today are becoming concerned that profit is now much more important than people. They are concerned that the mean salary of the contemporary chief executive is approximately 190 times the salary of the normal worker, up from 40 times in the 1970s. Nearly 50 percent of America's stock is owned by one percent of Americans. In fact, according to the Federal Reserve, 60 percent of American families own no stock at all.

Perhaps leaders today would be wise to study such leaders as Robert N. Johnson, the founder of Johnson and Johnson in 1886. His vision for his company was "to alleviate pain and disease." By 1908, this view evolved into a business strategy that put the satisfaction of employees ahead of profits for shareholders. J. Williard Marriott Jr. said the motivating factor in his company "is not the money" but the pride of accomplishing a task and doing it well. He points out that profit to shareholders naturally follows.

Coach Smith had an interesting way to "downsize." If he thought someone wouldn't ever play and sensed that to be very important to him, he'd not only encourage him to transfer but ardently help him find another school. He'd always be listed thereafter as a Carolina letterman, be a part of the family, and receive annual notes from Coach Smith. One such transfer encouraged a high school hot shot in his area to attend UNC, not the school to which he had transferred. That's the way to downsize! The law of loyalty still works!

Winston Churchill once said, "The inherent vice of capitalism is the unequal sharing of blessings. The inherent virtue of socialism is the equal sharing of miseries." There's no magic solution for how to prioritize people and profit and still keep shareholders happy. But I think one way is to examine Coach Smith's reciprocal law of loyalty.

Dean Smith coached for almost 40 years with unparalleled success. The results are now legendary, for the ages. They will be talked about and analyzed for decades to come. Why was he so successful? Because he placed others before personal gain. He lived first by the law of reciprocal loyalty.

By the way, when I left his office that spring day when he granted me permission to write this book, I shook his hand and exchanged final pleasantries. You know what his final comment to me was?

"As you develop this project, if you ever need me, call."

I knew he meant it.

Thought for the Day

If you are loyal to people, they will be loyal to you.

Game Plan

- Put people first

- Accept others unconditionally

- Care for them over a lifetime

- Be honest with everyone

- Have empathy for all

- Care for people who produce the profit

Team Practice

- What does loyalty mean to you?

- How do you demonstrate loyalty in your personal life?

- How do you demonstrate loyalty at work?

- What can your organization do to foster loyalty among customers, shareholders, and employees?

LOYALTY PROSPERS IN A FAMILY ENVIRONMENT

"I'll never be your real father, but I guess we do have a large Carolina family."

It was no different than any other practice session, at least that's what we thought. The 1971 season had been a surprise. No college basketball pundit ever dreamed that at this point in the season North Carolina would be on top of the Atlantic Coast Conference standings. Yet we were, a testament to Coach Smith's leadership ability and our playing together as a team.

We were all seated in our chairs that day, ready for Coach Smith to enter. We regularly assembled like this, either to go over the practice plan, study an upcoming opponent, or watch game film. The coaches entered the room and everyone fell quiet. But Coach Smith did not begin talking. Something was eerily wrong. He remained quiet for several seconds. Tears filled his eyes. We had never seen him like this. He cleared his throat, in obvious discomfort. The silence was suffocating.

"Gentlemen," he finally began. "This is very difficult to talk about. But we're all family here." Every man inched to the edge of his chair.

Personally, I expected Coach to share that he was accepting a job somewhere else. Or perhaps someone on the team had gotten into trouble and needed to be disciplined. I would never have imagined he was about to share that *he* was the one in trouble.

"I know that if I'm struggling, it is going to affect you," he said. "I wish it wasn't so, but I know it is. Since we are family, I want to share with you what's going on in my personal life." He then shared with the entire team how he and his wife were having problems in their marriage. He said it had been going on for some time and that it was tearing both him and his wife apart.

Then, in the final phrase, he admitted he didn't know what eventually would happen. They were seeking counseling, but he freely confessed that the marriage might very well end in divorce. Then he bravely asked if anyone had any questions. He said he wanted to be above board in every possible way, and if anyone had any reasonable questions, he would try to answer them as honestly and forthrightly as possible.

I don't remember if anyone had any questions. Frankly, I don't remember much more about that afternoon than what I've described. I remember feeling sadness for him, his wife, and the children. They did ultimately divorce, and he shared that, too, when it finally happened. It was a significant failure for him, one I'm sure he wishes he could change.

But what I do remember very vividly about that day is the fact that he openly shared his own private struggles because he believed we were a family. He believed that his personal life affected us, so we needed to be abreast of what was happening in his life.

As I have examined Coach Smith's leadership skills, I have come to realize that one of the reasons for his great success is that he created a family environment for his players. In fact, he created a family before he created the team. That's the context in which loyalty prospers: family.

Functional families care about one another and openly share both their failures and their successes, their happiness and their hurts.

The first thing Coach Smith did to create that family environment was to be vulnerable before his players and staff.

John Maxwell, in his book *Developing the Leader Within You,* recognized this same principle. He wrote:

> Long ago I realized that in working with people I have two choices. I can close my arms or I can open them. Both choices have strengths and weaknesses. If I close my arms, I won't get hurt, but I will not get much help either. If I open my arms I likely will get hurt, but I will also receive help. What has been my decision? I've opened my arms and allowed others to enjoy the journey with me. My greatest gift to others is not a job, but myself. That is true of any leader.

This is what Coach Smith was doing when he shared with the 1971 team about his own marital problems. He gave us the gift of himself.

Through the years, the family atmosphere Coach Smith created has evolved to the point where he has become a surrogate father to many of his former players.

Being a Surrogate Parent

Take Michael Jordan, for example. After his junior year Jordan left UNC to enter the NBA. "I was unsure, nervous, scared — going into a situation I didn't know if I was ready for," he told me. "But Coach calmed me down with a fatherly attitude, taking me under his wing and teaching me a lot of things about being an adult."

Then came perhaps the most trying moment of Jordan's life. His father was mercilessly and senselessly gunned down while sleeping in his car. Since that happened, Jordan has turned to Coach Smith over and over again for counsel and condolences. How does Jordan characterize his relationship with Coach Smith? "Since my father's death we have grown even closer," he said. "He's very much like my father to me. I love him."

Jordan may be the most famous player to regard Dean Smith as a surrogate father, but he is far from the only one.

Buzz Peterson, the 1981 North Carolina high school player of the year and present head basketball coach at Appalachian State University, also views Coach Smith as a father figure. "Every major decision I have made in my life — sports, marriage, everything — I have gone to him. When I was about to be married, he listened to me and gave advice. You almost feel like you are one of his kids.

"When I won my first conference game here at Appalachian State and I walked into my office early the next morning, the phone was ringing. It was Coach Smith congratulating me on my first conference win. That meant a lot to me. It was as exciting for me as the win itself."

Perhaps the most poignant story I heard came from Pat Sullivan, a former player and a graduate assistant under Coach Smith. Sullivan's alcoholic father left the family when Pat was about 15. "During my sophomore year," he told me, "I was really struggling with it. My mom was great. She handled it well. But I just didn't feel comfortable talking to my mom about something like that. I didn't know where to turn. I was also angry. Did he not love us? I just didn't understand."

Then Coach Smith came to Sullivan and initiated a conversation about his father. They started to meet regularly, to help Sullivan work through his feelings.

"He told me my dad had a disease," Sullivan said. "It wasn't that he did not love us. It wasn't that he chose alcohol over the family. Coach Smith gave me a bunch of tapes to listen to. Some of them were spiritual and some of them on the medical side. Then, every week or two, he would call me into his office and simply ask how I was doing. He asked me if I needed to talk to some of his friends who were psychiatrists. Without him, I would have stored a lot of grief and anger in my heart."

Gradually, Coach Smith convinced Sullivan to contact his father. "He made me think about how hard it probably was for my dad not to talk to me, how hard it must be to try to overcome a problem with no one supporting you. That really got me thinking. I realized I needed to love him even though he was sick. So I wrote him a letter and we corresponded after that. I was really glad Coach Smith encouraged me to do that."

Sullivan's father passed away during his son's senior year. They had never had the chance to talk personally again, but they had stayed in touch through mail. "I came home late from the movies one night and received the news from my roommate," Sullivan said. "The next morning, Coach Smith wanted to see me. He said at least my dad wasn't suffering any more, and I would be able to experience some closure on the situation.

"Later, I realized that in all those times we talked before my dad died, Coach Smith had been preparing me for it. By helping me deal with my anger and encouraging me to contact my dad, he was preparing me for whatever might happen, even his death. Coach refused to let me feel guilty. He simply helped me understand that my dad was sick. That was the greatest thing he helped me understand."

When I asked Sullivan if Coach Smith was like a father to him, he immediately responded, "Oh, yes. I look at him like my father. He knew about my dad's problem during the recruiting process. I think he knew even then that he would need to care for me during my years at Carolina. He is just so caring."

Similar sentiments flow from one of my lifelong friends, Bill Chamberlain. Few people would have expected us to become close. Chamberlain was a gifted, highly skilled, six-foot, six-inch African-American forward from the inner city of New York; I was a six-foot-seven white preacher's kid from the suburbs of Orlando, Florida. But, for whatever reason, we became fast friends at Carolina. He spent several hours with me sharing about his relationship with Coach Smith for this book.

Chamberlain was the most valuable player in the 1971 NIT tournament. He scored 34 points in the final game, exhibiting a dazzling display of skill and athleticism. He went on to play in the old ABA and the NBA. When he talked about his relationship with Coach Smith, there was a hushed awe in his voice, an almost reverent tone. At times he even became misty-eyed. "I remember," he said, "how much my parents liked him. He came across as a person with great character and integrity, unlike many of the other recruiters. His approach was humble, warm, and genuine. He came to my parent's apartment in Harlem, which I'm sure was not an easy trip for him!"

Chamberlain shared some of the different episodes in his life when

Coach Smith's friendship meant a great deal to him. "Probably the most difficult time in my life was when my wife of seventeen years, Wheatley, died in November 1988. We were very close and really loved each other. She had just given birth to our second child. About five weeks later, a congenital brain aneurysm erupted and she died. That night Coach Smith was on the phone to the hospital. He was there for me.

"It's like a blur right now as I talk about it because of the pain. But Coach was constantly there," Chamberlain said. Coach Smith called the hospital, came by the house, and attended the funeral. "He basically held my hand. I was an emotional wreck. We had no previous knowledge she was sick. We were amazed that she didn't die in childbirth, exerting so much pressure. But she didn't. And when she did, Coach Smith was there, by my side, caring for me, loving me like a father loves his son.

"During all my life's trials and circumstances, Coach Smith was like a father to me. I don't know too many players who go to a university and feel like their coach is a father they can call whenever they need him. But I feel this way about Coach Smith. He will be like my father until one of us leaves this Earth. There's nothing I won't do for him, and I sincerely believe he feels the same way about me."

We have already seen how the family environment created by Coach Smith fosters the kind of reciprocal loyalty Chamberlain talked about. But one thing we have not examined is where this whole concept of family originated.

Treating Each Other Like Family

That's an important question, because this feeling of family extends to anyone who has ever played for Coach Smith. For example, I had a difficult time trying to obtain an interview with James Worthy. He was a very successful NBA player and is now a nightly sports commentator for college basketball's television broadcasts. He is a very visible figure, with the NBA and many staff people protecting him from a clamoring public. All my attempts to have him comment on this project failed.

Finally, Mitch Kupchak called Worthy and told him that I was a former player and what I was trying to accomplish with this project.

Worthy readily agreed to see me. When we finally did the interview, he apologized for my difficulty in reaching him. He said, "If I had known you were in the family, I would have agreed to meet with you immediately."

When I interviewed Coach Smith, I probed him regarding his efforts to create this kind of family environment. He admitted he had intended to develop that atmosphere. "It probably goes back to the way I was raised," he told me. "We are all products of our environment in one way or another. I was raised in a relatively strict home. I spent four hours on Sunday in church, even though I oftentimes didn't want to go. But I learned most all my values from a very loving mother and father."

Bill Guthridge, Smith's longtime assistant and eventual successor, agreed with this assessment. When I asked Coach Guthridge about the Carolina family feel and why it existed, he immediately surmised that Coach Smith brought his personal family commitments into the UNC family philosophy. The closeness of his own family influenced his approach to coaching and his emphasis on treating each other like family.

John Lotz, another of Coach Smith's assistant coaches, also believes that Coach Smith's understanding of family was the foundation for leadership principles like loyalty and placing others above self. Lotz said, "I have no doubt it came from his own family. His mother and father were really Christians in the true sense of the word. We are talking about a different era — the thirties, when Coach Smith was being raised. They were strong Baptists and believed absolutely in doing the right thing. His parents were both schoolteachers and undoubtedly hammered these principles into him from an early age. They taught him to do the right thing and then to teach others how to do the right thing."

I believe Coach Smith learned most, if not all, of these principles about the value of family through his own family. These principles gave permanence and power to him, and he passed them on to us. They were delivered to him within the context of a family. He delivered them to us within the same context.

Bill Chamberlain shared another story with me about the family environment Dean Smith created at Carolina. As family members are apt to do, Chamberlain created some real headaches for Coach Smith.

One occurred during his sophomore year, when Chamberlain became involved with the Black Student Movement and the cafeteria workers' strike.

"The university had asked them to work thirty-nine and one-half hours per week," Chamberlain recalled," so they wouldn't have to be paid medical benefits. Other white workers weren't treated that way, and I simply thought that was unfair. I threatened not to play, even to transfer, if their needs were not addressed. Coach never tried to dissuade me from my commitment, even though I know he must have been wondering what to do.

"One day I went by his office unannounced to talk about the strike. He was in a meeting with the chancellor of the university. When his secretary buzzed to tell him I was outside, Coach asked the chancellor to leave so he could talk with me. Interestingly, he totally supported my position. He even ended up signing a petition demanding rights for the cafeteria workers, which they eventually got.

"When I left his office, the chancellor was still sitting outside. Then he went back in Coach Smith's office to continue their conversation. Can you imagine? A player causing him as many headaches as I did being more important than the chancellor! But we were more important to him than anyone except his own personal family. Yet, come to think about it, we were his family!"

As I listened to this story, a question kept sweeping over me: would any of my present employees ever say this about me? I thought especially about those who are younger on my staff, some of whom come from broken homes and dysfunctional families. Do they look to me as a potential father figure? Do I give them reason to do so? What could I do to make my work environment more like a family instead of a mere organization?

Evidently I'm not the only leader to be asking such questions. One man who is trying to create a family environment in a corporate context is Don Carty, CEO of American Airlines. According to Knight Ridder reporter Dan Reed, Carty is trying to change a long history of autocratic management and to make American a company that its people can love because it is a company that cares about and responds to their needs. To that end, he has spent much of his first seven months as CEO preaching to workers and managers alike about the importance of building not only professional skills and competencies, but also the enthusiasm and the love and respect for each other that he believes has been missing within America.

As more and more Generation Xers, many of them from negative family structures, enter the corporate workforce, managers and leaders need to be consciously creating a positive family environment. It's impossible to calculate how much more productivity takes place on a team or an organization when people feel like they are family, that they belong to one another.

But how do you go about creating a family environment? So far we've covered some of the general principles: being vulnerable, becoming a surrogate parent, treating each other like family. Let's look now at some of the practical things Coach Smith did to help create and develop this family feel.

Developing the Family Feel

Dave Hanners offered some interesting perspectives on Coach Smith's family approach to coaching basketball. Not only was Dean Smith like a surrogate father for the players, Hanners suggested, but he also set up, either intentionally or intuitively, a system where other members of the immediate and extended family played roles in the program. For example, assistant coach Bill Guthridge became the players' favorite uncle. He was much more relaxed than Coach Smith, with a gentle and engaging sense of humor. One of my favorite stories about Coach Guthridge's sense of humor involves Michael Jordan. At the zenith of his popularity in the early 1990s, Jordan was in Chapel Hill in the basketball office. Coach Guthridge ran into him in the hall and wryly said, "Michael, I haven't seen you in a while. What have you been doing since you left Chapel Hill?" Because of Guthridge's gregarious, humorous personality, some of the players felt more comfortable going to him with different problems. This may be one reason why the transition was so successful when Coach Smith retired. The players lost dad, but their favorite uncle stepped in to replace him.

Then there is Phil Ford, one of Coach Smith's greatest players and an assistant for many years, another uncle who brings something else to the family. He's a bit younger, therefore he can joke around with the players more easily. Hanners said, "Phil is great at loosening the players up. He runs out on the court with them at practice, telling them that he is number-one. He points to his jersey, retired over one of the baskets, and tells them that when he played they had a play called '12 lob.' They would just throw the ball toward his jersey and he would go up and get it and slam-dunk the ball. The kids get a kick out of that." Hanners suggested to me that when Coach Smith chose his assistants, he looked for personality traits he didn't have, in order to give balance and better meet the needs of the players.

"I think he even chose secretaries with the family idea in mind," Hanners continued. "To me, they are like four surrogate mothers or aunts. They possess the maternal instinct. When the guys come in the office, they tell the secretaries things they will never share with the coaches, things like problems with their girlfriends. Sometimes they don't want us to think that they have everyday problems. I believe Coach Smith knew the family needed moms, so he hired secretaries who are not only wonderful administrative assistants but who could also supply the maternal side of the family environment."

Hanners had a final insight into how Coach Smith helped develop the family feel. "I even wonder if in the design of the office space in the Smith Center he didn't think through developing this family thing. The kitchen is in the center, as are the players' mailboxes. In order to get a drink or get their mail, they have to walk by the secretaries' desks. I've always wondered if that were intentional, forcing the players to deal with their need to interact with a mother figure. Many of these guys come from fatherless homes and mom is the strongest person in their lives. Perhaps this design just had the right feel for him in developing this family commitment among us all."

Think about these practical things Dean Smith has done to create a family environment. Do you see these same ideas in your sphere of influence? How many leaders would recruit a staff knowing certain ones might fulfill different roles in the family? How many would begin to design office space in new buildings in order to maximize a family feel? What a revolutionary thought!

Long before the Smith Center came into existence, however, Coach Smith was nurturing a family environment. During my interview with him, he gave me another insight into how he tried to create family. He reminded me how, every Thanksgiving, he would invite any player who wanted to come over to his house for Thanksgiving dinner.

"Oh, yes," I said. "I did that a couple of times."

He then told me he personally would have never gone over to Coach Allen's house for an event like that when he was playing under him at the University of Kansas. "I would have preferred to be with my friends."

"I was just trying to get more playing time!" I replied.

We laughed. He said the Thanksgiving tradition was an attempt to create a family atmosphere among the players, "although I never wanted it to become a buddy-buddy affair. That was the tension for me. I wanted a family atmosphere, but I knew we couldn't be too friendly at this point. That would happen later, after you graduated."

Caring for Your Personal Family

During this conversation about family, something absolutely amazing happened. The phone rang. Coach Smith looked puzzled for a moment. He said, "I don't understand. I gave explicit instructions not to be interrupted." The phone stopped ringing. We continued the conversation. Then it started ringing again. He was not puzzled any longer.

"Excuse me for a moment," he said. "That must be my private line. It's either one of my children or another former player. They're the only ones who have my private number. You're the only ones who can get to me any time you want!"

He picked up the phone and said, "Hello." Then he smiled. "Hi, Kristen." He covered the phone and said, "It's my daughter. I'll be right back with you." Then he spent the next several minutes counseling his teenage daughter about something that was important to her.

I laughed to myself. I had been furiously studying different articles written about Dean Smith trying to find a way of illustrating my conviction that his former players are like family to him. I had looked everywhere but couldn't find one. Then he gave me the illustration during the interview. Coach Smith said the only people who possessed his private telephone number were his own blood children and players like me!

From his perspective, we're all in the same general category: we're a part of his extended family. That's the way he looks at us. That's why, if we ever need him, we can simply call. That's why we all love him so much.

Do most bosses feel this way about their employees? Or do they feel people are objects to help them reach the bottom line? What would happen in workplaces if employers fervently tried to create an atmosphere of extended family? What would happen if employers created an environment of honesty where all employees, the boss included, could at times open their hearts, share their struggles, and know they would be embraced, not rejected? Employers, do your employees look to you as a surrogate parent? Are your employees learning to treat each other like family, and learning to care for their own personal family, by following your example?

Through my years as the leader of a rapidly growing and changing church, I have learned that if my staff's families are not functioning properly, the staff will not perform well in their jobs. Therefore, I have tried to take this leadership secret from Coach Smith and initiate a family commitment among the staff at the church I pastor.

How do I do this? I try to create times away from our work and all of its tensions, times where the staff simply get to enjoy each other. Occasionally, four times a year, volunteers answer the phones while everyone goes to the local coffee shop for fun and fellowship. The leader over the different divisions must always buy. We'll also have picnics at the park during the week together, go bowling, or go to a movie together. One leader regularly takes his staff to Laser Quest, an arcade where people shoot laser guns at one another. I imagine this is a great opportunity to work out frustrations!

Another thing we do weekly is to divide into groups of six or so for the purpose of sharing any hurts or pains in our lives. Then we pray for one another. It's amazing how this 30-minute weekly meeting together significantly increases our family feel. You also have managers and support staff and maintenance people together sharing one another's burdens. Barriers break down quickly when you're helping someone else carry his huge problem.

However, probably the wisest thing I've done in fostering a family environment is to force, yes, mandate, that my staff take a day off every week to be with their families. I hold them accountable for this, and I become angrier at a careless oversight in this area than an inadequate monthly report. It's because I understand just how important this personal time is for establishing a stable, successful family.

For 19 years, I have had a standing appointment with my wife. It has reaped tremendous rewards. She knows that once a week, every Friday over breakfast, we will have two to three hours together to talk about whatever we need to talk about. On many occasions, it has been marital salvation. My staff could share similar testimonies. In all my years of ministry, we've not had one staff divorce.

For my staff, this mandatory day off every week communicates to them the importance of building their own families. If they have healthy families at home, then they not only help develop the family commitment at work, but they will perform better without personal distractions draining their focus.

Some are saying today that business is at war with family life. Not so at Half Price Books. It is presently the largest used-book dealer in the United States. What has been its key to success? By moving into cities where its employees and their family members desire to move. Again, developing this emphasis on personal family life will be especially meaningful to leaders who must manage GenXers. With their broken homes littering their past, they will be especially desirous of the ability to nurture their own families. Moreover, with women moving into corporate leadership positions, work and family life have become mandated with such features as working at home, flexible hours, and daycare at the work place.

Charles Handy is one of Britain's leadership gurus. In his latest book, *The Hungry Spirit, Beyond Capitalism: A Quest for Purpose in the Modern World,* Handy studied how contemporary organizations can adapt to modern situations. In a chapter called "The Citizen Company," he concluded that businesses must operate like communities. He described people who work for these companies as "citizens" in today's workplace. I think he may need to go a step further. We're not only communities with citizens, but families with individual family members — and the workplaces are either functional or dysfunctional!

Continuing the Family Relationship

The wall of the kitchen near Coach Smith's office is covered with photographs of former players, their wives, and their children throughout the years. A picture of my own three children is there, with Coach Smith holding my youngest, Michael, when he was just a few months old.

One particular picture is insightful. Michael Jordan's son, Marcus, is seen as an infant wearing pajamas. A phrase written on the pajamas nicely encapsulates the principle covered in this chapter: "All I do is eat, sleep and root for the Tar Heels." Marcus, too, is a part of the family!

And the most important part of this family relationship is that it continues long beyond a player's days at Carolina.

One of the most telling of all the stories from former players regarding their feelings about being a part of the UNC family came from Rick Webb, a seldom-used substitute who played for Coach Smith in the late 1960s. Here is the story Webb shared with me for this book.

"On October 5, 1996, I was involved in a life-threatening car accident. I was in intensive care for twenty-three days, undergoing seven difficult operations. Although I truly believe I was saved only by God's grace, my experiences under Coach Smith's leadership and being a part of the Carolina basketball family helped me recover.

"Although I played very little, tough practices and arduous conditioning reinforced important life lessons: humility, tolerance, patience, compassion, understanding, consideration, kindness, and, most important, love. I also learned the power and peace associated with prayer. Coach Smith was a great believer in prayer before and after games.

"The Carolina basketball family was there to support me throughout my recovery. Coach Smith wrote and checked on me regularly. Other players really cared for me with their prayers and presence in my time of need."

Everybody reading this book — everybody on the planet, it seems — knows who Michael Jordan is. Few would recognize the name of Rick Webb, however. He was never a superstar, just a seldom-used college basketball player who would have been long forgotten in the ordinary scheme of things. But the Carolina basketball family is not ordinary. And

30 years later, Rick Webb is still a part of the extended family, still as loved and respected and cared for as Michael Jordan. That's because Coach Smith made us a family.

"Most athletes learn how to endure and play through physical pain and suffering," Webb told me. "But coping with the mental and psychological aspects of debilitating injuries requires you to draw from experiences learned through life's many trials and tribulations. My experiences with Coach Smith, his influence, and the Carolina basketball family, helped me gain the strength, determination, and patience necessary for my continuing recovery and changed lifestyle."

Is there a leader in the world who would not love to have that statement made about them by someone who has been under their tutelage? Wouldn't it be thrilling to see how your leadership has positively affected someone during life's trials? This influence evolves most naturally in a family environment of caring for one another. It's an environment that the leader creates.

Every leader who desires to be effective should ask, "Are my people my most important product? Are they like a family to me? Do they care for one another like a healthy family does? Are the people under my leadership learning principles that can be used when tragedy hits? Would they describe our workplace as being like a family?"

Charles Dickens once said, "No one is useless in the world who lightens the burden of another." I'm convinced that most often takes place within the context of a family commitment. I believe Coach Smith understood this too.

After all, leaders come and go. But families will always be necessary.

Perhaps Phil Ford summed it up best when he said, "I always tell Coach that he's the only father in the world with three hundred children, and only five of them are his own."

Thought for the Day

Loyalty prospers in the context of family.

Game Plan

Create a family environment by:

- Being vulnerable

- Being a surrogate parent

- Treating each other like family

- Caring for your personal family

- Continuing the family relationship

Team Practice

- What do you do to create a sense of family in your team?

- How do you demonstrate vulnerability?

- In what ways do you treat each other like family?

- How do you demonstrate concern for others' personal family?

FRIENDS ARE FOREVER

"But when you leave, you're my friend."

When I asked Coach Smith to describe his leadership style, he never paused. "I was a benevolent dictator. I was the leader. There was no doubt about that. I came up with the practice plans. I controlled everything. But I hope I did it all with some benevolence. I tried to control with compassion."

I had to smile. He did run everything with an iron grip. There was no dialogue in practice. He did not seek our input regarding issues. It was either his way or the highway! Coach Smith would never hesitate to throw someone out of practice, or make them run extra sprints if he thought their actions were hurting the team.

No, there was no doubt about it. He was unquestionably in control. Yet he *was* a benevolent dictator. We knew he deeply cared for us, individually and collectively.

Coach Smith reminded me that each year he let us become just a little bit closer to him. "Wasn't it your senior year, David, that we started letting the seniors make some of the rules and regulations outside of practice?" I nodded.

"Well, I knew that most freshmen come on campus as high school hot shots, and I had to begin to knock some of that out of you. That's why on road trips, freshmen had to carry the projector and do other grunt work. That's why sometimes I would be extremely hard on you as a player. In a real way, I had to tear you down to build you back up. Then, as seniors, you became leaders yourself. You had earned the right to be closer to me."

What he said rang true with me. That was exactly what happened in my years under his leadership.

"But," he continued, "after you left, after you graduated, you became my close friends. Everyone talks about my loyalty to my former players. But I don't treat you any different than I would a close friend. Since you're my friend for a lifetime, of course I'm going to be there when you need me. Of course I'm going to care for you. And I hope that you would do the same for me, simply because we're friends."

In the last chapter I showed how many former players consider Coach Smith a surrogate father. When I asked if he thought of himself in this way, his answer was immediate. "No, I couldn't replace your parents. They did the job of raising you. You are who you are primarily because of them, not me. I look at you and all the former players as my friends. I am your ally, your friend."

I would respectfully disagree with Coach Smith on this point: he is like a father who grew to become our close friend.

But perhaps he is stating something that is even more important than the family feel he created among us. Perhaps he is stating that, beyond family, we possess something that is greater to him: friendship. Above everything else he wants us to be his life-long friends.

My conversation with Coach Smith made me reflect on my relationship with my own father. I grew up in a loving family. However, make no mistake about it, my dad was the boss. He was a benevolent boss, but he was still the boss. In my early childhood years, I remember him as this huge figure. He was in control and I was supposed to obey him. I knew he loved me. I knew he cared for me. But there was still some distance, caused mostly by my awe and respect for him.

Then, as I moved into adolescence, I experienced him more and more as my father. We started doing more things together. He would come to my games. We would share thoughts about different subjects. We grew closer, and as the years passed I moved from experiencing him as a benevolent dictator to knowing him as a loving father.

Now, as an adult, I know him as one of my closest friends. The depth of our relationship far transcends his being the one responsible for raising me, or giving me guidance, as a father is supposed to do for his child. Now, he is simply my close friend.

Similarly, that is what former Carolina players have known with Coach Smith. He is a father figure who became a close friend.

And the basis of this friendship starts with the fact that he accepts us for who we are and respects us as individuals.

Accept People for Who They Are

His acceptance of and respect for people as individuals is apparent in episodes such as the recruitment of Danny Manning. When Manning was a senior in Greensboro, North Carolina, everyone thought he was a lock to attend North Carolina. However, Larry Brown, then head coach at Kansas University, hired Ed Manning, Danny's father, as one of his assistants. The younger Manning committed to Kansas soon thereafter and later led the Jayhawks to the national championship.

Many Carolina people have never forgiven Larry Brown for the Danny Manning situation. They thought it cost UNC many victories and possible national championships. It's one of the first things they bring up when referring to Larry Brown. But Coach Smith never mentions it. Whenever he talks about Larry, it's always with great respect. Why? Because they are friends and that's the way friends treat one another.

This kind of friendship has a higher priority for Dean Smith than celebrating victories. When North Carolina beat Georgetown in 1982 for the national championship, most fans missed something that happened on the court as the Tar Heel team erupted in celebration. Coach Smith immediately looked for John Thompson, Georgetown's head coach and his close personal friend and assistant on the 1976 Olympic gold medal team. Coach Smith ran to Thompson and hugged him. Reading his lips, you could see him ask, "Are you okay?" His first reaction was empathy for his friend, not joy for the national championship. Only after Thompson acknowledged that he was okay did Smith return to celebrate with his players and assistants. No wonder John Thompson remains a close friend to this day!

One player who has experienced this kind of acceptance and forgiveness from Coach Smith is Phil Ford, undoubtedly one of Smith's greatest individual and team players. Ford graduated from high school in Rocky Mount, North Carolina, with amazing credentials. His basketball acumen was outstanding. Practically every school in the country tried to recruit him, and many different coaches all promised him a starting position and plenty of playing time. That's quite alluring for any high school star. It's a difficult carrot not to bite when thinking about signing with a school.

Then Coach Smith came to visit him. Ford had always been a North Carolina fan. But he also knew he was a fabulously gifted point guard who could impeccably run Coach Smith's famous Four Corners offense. So he waited for the pointed pitch, specifically how he would almost certainly start and be given tons of playing time in his first season.

To Ford's astonishment, Coach Smith promised nothing. Instead, he told Ford he might have to play on the junior varsity his first year in order to grow as a player and totally understand the system. The only promise Coach Smith made was that he would be treated fairly.

"That kind of set me back," Ford later recalled. Indeed, he didn't like it one bit. However, slowly but surely, he began to see this honesty as something positive, especially with help of his mother. She said, "Phil Jr., if he's not out here promising you that you will start, that means that if you go there and work hard and do the best you can, then he won't be out promising your job to another high school player." Acknowledging his mother's wisdom, Ford said, "If you think about it, that made a lot of sense."

Ford did sign with Coach Smith and North Carolina. His career was spectacular. Not only did he lead Smith's teams to dozens of victories and to ACC championships, but to the championship game of 1977. He became an All-American and a John Wooden Award winner as a senior. His future sparkled. He was a first-round draft choice in the NBA and became rookie of the year in 1978.

Forgive Human Frailties

The future seemed limitless for Phil Ford, until his third season as a professional. A broken orbital bone of his left eye caused double vision. He could never regain the magic in basketball that had led to so many successes. Slowly, depression crept over his soul. He turned to alcohol. He consumed more and more. It didn't take long to realize that full-blown alcoholism had ensued. His career began to erode. He was being pushed out of the league and onto the streets. It was the darkest moment in Ford's otherwise brilliant life.

Yet it was also at this moment that Ford discovered Coach Smith was not just a benevolent dictator or his surrogate father, but his friend. When word reached Coach Smith about Ford's dark despair, he immediately picked up the phone and tried to track him down. He wanted to meet immediately and find out what needed to be done for Ford to become well.

Ford described it this way. "Coach Smith saved my life. It was like he was saying to me, 'Hey, I'm here for you. It's going to be me and you. You and I will solve this problem together.'" Hope began to flood his soul. He saw that life still had purpose and that, with Coach Smith's help, he could overcome this demon tormenting him.

Coach Smith began making phone calls to rehabilitation centers around the country until he found what he thought was the best one. Ford entered the clinic and began the long, difficult road toward recovery. That was more than 10 years ago. A couple of years after the recovery process began, with his life back on track, Ford became an assistant coach at UNC, where he stayed until Coach Smith's retirement in October 1997.

Why would Coach Smith do this? Yes, Ford was a former player, an awfully good one. Yes, he was part of the Carolina family. That's important. But I would suggest that the primary reason Coach Smith believed in and helped Ford is that he is his friend. That's the way friends act. They forgive our human frailties and reach out to help us when we need it.

When James Worthy, North Carolina's All-American forward in the early 1980s and later an all-pro with the Los Angeles Lakers, talked about Coach Smith as his friend, he said, "You notice it right away. There's nothing you can't talk to him about. The door is always open to his office. If you needed a day off to study for a final exam, he would give you the day off to study.

"But the friendship really happens after you graduate, when you are living life on your own. You really grasp how much he cares after you leave. I am much closer to him right now than I have ever been, and the closeness grows every month. When I was playing, he still sent me good luck mailgrams on opening night. He remembers anniversaries when *we* can't remember them. And it's not public relations. It's sincere. It's Coach Smith. He is our friend and he regularly communicates it."

After James Worthy made headlines with a much-publicized bad decision, another former player expressed his exasperation with Worthy to Coach Smith. Smith quickly defended Worthy, saying that no one could really understand all the pressures and temptations of being an NBA superstar. He, too, lamented Worthy's poor choice, but he was very unwilling to throw stones. Coach Smith encouraged empathy toward Worthy, not judgmentalism.

Desire the Success of Each Individual

Another way Dean Smith expresses his friendship is by wanting the best for his players as individuals, desiring their success, no matter what it costs the team. Yes, the team was all-important. But we heard him say regularly, "The individuals on the successful team are the individuals who receive the most attention."

Justin Kurault, a team manager in the late 1980s, shared insights with me about Coach Smith's friendship for his players and managers during his tenure. Ostensibly, Kurault was not essential for the program to remain in the top 10. Yet, at the end of his senior year, Coach Smith took aside Pete Chilcutt, Rick Fox, and King Rice, his senior starters, and Kurault, the team manager. He asked the four of them how he could help them fulfill their life desires.

Kurault told Coach Smith he wanted to coach. Coach Smith responded, "Well, if you don't want to make any money, I'll see what I can do for you."

"So I spent the summer working Coach Smith's camp and a couple of other camps. Finally, I found out that Coach Smith helped me get the assistant's job at Davidson. It's hard to believe he would do all that for someone like me — just a manager. But he told me, 'You're my friend. That's what friends do for one another.'"

Richard Vinroot, a letterman in Coach Smith's early years and former mayor of Charlotte, North Carolina, told me this story about how Coach Smith placed his respect for individual players even above victories against Atlantic Coast Conference foes. When King Rice was the starting point guard, he went through a very difficult week. He had a campus altercation that resulted in his arrest, and he had a short stay in jail.

That week, Carolina was playing Maryland in Chapel Hill. At that time there was no proof that King Rice was culpable, so Coach Smith allowed him to start.

He played terribly. Carolina lost. Tar Heel fans are usually loyal to a fault, but they mercilessly booed King Rice when Coach Smith left him in the game.

Afterward, Vinroot was in Coach Smith's office. He was frustrated with the loss and launched into a diatribe against Rice. Coach Smith's irritation slowly but surely rose. He finally said, "Richard, you don't know all that King has been through this week. You don't know his frustrations and what is going on in his mind. Yes, I started King tonight and played him practically the entire game. But, frankly, King's self-esteem at this point is far more important to me than whether we win a basketball game."

Isn't that amazing? Coach Smith was more concerned with one player's self-worth than winning a basketball game. By the way, King Rice went on to win many games for Coach Smith and Carolina. Today he's also successful in his chosen career. Could it be at least partly because of the confidence he gained from Coach Smith in this Maryland game? One game was sacrificed to help win many others and to help a kid grow in his life.

Justin Kurault added this insight about the King Rice incident. He said that after the campus altercation, Rice was so embarrassed about it, he didn't respond to two different attempts by Coach Smith to reach him. When they finally met together, Coach Smith firmly reminded Rice that he cared about him as a person first. Coach Smith also told him that he was his friend, and he would stick by him no matter what.

One of my most intriguing interviews in working on this project was with Bob Knight, head coach of the Indiana Hoosiers. North Carolina squared off against Indiana in the 1981 national championship game in Philadelphia, Pennsylvania. Knight has repeatedly received flak in the press for his antics and treatment of players.

Coach Smith had mentioned to me that he and Bob Knight were friends so, on a lark, I wrote Knight and asked if he would like to comment about Coach Smith's leadership for this project. He responded immediately and said he would really like to express his thoughts about Dean Smith.

The interview took place on a snowy day in early March 1998, in Bloomington, Indiana. It was on a Monday of the first week of the NCAA tournament — not the best time for his total concentration. However, when he finally did sit down with me, Knight could not have been more cordial. He began by trying to teach me about theology and particularly the differences between John Calvin and John Wesley. Fortunately, we quickly moved to the real reason for the interview. (I think I could have beaten him in a theological debate, but I honestly did not want to try!)

When Knight began to talk about Coach Smith, his voice changed, becoming almost reverent. He said, "Over the years our friendship has deeply grown. When somebody asks how I get along with Dean Smith, I tell them we are good friends. And I also tell them that he is one of the few, if not the only, person I know, that the more I became acquainted with him, the more I wanted to know him."

Knight continued by telling me a story he had never told before. "We were eating in Chapel Hill," he said, "after an NCAA officiating meeting in Greensboro we both had to attend. The restaurant was very crowded and there was a light atmosphere. When the check came, Dean grabbed it. I said, 'No, I'm taking us to dinner.' And he said, 'No, I'm taking us to dinner.'"

Knight swore and said, "Dean, I am going to pay for this." He put his hand on Coach Smith's wrist and demanded the check.

"I told Dean I'd seen this kind of stuff from him before and that he could pay tomorrow night. We could argue about it again the next night too, but I was paying for dinner tonight. And I took the check from him.

"He didn't know that I heard him, but while I was giving the credit card to the waiter, he leaned over to my wife, Karen, and said, 'You know, he is the only person in the world that I would let do this.' That's the way Dean is. He's unbelievably generous.

"What I was saying by paying for that dinner was that I really appreciated being with him. And by letting me pay, he was saying he really enjoyed being with me too. I thought that was really a nice thing for him to say about our relationship."

Coach Smith and Knight have known each other now for 33 years. They are close friends. At no time was this in greater evidence than the summer of 1998, when *Sports Illustrated* published a rather scathing article about Coach Knight's antics and treatment of players. The next week, in the letters to the editor, who wrote a letter to defend his friend? Dean Smith. He said:

> Coach Knight was and is a brilliant technical coach and teacher of skills.
>
> Knight will not cheat in recruiting, although many coaches in the Hall of Fame with him have been on NCAA probation.
>
> Knight demands that his athletes get their degrees.
>
> Every school would like to have a coach who wins games, whose players have been recruited legally and who graduate, and who brings in millions of dollars to support the many men's and women's programs that cannot support themselves.
>
> I am not aware of any player who has graduated from Indiana who is not grateful to Coach Knight for his experience with the Indiana basketball program.

When Richard Vinroot criticized Bob Knight over his news-making antics with players, Coach Smith angrily came to Knight's defense. He pointed out many of the things Knight has done and continues to do for his players.

For example, after Landon Turner, a star in Indiana's 1981 national championship season, was crippled in an automobile accident, Knight came up with money to help defray his medical expenses. He continued to counsel Turner through a time of deep, dark depression, when Turner learned he would be in a wheelchair for the rest of his life. Smith wanted Vinroot to know the kind of positive things Knight had done that did not receive publicity.

Wouldn't any of us do the same thing for a true friend? Wouldn't we publicly defend a friend if we thought he was wrongly accused? If a close friend of ours had fallen into alcoholism, wouldn't we do anything within our power to help him return to a normal life? Wouldn't we want to help a close friend find a job and fulfill his career ambitions?

We would do that for our friends, but what about our employees? Why do we not allow them to get close to us?

Allow People to Get Close

Yet think about what would happen if employers, over the years, allowed employees to become friends.

Certainly there will always be the tension of how to be a boss and a friend at the same time. Someone naturally has to be the captain of the ship. But should this prevent a meaningful friendship from taking place, a friendship that could enhance, not hurt, the bottom line?

I believe there is a way to do both!

In my own ministry, I oversee dozens of people. The 15 who work most closely with me are called "the program staff." Daily we interact and struggle with difficult issues. They are very gifted, competent people who have been working with me for as few as six and as many as 12 years.

Yet, through time, they have not only been close work associates, but have become my closest friends. If I am hurting, I could go to any one of them and seek help; they would gladly give it to me.

Yes, I am the leader. They understand that. If tough decisions need to be made, I must make them. Yes, I do their annual performance evaluations. Indeed, yearly I call a select few of them into my office and they do a performance evaluation on *my* leadership! This has proved to be extremely helpful to my personal and professional growth. I know they are concerned about my leadership. They want the church to succeed. And I receive their input because I know it is coming from people I value as my friends.

Conversely, I sometimes have to say difficult things to them, pointing out areas that need improvement in their ministry. But that's understood. They understand that's the way the system has to work. But they are also my friends, and this close friendship allows us to work more competently together. We believe in each other. We care enough to confront when necessary. But we also love each other because we are friends.

We also hang out together. We love to spend time together as families. Annually, we spend three days at the beach together. My son's closest friend is the son of one of my staff persons. We simply like each other. And it has carried over to the workplace.

I believe that employers and employees can be friends. It is the foundation of the best possible working relationship. But for this to happen, you must see people as your highest aim, your most important product.

It's my conviction that out of these meaningful friendships your best product is produced. Ronald R. Fogleman, the Joint-Chief-of-Staff for the United States Air Force, once said,

> You ought to treat your machines as if they were people, but never treat your people like machines. You need to care for your resources, but you have to treat people like people. To become successful leaders, we must first learn that, no matter how good the technology, people-to-people relations get things done. People determine our success or failure.

When win number 879 occurred in Winston-Salem in the NCAA tournament in March 1997, allowing Coach Smith to move ahead of

Adolph Rupp as college basketball's all-time winning coach, every former player who could be there was present. I had already committed to being with my family in the mountains, or I would have been there too. As I watched the game on television and saw the record become his, my eyes were moist. I was profoundly happy for him and excited to know I had been a part of his program. Mostly, however, I was proud that I could call him my friend.

Right before the game ended, the former players who were there slipped out of the stands and lined both sides of the tunnel leading to the locker room. As Coach Smith left the coliseum, his eyes also became moist as he noticed each former player. He stopped and shook their hands. He knew they had all helped allow this moment to occur. Overcome with emotion, he thanked all of them for what they had meant to the university and to him. He thanked them for being there and, mostly, for being his friend.

Perhaps Phil Ford best summarized it for all of us who played for Coach Smith when he said, "I had a coach for four years, but I got a friend for life."

Thought for the Day

A friend is always there, no matter what the situation.

Game Plan

- Accept people for who they are
- Forgive human frailties
- Desire the success of each individual
- Allow people to get close

Team Practice

- What actions do you take to build lasting friendships?
- To what extent can a leader be friends with his/her followers?
- How important are friendships in the workplace?
- What could your organization/team do to build stronger relationships?

THE TEAM BEFORE
THE INDIVIDUAL

"The individual must submit his talents for the sake of the team."

At the beginning of his career, many critics doubted Dean Smith's coaching ability. His early teams did not succeed. After a particularly painful ACC loss in the early 1960s, some of the student body even hung him in effigy. He ostensibly turned it around from 1967 to 1969 with three straight Final Four appearances. But many still felt Smith achieved this because of his ability to recruit talent, not because of his coaching ability.

Then came the 1971 season, my senior year. The pundits predicted doom and gloom for Carolina basketball. Charlie Scott, our All-American, had graduated following a disappointing 18–9 season. His replacement was an aggressive, fearless point guard named George Karl (now coach of the NBA's Milwaukee Bucks). On the surface, it seemed like a replacement that would make the team worse, not better. We were slotted to finish next to the last, right above Clemson.

Before the season began, Coach Smith preached that teams, not individuals, win games. He constantly exhorted us to play as a team, to believe in his vision of the team. He said that if we did, we would surprise everyone. He was so convinced that no individual was greater than the whole, that every player bought the idea. None of the critics imagined we would succeed like we did. Yet we were ranked in the top 15 teams that season, winning 26 games, the Atlantic Coast Conference regular-season title, and the prestigious NIT championship in New York.

Art Chansky, in his book *The Dean's List*, which chronicles all of Coach Smith's seasons, said the 1971 season did two things for Carolina basketball. First, it showed the philosophy of team above the individual worked. With no apparent superstar, the team was imminently successful. Second, it convinced every Carolina recruit thereafter that if they played by the Smith philosophy, they would win games. They caught the vision.

Bobby Jones told me, "Coach Smith somehow, someway, made us believe that if we followed his philosophy we would win. By the time I was a senior, if he'd told me to go to the corner and stay on my hands and knees until the play was over — if he said we would win by doing that, I would have done it. We knew putting the team above the individual worked. We knew that was his vision. And we did whatever he told us because we believed in him."

In my opinion, this concept of team may be Coach Smith's greatest gift to basketball and society. It doesn't matter whether you're coaching a sports team, managing a corporation, being a parent, or leading a Boy Scout troop, creating a cohesive team is critical.

In his book titled *Business as a Calling*, the respected lay theologian Michael Novak quotes David Packard of Hewlett-Packard: "When a group of people gets together and exists as an institution that we call a company, they're able to accomplish something collectively they could not accomplish separately. Together they make a contribution to society."

When a leader melds a group of people into a team, and when the leader inspires that team with a vision, then great things begin to happen in an organization. The team will be far more productive working as a unit than as individuals. B.C. Forbes, founder of *Forbes* magazine, once said you spell success: T-E-A-M-W-O-R-K.

Critics have tried to demean Coach Smith's dogged vision of the team as being more important than the individual. A regularly recurring joke has been that Dean Smith is the only person ever to hold Michael Jordan to fewer than 20 points a game.

When I asked Kansas coach Roy Williams about this, he became mad. "The people who make those kind of comments don't know what they're talking about. Michael was double- and triple-teamed at every opportunity. Then the shot clock was initiated during his college years. In 1982, when we won the national championship, we averaged scoring in the sixties. Everyone was trying to control tempo by controlling the basketball. Plus, we saw zone after zone, and Michael had not yet developed his great jump shot. But go ask Michael about his greatness and the foundation he learned under Coach Smith. He is a great player today because he learned to play team basketball at North Carolina."

As much as Coach Smith's former players genuinely love him, that affection was only partly responsible for his success. We played hard for him because we believed in his vision. We believed it won basketball games. We believed his philosophy worked. And his record of 879 wins proved it beyond a doubt.

What was Coach Smith's vision? It's very easy to encapsulate: "No individual person is greater than the team." He would frequently say to us, "If you want personal recognition, you should play tennis, golf, or run track." He was totally convinced that the team playing together is the goal of basketball. He even told me, "I wish that some year some coach who had gone twelve and fifteen would be named coach of the year, just because he did a wonderful job coaching the team. It's society that stresses wins and losses. But that's not what's most important: it's the individual submitting himself to the team."

Even before the team is assembled, the leader must realize that it is his vision that gives direction. Then he must surround himself with gifted, competent people to achieve this vision.

Justice Oliver Wendell Holmes once boarded a train in Washington, then realized he had lost his ticket. The conductor recognized him and said, "Don't worry, sir. I'm sure when you find it, you'll send it in."

Justice Holmes replied, "Young man, the question is not 'Where is my ticket?' but rather, 'Where am I supposed to be going?'"

Coach Smith clearly knew where he was going: the team would be more important than the individual. The team would win games. This was his vision, and he stated it almost daily.

Management gurus say that a leader needs to restate the vision every 28 days to keep the team focused on it. I have learned in my own organization that our vision similarly needs to be repeated at least that frequently, or people tend to forget it. We therefore talk as often as possible about the vision of being a contemporary church trying to express old truths in new ways. We use bulletins, inserts, up-front announcements — whatever possible — to communicate the vision.

Coach Smith did the same. I can hardly remember a practice session without the vision of the team above the individual being stated in some way. Often the thought of the day, printed at the top of the daily practice plan, had to do with this vision. The assistant coaches regularly stated it. While studying game film, we would hear the team vision quoted over and over again.

Every year it was this vision that united each new team. This vision was reflected in a sign that hung over the door leading to the court in Carmichael Auditorium. It simply read, "United we stand, divided we fall."

Teams win games. Individuals playing selfishly lose them.

Burt Nanus, president of Visionary Leadership Associates and professor emeritus at USC Graduate School of Business Administration once said, "Every leader needs a vision. And the process never ends. The role of direction-setting never ceases. The leader is constantly reassessing the vision, refining it, and allowing it to evolve and grow."

That's what happened in 1971. We totally believed in Coach Smith's vision of a team. We truly believed that if every individual subordinated his gifts for the sake of the whole, we could accomplish anything we desired. The vision created synergy and the victories piled up. Every team under Coach Smith's tutelage has similarly caught his vision.

I had the privilege of being in Chapel Hill when Vince Carter announced his decision to forego his senior season and turn professional. It was not the best decision for the North Carolina team. However, it was the best decision for Vince Carter, and that was why Coach Smith encouraged him to do it. During the press conference, Vince shared why he was going to the NBA. He went on and on about how it would help him fulfill personal and professional goals.

Finally, Coach Smith interrupted Vince in mid-sentence. "He'll also help the team," Smith said. Everyone associated with the Carolina program chuckled. Even during Vince's momentous occasion, Coach Smith could not resist reminding his superstar that the team was what is most important.

Let's look now at some of the different ways Coach Smith allowed this team concept to develop. Most, if not all, of these ideas are transferable to different leadership situations. They have been for me in the church.

Teach What's Important in the Vision

I asked Coach Smith how he initiated this concept of team first into practices so we could best understand it. How did he teach the vision? "You should know that one," he responded. "It begins on the defensive end. If a team plays good defense, it can always be in a game."

We spent the first three weeks of preseason practice mostly learning team defense. He taught us "help" defense, how we all needed to help one another. Then he taught pressure defense.

Coach Smith used a particular trick to prove the need for pressure defense to initiate the action. He would hold a dollar bill between his thumb and forefinger. He then bet us that we couldn't catch the bill when he dropped it. Of course, we all tried to do it. And each time we failed. It was a demonstration of his cardinal basketball theory: "Action beats reaction."

That's probably why Coach Smith considers himself primarily a defensive coach, why he advocated strong, man-to-man, pressure defense. He said, "The offense will always have the advantage against a defense that just sits there waiting to be attacked, waiting for somebody to take a shot. So, if you're on defense, you've got to go get the ball. Let's not take what they are going to give us; let's take what we want."

After I played for three years in the European professional leagues, John Lotz, who had become the head coach at the University of Florida, invited me to become a graduate assistant in his program. I gladly agreed. I was with him for two years and received a graduate degree in counseling while there.

During my first year at Florida, Coach Smith spoke at the Gator team banquet. At the beginning of his talk, he noticed that I was sitting in the audience. He said, "Oh, I see that one of my former players is here and working on the staff, Dave Chadwick. I want to tell you that Dave was one of the finest offensive players ever to play at North Carolina. He could really score."

My chest widened. I was so proud to hear Coach Smith say these things about me. I looked around to see who was glancing at me.

Then he continued, "But, unfortunately for Dave, I'm a defensive coach."

My balloon popped. I melted in my seat. Everyone laughed — at my expense!

But Coach Smith was right. I could score, but defense was difficult for me. And he was a defensive coach who believed the concept of team began with defense. He taught this from the first day of practice forward.

That's not to say that offense wasn't important. He also taught that no matter how good the defense was, the other team would score. But he knew that if we played good defense, we could stay in the game.

Coach Smith's offensive schemes are as carefully studied and copied as his defense. Let's face it, he's a brilliant coach, offensively and defensively. However, in teaching the team concept, he began with defense because it was the most important part of the vision. He could never know, from night to night, if the offense would score. Players who are gifted offensively never know from one night to another if they are going to have the touch or be in the zone. Coach Smith knew, though, that a team could play hard defensively every night. This could be a constant. He therefore developed the team concept first by focusing on defense.

Jack Welch, CEO of General Electric, believes in this idea of focusing on what's most important with your team. Since Welch took over in 1981, GE has moved from a cumbersome bureaucracy with 350 different businesses to a burgeoning enterprise focusing on just 17 businesses. As a result, GE's revenues rose to a record $90.84 billion in 1997, a 15 percent increase over the previous year's revenues. More important, its profits rose to $8.2 billion, an increase of 13 percent. Moreover, near the end of 1998, GE's total market value neared a staggering $300 billion!

An interesting question for all leaders would be: how do you teach team above the individual in your workplace? Coach Smith began with defense. This was a constant, easily controlled by consistent effort. What would that be for you?

In my workplace, it would be Sunday morning worship. It is regular and predictable. No matter what, Sunday comes every week. It is the engine that drives everything else in the church. Therefore, we spend much time on the staff making sure we're united in what we're doing on Sunday mornings and why we're doing it. Everyone is committed to excellence. That commitment fosters teamwork. We know that every individual is needed to make Sunday morning work. But we also know that no individual is greater than the whole.

As a Leader, Take the Hits

Another way Coach Smith developed the team concept was his commitment that *we* won games and *he* lost them.

He never demeaned a player in the press, even if it might be justified because of a mistake. He did not want to do anything to disrupt the team. And if a player made a mistake, Coach would assume that somehow he had not properly communicated to that player what he should have done.

As a result, the players felt protected. It fostered trust among us when we knew that, as coach, he was willing to take the hits for the team.

I can't begin to emphasize the need for trust for any team or organization. It can be easily lost and difficult to regain. Gaining trust takes hard work, commitment, perseverance, and loyalty. Donna Wyatt, who leads the initiative for Team Development for the North American Division of the Colgate-Palmolive Company, said this about the "payoff" of trust. "In an environment of trust, people begin to tap into their potential and create outcomes that benefit themselves and their organizations...And it is the extraordinary leader — who is both powerful and vulnerable, trustworthy and trusting — who is the architect and resident of the trusting organization."

The extraordinary trust that existed between Coach Smith and his teams came out of his commitment to lose games and let his players win them. He steadfastly refused to embarrass any of his players at any time. In fact, if we made a terrible mistake in a game, he would always wait to take us out. He did not want the fans to think that he was yanking us because of a mistake. He knew that would embarrass us.

In 1971, my senior year, we had won the regular-season ACC championship. South Carolina was still a part of the conference then and our most bitter rival. We had split two games with them during the regular season. We met in the finals of the ACC Tournament to decide who would represent the ACC in the NCAA Tournament. It was a winner-take-all tournament, the pressure of which no contemporary team knows.

With six seconds to go, we were ahead 51–50. Our 6'11" center was jumping against their 6'3" guard. We thought we had the game won. Coach Smith went over all our assignments in the huddle. Somehow, though, not everyone understood what we were supposed to do. The ball was tipped to the wrong spot. South Carolina scored, and we lost 52–51. We were devastated. For many Tar Heel fans that loss stands out as one of the most disappointing losses in Carolina history.

I was in the game when the tip went awry. For years, I did not even want to talk about the game. It was that painful. Finally, a few years ago, when I was visiting with Coach Smith, my curiosity overcame me. I asked him about that game and if I had done anything wrong to cause the loss. He went over every detail of the play. He showed me what he had been trying to do. Then he said, "I wanted you to be here. But that wasn't your fault. That was my fault. No one was really where I wanted them to be. I accept full responsibility for that loss. I didn't communicate well enough as a coach."

I seriously doubt that it was all Coach Smith's fault. We probably did not listen as closely as we should. But I did find it fascinating that more than 20 years after it happened, he was still protecting his players and the team, still taking full responsibility for the losses. *Players win games. Coaches lose them.* The unity of the team is what is most important!

Recognize Potential and Reward Effort

Another thing Coach Smith did to create the team vision was to recognize potential and reward effort. I believe he was always thinking about next year's team when examining a player's potential. He looked for ways to encourage individuals to become better players and contribute to the team.

Pearce Landry tells an interesting story that illustrates this point. He was a Morehead Scholar, recipient of a very prestigious scholarship awarded to outstanding high school students who show giftedness in academics, athletics, leadership, and service. During his sophomore year at Carolina, he played solely on the junior varsity team.

In February, Carolina played Notre Dame. Coach Wiel, the junior varsity coach, came up to Landry before the game and told him that if the game was a blowout, Coach Smith wanted Landry to dress and earn a few minutes playing with the varsity team. He had played in practice against the varsity, but this was beyond his wildest thoughts.

Sure enough, in the second half, Carolina blew the game open. Landry was sitting in the stands wearing a suit and tie. With about 10 minutes left to play, Coach Wiel turned toward the stands and told Landry to run to the locker room and change. "I sprinted out of the stands and back into the tunnel to the locker room," he said. "The assistant manager handed me a uniform with number fifteen on the back. I slipped it on and got back on the court with about four minutes to play. Finally, with about fifty-five seconds to go, I entered the game. That was my claim to fame that year."

"What was Coach Smith trying to accomplish by putting you in for the last minute of the game?" I asked.

"You know, I think he was trying to say to me that there were good things ahead of me if I kept on working. He was trying to give me a little taste of varsity competition so that in my junior and senior years I might be a good practice player. He was also saying, 'Thanks for helping the varsity in practice.' I simply think he was looking ahead to the next two years."

For his junior year, Landry remained pretty much a practice player. He got to play in one important game against LSU on national television. But he kept working and kept getting better. Then his senior year, Larry Davis transferred, Pat Sullivan blew out his back, and suddenly Landry was the sixth man.

"Then I remembered that game against Notre Dame my sophomore year," he said. "That began to boost my confidence. Had Coach been looking to the future, thinking that I might improve enough to help the team, and he wanted to give my confidence a boost? I think so."

Napoleon once said it amazed him that men were willing to sacrifice their lives in order to have a few medals pinned on their chest.

Recognizing potential and rewarding effort pays off in the corporate boardroom as well as on the basketball court. A good leader sees the potential of workers and how they can develop to help the organization in the future. Are you presently doing this as a leader?

I have learned that the best pool for potential staff people are our interns. Yearly we bring on board young people just out of college or those who have just entered ministry. In 18 years of ministry, our staff has increased from two full-time employees to more than 40. The single best resource has been these interns. When they come on staff, I have a hidden agenda to develop them for future teams. The results have been extraordinary.

We expose the interns to every area of church life. When they show exceptional ability, we find out their primary interest and give that to them as a full-time responsibility. Invariably, they then desire to stay on staff and pour their hearts into this ministry.

Like Coach Smith putting a junior varsity player in for the last minute of a big game, we look for ways to reward our interns by getting them involved in meaningful work and giving them a chance to show their potential. It's a powerful strategy.

John F. Welch Jr. is chairman and CEO of General Electric Company. In his 1995 annual report, he described the leadership challenge of getting everyone in the company involved. He wanted to give GE's 222,000 employees "what the best small companies give people:

voice." To do that, GE came up with a plan called Work-Out. Welch wrote:

> Work-Out was based on the simple belief that peo-
> ple closest to the work know, more than anyone, how it
> could be done better. It was this enormous reservoir of
> untapped knowledge, and insight, that we wanted to
> draw upon. People of disparate ranks and functions
> search for a better way, every day, gathering in a room
> for an hour, or three days, grappling with a problem or
> an opportunity, and dealing with it, usually on the spot
> — producing real change instead of memos and prom-
> ises of further study.

While most people think factories should run with machine-like precision, Charlene Pedrolic, the manufacturing chief at Rowe furniture in Salem, Virginia, tore apart the assembly line. She sent gluers, staplers, and seamstresses away and ordered them to build their sofas as they best believed it should happen. The result? Productivity, profit, and employee satisfaction jumped through the ceiling.

Bob Nelson, vice president of Blanchard Training and author of *1001 Ways to Reward Employees*, says one of the primary ways an employer can motivate people today is "to involve employees in decisions, espe-cially when those decisions affect them." It gives them a sense of own-ership in their work and the work environment.

That may be the latest advice from the business world, but it's some-thing Coach Smith was doing in college basketball almost 30 years ago. Who made the rules and regulations for each new season? The seniors did. He believed they would know best what the team needed. Because he trusted the seniors to make the rules, they felt more ownership. The other members of the team felt they could give input as well. They felt represented. The team was enhanced.

I personally practice a lot of management by walking around. But I've tried to take this a step further for greater effectiveness. While I'm interacting with staff people, as I find them doing something good and commend them for it, I also regularly ask, "Hey, about this problem in the church, what do you think might be a solution?" Not only have I sometimes received some great solutions, but also the workers regularly feel like they are a part of what's going on.

It's just another way of recognizing potential and rewarding effort.

Know Your Team Members

Another way Coach Smith helped develop the team was by knowing the players and communicating honestly with each member of the team.

In some ways a coach needs to be a master psychologist. He has to try to understand each player's personality, his unique psychological make-up. This information is critical to know in order to make the proper decisions for the team. I experienced Coach's Smith unique ability in this area first-hand.

As shared previously, I worked hard preparing for my senior season. I readily understood that the two players with whom I would be competing were better players: Bill Chamberlain and Dennis Wuycik.

Yet during preseason practice, I outplayed both of them daily. Coach Smith started me the first three games of the season. We won all three, and I was averaging 16 points and eight rebounds per game. The fourth game was against Creighton, a nationally ranked team. I started that game, too, but was taken out after about four minutes; Chamberlain played most of the rest of the game. He played extremely well and we won.

The fifth game saw Chamberlain become the other starting forward, and he remained in that spot for the rest of the season. I started 11 games altogether, filling in when someone was hurt or disciplined. It was a very fulfilling season, although I always wondered why I was moved to the sixth-man role when I clearly outplayed the others in practice.

When I was a graduate assistant at the University of Florida, I summoned the courage to ask Coach John Lotz why this had occurred. He had been an assistant when I played at UNC. I was not bitter, not holding a grudge, I told him. I was simply curious.

Coach Lotz paused for a few moments. Then he finally said, "David, that was a very difficult decision for Coach Smith. You know how he preaches that your game time is related to how you play in practice. But one day he came in and simply said, 'Dave will accept coming off the bench and having a lesser role. It'll be more difficult for Bill to accept since he's such a gifted athlete. Bill will play harder if he's a starter. It will be better for the team if David comes off the bench.' And that was that."

I was not hurt or miffed when Coach Lotz told me how Coach Smith had made the decision. In fact, something deep inside said, "You know, he's right!" It was undoubtedly a good coaching decision, based on the fact that Coach Smith knew the psychological make-up and talent level of his individual players. But his decisions were always made for the betterment of the team. I think he knew I would accept that.

How did Coach Smith get to know his players so well? It started during the recruiting process. James Worthy shared with me how, during Coach Smith's recruitment visit, Coach Smith talked about five minutes to Worthy and then spent most of the evening conversing with his parents. He talked with them about the scholarship, life, and his experiences growing up in Kansas. He spent very little time talking about basketball. At the time it was puzzling to Worthy. "Later in life," Worthy said, "I realized what he had been doing. In getting to know my parents, he was getting to know me. That was the best way he knew of to get to know the recruits."

Leaders, do you know the psychological make-up of your individual team players? There are many tools on the market to help you (i.e. DISC inventory). My entire staff has taken the DISC inventory so we can all understand one another better. Personally, I have found these tools invaluable to understanding my staff, my own make-up — even why sometimes I respond to my wife the way I do! — and the decisions I must make as a leader for the betterment of the team. It has also been very helpful for me to know their family backgrounds. It helps me know them and how they may respond to different situations.

When you understand your team members, then you can develop a relationship with them based on openness and honesty. That's something else I learned from Coach Smith. Not only did he know each player inside and out, but he was always honest with them. It was another way of developing the team.

Regularly, he would cry out in practice, "Know your limits." He would then carefully outline the specific giftedness and limitations of his individual players. Only certain players could shoot three-pointers, or handle the ball on the break. If he didn't think you could do these things, he wouldn't allow you to try. This honesty, accepted as truth because we all wanted what was best for the team, was extremely important.

Before and during the season, Coach Smith would specifically share with each player the role he played. He was honest and plainspoken. At the end of each season, Coach Smith made a personal appointment with each player. He clearly outlined individual strengths and weaknesses. He forthrightly pointed out where they were with the team and how much playing time they would probably receive the next season unless they improved. Then he challenged them to start building on their strengths and improving their weaknesses. Amazingly, he would be so honest that he would even tell a player if he thought he'd never play. Then, if the player concurred and desired to transfer, Coach Smith would help him.

This honesty, I believe, is absolutely crucial to how he developed the team. It helped avoid unnecessary rivalries by clearly defining each player's role on the team. It helped avoid childlike outbursts of "that's not fair!" Each player knew he was appreciated for his own unique contribution to the team.

Some people believe that only positive encouragement and comments should be given to members of the team. They suggest that when a boss sees mistakes in judgment and errors, he should only look for something good to say and not discourage a member of the team with criticism.

Coach Smith would not agree! In practices, during games, and at the end of the season, he would be brutally honest with us. If he had to say something to us in a game, he would always kneel in front of us and quietly talk to us one on one. He was committed to never embarrassing us in front of a crowd. Coach Smith believed that criticism should be given constructively. Moreover, he would give this criticism without favoritism.

Buzz Peterson remembers when Michael Jordan was receiving all the publicity and glamour. "Coach Smith thought it was going to his head. Therefore, from time to time in practice, he would really get on Michael to keep his head level and the team as most important."

Dave Hanners remembers one moment when he experienced Coach Smith's biting tongue. Hanners was a freshman in his very first practice. "It was the first year freshmen were eligible," he said. "He did not want us in the practice in the first place. We all came into the circle at the beginning of practice. It was very sunny outside. I'm from Ohio, and I couldn't believe how bright it was. The light was coming through the windows. I was looking off at the sun, and Coach looked at me. Bang! He got me. He said, 'Dave, what is the emphasis of the day? You seem to know everything and don't need to pay attention. If you don't need to listen, you must already know the emphasis of the day.'

"That put me at a loss. I stuttered. And guess what? I never again looked at anything but Coach when we came to that circle. And I never forgot the emphasis of the day!"

When criticism is thoughtful and sensitively delivered in a timely manner, it can have a positive purpose. Coach *never* scolded, berated, demeaned, or humiliated us. He did become angry at the wrong behavior, but not at us. I think he knew that approval and disapproval are both realities, and it was his job to give both. The way he did it always honored his life principle that we, his players, were his most important products.

When I interviewed Bob Knight, I asked if he thought Coach Smith's greatest strength was loyalty. He said no. Knight thought the better word to describe Coach Smith's greatest asset was *honesty*. "Someone can be loyal to bad things," he said, "but honesty cannot. Honesty is the greatest of all the virtues. Our mutual honesty is what has caused the mutual respect we have for one another."

Coach Smith had this same commitment to honesty with potential recruits. For example, most people thought Kenny Anderson, now with the NBA's New Jersey Nets, would come to Carolina. Many think the reason he didn't come was because of Coach Smith's honesty. Anderson was asking two questions of all the coaches recruiting him. Phil Ford and Coach Smith met with Anderson to try and answer his questions.

The first one from Anderson was, "Coach, will I start as a freshman?" Ford leaned back in his chair, anxious to hear the answer to that one.

Coach Smith responded, "Kenny, if you are as good as people think you are, and if you show the confidence that you have shown at this stage of your career, then the playing time will take care of itself. You don't have to worry about that."

Then came the second question. "Will you let me run the show?" Anderson asked. Ford's back straightened up on that one. He said, "Even I wanted to hear Coach's answer!"

"Kenny," Coach Smith replied, "we have done this for so long I hope you will trust our judgment on matters. My door is always open for discussion. If you have any questions about anything that we do or don't do on the floor, I hope you'll always come in and talk with me about it."

Kenny Anderson went to Georgia Tech. He said he didn't want to be just another horse in Coach Smith's stable. Coach Smith believed the team was greater than the individual. And this principle would not be abrogated, even for a point guard as gifted as Kenny Anderson. Therefore, Coach Smith had to be honest with him, not making any promises during the recruiting process that he couldn't keep later. His honesty may have cost him a talented recruit, but it was best for the team.

Dr. William Schultz, a psychologist who developed strategies to increase productivity with Procter & Gamble and NASA once said that the key for success lies in how well people work together. He went on to say that, in his opinion, the key to people working together is mutual trust and honesty. He concluded, "If people in business just told the truth, eighty percent to ninety percent of their problems would disappear."

It is this principle of honesty that leads to my yearly performance evaluations of my staff. We both clearly understand what's expected of each other. There is open honesty from me to them and, when necessary, from them to me. Actually, I rather enjoy these evaluations. When you have an effective staff, most of the time is spent affirming the great job they are doing and trying to find together how they can do it even better.

Coach Smith taught me the necessity of open candor in leadership.

Create Little Teams on the Big Team

We were playing Georgia Tech in the old Charlotte Coliseum in 1971. We had the better team and were expected to win easily. However, Georgia Tech came out highly motivated, and with 10 minutes left in the first half, we were down by 10.

Dennis Wuycik gave the fist, signaling that he was tired and needed to come out of the game. Coach Smith sent me to the scorer's table. Then Lee Dedmon gave the fist. Craig Corson, the back-up center, followed me to the scorer's table. Then George Karl. Coach Smith was already greatly exasperated with their uninspired play, so he muttered under his breath, "Oh, what the heck!" He told the entire second team to go into the game and replace the first team.

We entered the game with fresh legs and great enthusiasm. Within three minutes we had taken the lead from the Yellow Jackets. Coach Smith then put the starters back into the game. They now had fresh legs and were greatly inspired — and a bit embarrassed! They blew the game wide open.

That game started something that lasted for many years. It was called the Blue Team. This was the second unit that, for most teams, just sits on the bench, watches the games, and serves as cannon fodder for the first team. However, from then on, Coach Smith would regularly substitute the Blue Team in mass force for the first team, with startling results! We almost always held the score until the first team reentered the game, and sometimes we increased the lead.

However, we discovered something much more important than the score. If you give a player a few minutes, even if it's only in the first half when the pressure's not on, he will be ready if you need him in the second half. And, even more important, he will feel that he is a part of the team. After that Georgia Tech game, a new spirit of unity engulfed our team. I'm thoroughly convinced that one of the primary reasons for that team's extraordinary and inexplicable success was the fact that all of us felt we were a part of the team. We believed in Coach Smith's vision for us.

Moreover, the Blue Team had an identity. We even developed our own handshake, one that could only be used by Blue Team members, with our fingers all crunched together as we touched fingertips together. We became highly offended if a player other than a member of the Blue Team used this handshake.

Bill Guthridge, who was then assistant coach, usually coached the Blue Team when we played against the first team. Therefore, we allowed him to use the handshake. In fact, when I visited Coach Guthridge to interview him for this book, he walked out of his office and extended to me the Blue Team handshake — 27 years later!

Thinking back, I realized we had created a team within the team. They were separate teams, yet connected, still with the overall vision of winning together as our goal. We discovered that a team could have smaller teams within the larger team, while still accomplishing the team vision. I remembered how Coach Smith used to break us down into teams of big men and small men to play against each other. Each group developed its own sense of team. When we worked three on three in practice, the vision of teamwork was preached. Coach Smith would sometimes watch preseason three-on-three drills. If he ever saw selfish play, he would find a way to get the message to us.

I do something similar. We have several divisions that oversee the life of the church. We do many things together as a larger staff, activities that promote reciprocal loyalty, create the feel of family, and help us become close friends.

However, as the staff has grown larger, this is increasingly more difficult. Therefore, we try to create smaller teams within the big team. I encourage each division leader to do with their division team what we do as a larger team. They go out for coffee and movies together. They take their own division retreats together. It helps everyone feel like they belong, and the larger team is then made stronger.

Creating little teams within the big team is one of the most important things you can do to promote team unity. And helping every player, or staff member, feel they belong to the team has a snowball effect, building and building on itself with greater and greater results.

The same concept is still working in the Carolina basketball program. And not only has it unified the team, it has spilled over to the fans.

One of the most amazing scenes in the 1997–98 season occurred in the home game against Florida State. UNC may well have played its best game of the season. It was a blowout against a very good Seminoles team. With about 12 seconds left, Scott Williams, the son of Kansas's Roy Williams, was playing during what is known as mop-up time.

The game had obviously been won, but the crowd and the entire team were intensely into the game. Why? Because Williams does not get to play very much and had not scored a basket in his varsity career. Finally, he drove to the basket, threw the ball into the air, and whoosh! In it went. The bench erupted. They acted as if he had just hit the game-winning basket in the national championship. The players, and even the fans, all knew how important every man is to the team.

Justin Kurault experienced this reality of everyone feeling equal and a part of the team, even though he was the team manager. "There is no one person who is bigger than the program," he said. "Coach put us right there in the locker room with the players. We had a locker just like the players. In fact, ours was a little bigger, to store some of the stuff we needed to do our job. We received the same warm-ups to travel in. When the team received pictures at the end of the season, so did we. I was lucky enough to win three ACC Tournaments, and the managers received rings just like the players."

In their book *The Wisdom of Teams,* Jon R. Katzenbach and Douglas K. Smith wrote:

> Teams are not the solution to everyone's current and future organizational needs. They will not solve every problem, enhance every group's results, nor help top management address every performance challenge. Moreover, when misapplied, they can be both wasteful and disruptive. Nonetheless, teams usually do outperform other groups and individuals. They represent one of the best ways to support the broad-based changes necessary for the high-performing organization.

How about your organization? Do people in your workplace have a chance to be involved? Does your lowest-level employee feel like he or she is a part of the team? If not, why not? Ask yourself what you can do to make them feel that they, too, own the vision. When workers feel they have input into key decisions, oversight, and the overall direction, they feel ownership and work harder to make the team's vision a reality.

Show Fairness, Not Favoritism

There is one final thing you can do to develop a team vision, and that is to treat each team member fairly. It's another leadership lesson I learned from Coach Smith.

According to Coach Guthridge, this might be Dean Smith's greatest genius in creating a team. Everyone knew that he treated his players fairly. So how could anyone argue with him if he chose to play one person more than someone else? They knew it was not an arbitrary decision.

How did Coach Smith accomplish this? Guthridge said the major way of ensuring fairness stemmed from the hierarchical system of moving freshmen to seniors. If you were a senior, you knew you would get every opportunity to play, even if a freshman was playing at the same level.

This conviction was at the heart of the struggles of the 1994 team. Four out of five starters returned from the '93 championship team. Three heralded freshmen also came on board. The freshmen were enormously talented. In practice they regularly challenged the incumbents. But the majority of playing time went to the seniors. If it were even, the seniors got the edge.

Eddie Fogler, presently head coach at South Carolina, says this states to the incoming players that you have to pay your dues in the system. It says to the freshmen, "Coming out of high school, you haven't put anything into this system." From day one, people learn that service to the organization has its benefits. And if you pay your dues, you will be rewarded.

Woody Durham, the Tar Heels' radio voice, pointed out an example of this respect for seniors that many people would not know about. Carolina played in the 1977 national championship game against Marquette. Coach Smith was coaching against Al McGuire. They are good friends and had learned much basketball from one another. The game was a chess match, with Carolina finally getting the lead in the second half. Then Coach Smith went into the Four Corners at a crucial point in the game.

Mike O'Koren was a fabulous freshman who had 34 points in the semi-final game against UNLV. He gave the tired signal and exited the game right before Carolina gained the lead. Bruce Buckley, now a prominent Charlotte attorney, took his place.

When Carolina regained the lead, Eddie Fogler leaned across Bill Guthridge and said to Coach Smith, "Don't you think we should take a time-out and get Mike back in the game?"

"Now think about this," Durham continued. "It's the national championship game. Coach Smith had been to three Final Fours in the late 1960s. He had taken another team to the Final Four in 1972. Comments were spreading nationally that perhaps Dean Smith was not a great coach because he couldn't win the supposed big one. Do you know how he responded to Eddie? He said he would never embarrass a senior like Bruce Buckley by taking him out of the game like that.

"Right after that, Bruce had a shot blocked and the momentum of the game changed a bit. That's not to say Carolina lost the game because of this decision. It is to say that Coach Smith was concerned with how his seniors were cared for, concerned with his loyalty to them, even in a national championship game!"

Freshmen don't like this hierarchy, nor do they understand it. But it's birthed in the conviction that this is the fair thing to do. It's best for the team. When you become a junior or senior, you especially appreciate it. And the team is more unified. It states in a subtle but loud way, "The team is more important than the individual."

For this book I asked Coach Smith if he had any regrets about how he taught team basketball. Would he change anything in the way he coached?

His answer was intriguing. "I don't think I delegated enough to my assistants. I always valued input from the players, but I probably didn't receive enough from the assistants. I love the way Coach Guthridge is doing it now. They have a three-hour staff meeting every morning to talk everything over. Everybody has ideas. Everybody has input.

"I used to have the practice plan and then spend about an hour talking about practice. I would say, 'Here is what we are going to do' instead of saying, 'What do you think?' I think I controlled too much. I knew I had a vision of how I thought a team should play and how to bring that about. But if I were coaching today, I'd probably allow more input from the assistants. They have good ideas too."

He may well be stating the obvious paradigm shift in leadership that has occurred during the last decade. In the 1970s and 1980s, the autocratic leadership style was still honored. The general was the general, and if he thought the hill should be taken, he simply ordered it and the underlings obeyed. Now, in the 1990s, many people feel qualified, educated, and competent. Those who are second or third in command simply find it difficult to obey the top person if they think there may be a better way to reach the goal.

Nowhere is this better illustrated than the movie *Crimson Tide.* The commander, played by Gene Hackman, received the command to fire nuclear weapons on Russia. However, one checkpoint was missing. The second in command, played by Denzel Washington, fearful of a nuclear holocaust and confident of his own leadership ability, took command of the ship. He wasn't sure the commander was right. He demanded input.

The movie is a thrilling example of the leadership shift from the 1980s to the 1990s. Who was right? In a way, Gene Hackman was right, because every organization, especially the military, needs firm leadership, a person in control with authority and a vision. Yet, in another way, Denzel Washington was right, because competent assistants can and should give input. Their input could avert disaster, as the movie clearly teaches.

This shift in leadership style is largely attributable to Baby Boomers entering their forties. We're well-educated, independent, entrepreneurial, and were reared to question authority, even when authority is ours.

It's this shift that I think Coach Smith senses. If he still coached today, I'm sure he would make that shift easily and ably. And the team would still be the vision, and he would still be successful.

Coach Smith said to me, "Our philosophy, as you know, has been simple: play hard, play smart, and, most important, play together. And I don't think any player, five years after he has left this program has ever regretted coming here."

When people play for a coach whose vision is the team over the individual, they are learning something much larger and more important than playing basketball. They learn how to live and play together, how to get along with one another, how to be independent yet interdependent, how to be a team, how to live life as it's supposed to be lived.

At Carolina we believed in Coach's vision that teams, not individuals, win games. Dean Smith convinced us of this truth. We bought it. We lived it.

And it's difficult to argue with his success.

Thought for the Day

**The vision of the team is more important
than the individuals on the team.**

Game Plan

- Teach what's important in the vision

- As the leader, take the hits

- Recognize potential and reward effort

- Know your team members

- Create little teams on the big team

- Show fairness, not favoritism

Team Practice

- How important is teamwork to the success of your organization?

- What actions are you taking to build a strong team?

- How do you reward individual effort so that it
contributes to team results?

SUCCESS REQUIRES A FLEXIBLE VISION

"We don't have a system, but a philosophy that is flexible and innovates."

It rankles Coach Smith whenever his vision is called a system. "To me," he said, "that connotes that we're rigid, that we don't change with our personnel, and that's just not true. Now if you say North Carolina has a philosophy, I love that. We change every year, even though the basic vision remains the same."

He was a stickler for fundamentals, emphasizing them over and over. The approach might change, but the fundamentals stayed the same from year to year.

For example, in 1971, my senior year, Coach Smith knew we were predicted to finish at the bottom of the conference. So, on the first day of practice, he called us to the middle of the court. He held a basketball in his hands. He looked at all of us and said, "Gentlemen, this is a basketball." Then we began drills on dribbling, passing, rebounding, and shooting. They were drills we had done in junior high school. But Coach Smith knew that for us to be a good team, he had to reemphasize the fundamentals.

Every company, corporation, or church that is accomplishing anything of note has core values and fundamentals. And those basic elements need to be repeated, relearned, and reemphasized regularly, at least yearly. I contend that no innovation takes place outside of a commitment to these fundamentals. During his 36 years of coaching, every one of Coach Smith's teams had these fundamentals as a foundation.

I take every opportunity I can to return to Chapel Hill and reminisce about four of the happiest years in my life. So in 1993, the year Coach Smith won his second NCAA championship, it was a "no brainer" when I was invited to speak to a Christian organization on the UNC campus.

I decided to make it an event. I called the basketball office and got permission to observe practice. I then asked my six-year-old daughter, Bethany, if she would like to accompany me to my old college stomping grounds. She eagerly agreed, especially when she found out it would take her out of school a few hours early.

Speaking to several hundred students at the campus event was exhilarating. Bethany and I walked around the university and had dinner at "The Rat," a UNC institution. It brought back special memories that I excitedly shared with her. However, the highlight of the trip was the privilege of viewing practice.

We entered the Smith Center almost in a hushed, reverent awe. I shared with Bethany how this was going to be a new experience for me, too, since I had played in Carmichael Auditorium. This was my first practice in the Smith Center. As we settled in our seats, I looked forward to seeing how practice might be different some 20 years later.

You can therefore imagine my deep introspection as the next two hours unfolded in remarkable similarity to the many practices I had personally experienced years earlier. Practice began with a huddle at center court and a player reciting the thought for the day. Then came the drills to enhance the fundamentals. The drills were precise and exactly timed. The emphasis was on teamwork and unselfish play.

The thought for the day was repeated over and over. All of it struck a familiar chord.

Coaches Smith and Guthridge constantly adjured the players to listen to what they said and respond immediately and accordingly. More and more I felt a sense of déjà vu, that I was reliving a part of my past.

Teach the Fundamentals

For the next two hours, I heard Coach Smith say things I had heard more than 20 years earlier, phrases that emphasized the fundamentals of his understanding of how the game should be played. No wonder these things had become the foundation of the concepts I have used in my own leadership.

Let me give you a few familiar examples of things I heard during the practice session.

"You play like you practice." Over and over again I have stated to my staff that the one-time event is fine, but the best results are produced as a result of a day-in and day-out commitment to work.

"Little things win games." The big shot may get headlines at the end of the game, but equally important are the little things that set up the victory. When every member of the team, both on the bench and in the game, consistently practices the fundamentals for 40 straight minutes, it allows a person to take the big shot and score the win. How often I tell my staff, "The details do matter." If a company is successful only 98 percent of the time, the profit loss could be in the millions!

"Keep trying! Good things happen when you play hard." Surely this attitude, planted in practice, is the reason for the dozens of miracle comebacks engineered by Coach Smith throughout the years. In the huddle during a close game, he often turned to different players and emphasized this reality. "Just keep at it. Keep playing hard."

In the Eastern Regional final against Louisville in 1997, the Tar Heels watched a 20-point lead melt to three with about eight minutes to go. Coach Smith called the team together during a time-out and said, "This has been a great season. We've had a great run. Thank you for all your hard work."

The players were confused. They looked at one another. Was Coach Smith giving up?

Finally, Ademola Okulaja shouted out, "No! It's not over!"

Coach Smith looked at the rest of the team and asked, "Do you all agree?"

"Yes!"

Then he designed a play to score out of the huddle. They scored. It stopped the Louisville run and the lead was quickly built back to double digits. They coasted to a win and went to the Final Four.

"Being in shape doesn't mean you'll never get tired. It means you'll recover more quickly." In my opinion, this is a great fundamental of life to teach to those who work with us and under us. We all become tired in our work. We then feel guilty for being tired, thinking no one else ever tires. Fatigue is a reality, but we know we're healthy when we recover from it quickly.

Coach Smith always believed that the sign of being in good shape was not if a player became tired, but how quickly he recovered after becoming tired. If the recovery period wasn't fast enough, it signaled to him that we needed more conditioning.

If a person doesn't recover quickly from a mistake, that's a sure signal to us as leaders that they need more conditioning, more training. Continual mistakes may be the fault of the boss, not the worker!

"Freshmen, go get the ball!" Any time a ball rolled away, a freshman was expected to spring to it and bring it back. From the beginning of their very first practice, the freshmen, no matter how exceptionally talented or highly recruited they may be, were expected to serve the upperclassmen.

I wonder how leaders are today about teaching employees the value of serving and also of waiting for rewards. I've learned through the years that the best staff people are those who have first learned their own unimportance and are willing to give themselves to others for the sake of the vision and the team. The top staff people also have not fallen prey to the American lie of instant gratification. They are willing to work hard, persevere, and wait for the rewards.

A tug on my sleeve interrupted my musings during the basketball practice. Bethany had been watching Coach Smith run practice for quite some time. "Daddy," she said, "I like him. He's like my first-grade teacher, Mrs. Davis. Kind, but firm." I laughed inwardly. A child has the ability to see the truth very clearly and easily. She was exactly on target.

Coach Smith is firm on his commitment to the fundamentals that guide his team. These fundamentals are immutable. After 879 wins, it's easy to see how successful the annual teaching of these fundamentals can become.

In the church I pastor, our leadership team has worked hard to define six fundamental, core values. We regularly go over them together and with our church. We practice them over and over again. We are convinced that they are the foundation for the success of this church.

Why is teaching the fundamentals so important to success? Here's an illustration from 1970.

Charlie Scott, UNC's All-American guard, could do things with a basketball that would amaze people even today. He was a superb athlete with unbelievable ball-handling skills. One day in practice, he came down court and completed an amazing behind-the back, no-look pass that led to a basket. All the players paused and applauded the pass.

What was Coach Smith's response? He said, "Charles, the great player is the one who makes the hard play look easy, not the easy play look hard."

Coach Smith was simply restating his conviction that fundamentals, properly performed within the team, win games, not spectacular, individual plays.

Innovate as Necessary

But the fundamentals are also the foundation for innovation. And, in fact, unless these fundamentals have regular, even annual, innovations, they will not work.

The fundamentals of dribbling, passing, shooting defense, and rebounding represented Coach Smith's philosophy. But it was a flexible philosophy, and his innovations, that kept each team fresh and effective each individual season. A part of Coach Smith's genius is that he did innovate and change when necessary to accommodate his personnel.

Pearce Landry told me this story about Coach Smith's willingness to be creative. In 1995 Carolina was the number-one team in the nation. They had experienced only one loss. "We were about halfway through the ACC season and we came off just a horrible performance against Notre Dame. I can't remember the team. We ended up winning, but it was a team we should have beaten by twenty.

"We showed up at practice the next day and found out Coach had suddenly changed our whole defensive scheme. He told us we weren't going to run what we had been running to that point. He said we simply didn't have the personnel to do what we're doing. He knew that if we were going to be successful in the NCAA tournament, we didn't have the horses to play that kind of defense. So he switched to a more passive defense that put pressure on the three-point shooter. We ended up going to the Final Four."

Most very successful corporations know the value of innovation. Johnson and Johnson encourages new innovations and personal initiative. Then the successful experiments that are profitable and fit the company's core ideology are retained. They encourage multiple attempts at innovation and are unafraid of failure. They feel innovation and failure are twin sisters.

How important is it in business for a leader to have foundations that remain flexible enough for innovation? Peter Drucker once predicted failure within four years for any leading corporation that loses its proactivity.

Over and over again, in the history of corporate management, his thesis has proven to be correct. Fully half of the Fortune 500 companies between 1975 and 1980 no longer exist. Drucker has updated his prediction. He now believes it takes only 18 months to go from leader to loser. Even failure runs the risk of downsizing today!

Imparato and Harari give a startling insight into this leadership secret in their classic book, *Jumping the Curve*. After interviewing CEOs of various companies that averaged 15 times better than the Dow during the past 20 years, they concluded that the biggest threat to a company's survival is complacency. The refusal to be innovative is a terminal disease for corporate America.

Peter Drucker points out how the Japanese and Koreans are organizing innovation. "They've set up small groups of their brightest people to systematically apply the discipline of innovation to identify and develop new business. Innovation requires us to systemically identify changes...to abandon rather than defend yesterday — something most difficult for existing companies to do."

Converse was the shoe I wore in high school and college. I can still describe in detail what this canvas shoe looked like. Chuck Taylor's name was printed on the shoe. Everyone, and I mean everyone, wore their Chucks, as we all called them. It was the elite shoe for basketball players.

Here's a simple question: What happened to Converse? In the '80s and '90s Nike, Reebok, and other shoe magnates have left them in the dust. Converse had a great shoe for the '60s and '70s. But it failed to innovate. It is just now coming back with a contemporary canvas Chuck. But the failure to innovate left Converse in the back of the pack with a long way to catch up.

IBM once dominated the computer market but became complacent. Microsoft and other companies read the future more accurately, innovating and passing IBM, which then had to reorganize completely to try and catch up. If innovation does not happen regularly, the game will pass you by.

Twenty years ago, one bought hamburgers at a hamburger restaurant. McDonald's ruled. Then other fast-food chains started to innovate. They realized people wanted more choices — some for health reasons, others for more diversity in menu selections. Today practically all the franchises offer baked potatoes, chicken, salads, and Mexican options. Those who did not innovate were left behind.

Bank of America in Charlotte, North Carolina, has grown and merged with several banks across the country to become the second largest bank in America. Yet it has also been on the cutting edge of new innovations that have allowed continuing growth. For example, Bank of America placed ATM machines in as many places as possible. Recently, however, it began to see that more and more people wanted to transact business from their homes. Therefore, Bank of America went on the cutting edge of online banking and has led the way in this enterprise. If it hadn't, Bank of America would have been left behind.

American Airlines foresaw a way of encouraging more customers to fly their airline: frequent flyer miles. The company began awarding customers travel points when they flew American. More and more travelers saw the potential benefits and chose American. Now every airline offers this innovation.

Charles Schwab saw the potential of eliminating the middle-man for individual investors. A huge company was built on an innovation: bypassing the investment broker with a direct phone call to Schwab, with the additional savings passed on to customers.

Innovation is necessary for churches, too. Several hundred churches close every year. As pastors, many of us knew that something had to be done or America would become like postmodern Europe, with beautiful, but empty, cathedrals everywhere.

About six years ago I changed the vision of the church I lead. Previously, we had a vision of basically taking care of our own. That is certainly necessary; but unless the church is directed outward, it will die. We therefore transitioned ourselves to a more current, progressive church. We initiated contemporary music, drama, and other methodologies to reach people who were bored with church or thought it to be irrelevant.

This change in vision was one of the most difficult times in my ministry, an episode that I will share in more depth when I get to the topic of dealing with failure. During this period I received more criticism than ever before. My wife, Marilynn, helped by remarking that whenever anything new is born, it must go through a time of transition. She reminded me that in childbirth the most painful stage of labor is the final one, called transition, which occurs just before delivery. This is the time when the wife may say to her husband, "You're the reason this happened to me. I hate you!" She doesn't really mean it, but the pain during this transition time is unbearable.

People in the church were undergoing a painful time of transition. Did it finally stop? Yes, it did. Are we in a much better position now? Indeed we are.

The new vision is working. The innovation was necessary. We're now a church ready to face the twenty-first century!

Change is Constant

It's easy to keep on doing something that is successful and remain unwilling to change. But courageous leaders are unwilling to say, "If it ain't broke, don't fix it." They know they constantly need to break something in order to make it better, in order to reach even higher objectives.

Consider that, right now, we know only three percent of all the information that will be available to us by the year 2010. The world around us is constantly changing. The attitudes of Generation X and the following generation, the Millennials, are different from Boomers. We had better be willing to understand them — willing to innovate and change — or leaders and organizations will be left behind.

The contemporary market place leaves leaders no choice except to embrace innovation and change. Change will arrive monthly in tsunami-like proportions and will threaten to eradicate organizations overnight. Therefore, today's leaders will only be able to survive by encouraging their people, their most important asset, to act immediately on their knowledge and beliefs.

Wayne Gretzky, perhaps the world's best hockey player, said it this way: "You miss one hundred percent of the shots you never take."

Stephen Covey, in his book *Principle-Centered Leadership,* says, "A strategic leader can provide direction and vision, motivate through love, and build a complementary team based on mutual respect if he is more ...concerned with direction and results than with methods, systems, and procedures. While all of the producers are hacking their way through the jungle and their managers are sharpening their machetes for them and setting up machete-wielding working schedules and putting on training programs for machete wielders, an enlightened and courageous leader must sometimes cry out, 'Wrong jungle!' even though he can expect to receive the answer, 'Be quiet! We're making progress.'"

Coach Smith was annually willing to wail, "Wrong jungle!" He was always willing to innovate, to make his vision stronger with new concepts and ideas. Some of his innovations are now legendary. Coaches at every conceivable level now institute these different concepts to foster team play. Let me give you a few examples.

Thank Those Who Assist

The player who scores the point must point to the player who gave him the pass. Everyone recognizes the scorer; Coach Smith wanted to make sure all the spectators knew who gave the pass, because scoring two points was impossible without the pass. If someone failed to point, and Coach Smith noticed it while reviewing game films, the entire team would have to run extra sprints the next day in practice. When one player fails, the entire team is hurt, not just the individual.

Bobby Jones, the All-American forward in the 1970s, once missed a lay-up in a game. He still pointed to the person who gave him the pass. Coach Smith liked that. The next day it was instituted in practice. Now hundreds of teams, from youth leagues to the professional teams, do the same — whether the basket is scored or not.

Coach Smith was trying to teach us about life by learning to point to the person who gave us the pass, the person who made it possible to score. No great leader has ever reached any position of significant success without saying thanks to those who have helped him achieve it.

After win number 878 Dean Smith did not take time to bask in the glory of tying Coach Rupp's record; he was too busy thanking his former players. A national television audience watched him traverse the tunnel to the locker room, stopping every few feet to shake hands and greet the scores of players who had come from all over just to be there for the momentous occasion. By his actions Coach Smith was saying that we were the ones who had allowed him to achieve this success.

Was he sincere? I am absolutely convinced of it. Long before win number 879 ever came, he annually wrote all his former players and their families at Christmas, often thanking us for our friendship and what we have meant to him through the years. He would ask us to say hello to our wives, kids, and parents. This letter would accompany the media guide. I've received one every year since graduation in 1971. I had been in Ostend, Belgium, less than a month, beginning my first year with the European professional leagues, when I received a letter from Coach Smith thanking me for the four years I played for him.

Hearing the simple words *thank you* can have a powerful effect on employees as well as basketball players. Max Depree, in his wonderful little book *Leadership is an Art,* wrote, "What is it most of us really want from work? We would like to find the most effective, most productive, most rewarding way of working together. ...We would like a work process and relationships that meet our personal needs for belonging, for contributing, for meaningful work, for the opportunity to make a commitment, for the opportunity to grow and be at least reasonably in control of our own destinies. Finally, we'd like someone to say, 'Thank you.'"

Depree contends that effective leadership today cannot be leadership by control, but leadership by persuasion. One of the ways, he says, that people feel they are participating in the process is when the leader simply says, "Thanks."

A raise is not always the best way for a boss to say, "Well done." Most often workers want a simple "thank you," personally stated or on paper. Bob Nelson, who wrote *1001 Ways to Energize People,* said, "Raises are expected. Their value has been diminished." He goes on to say that employee validation does not have to be elaborate or expensive. E-mail or voice mail, or a verbal affirmation in a staff meeting can suffice. In a newspaper interview Nelson added, "If you think you're too busy to do this kind of thing, you need to reassess your priorities. Most people don't worry about their people until they're walking out the door. By then it's too late. Do it now! Don't wait until the annual banquet!"

Monthly I ask my program staff to submit names to me of people in their ministries who are doing outstanding work. I then sit down and write each one a thank-you card, specifically noting what they have done.

The recipient of one of those cards sticks in my mind. Grace, a 70-something-year-old grandmother who tirelessly works in our kitchen, came up to me one Wednesday night at our community meal. She had ketchup stains all over her apron. Her shoulders were a bit hunched over. She was obviously tired from her duty of serving food and clearing the tables. Yet as she approached me, she had a gleam in her eye. For the next few moments she effusively thanked me for sending her a thank-you note. She was overwhelmed that I would take time from my busy schedule to write her. And I'll never forget the last thing she said to me. "You know, David, I'm going to work even harder now."

In a recent staff meeting, I had just come from another meeting where someone outside my church profusely praised my youth pastor. Before the entire staff, I repeated what I heard. Fischer's face lit up! The next day he came to my office door to thank me for publicly thanking him.

Everyone likes for someone to say, "Thank you for the pass."

Help Those Who Sacrifice

Here's another one of Coach Smith's innovations that other coaches have adopted. When a player dived on the floor for a loose ball, the player closest to him had to run and help him up. One had sacrificed for the team. Therefore, another team member ought to come to his aid. If someone failed to do this, the entire team would have to run the next day in practice.

I constantly look for the person on my staff who is diving for the ball, that person who is going over and above the call of duty, who is willing to move outside his or her own area of responsibility to help someone else who is overwhelmed. When I see this kind of sacrifice, I love to reward it with a meal out, or movie passes, or a half-day off — anything that communicates that a sacrifice for the sake of the team will be properly rewarded.

We even have a Giant-killer Award, a statue of David slaying Goliath, for the one who tackles a difficult problem and finds a solution. The recipient gets to keep the statue in his or her office until the next giant arises. They also receive another small benefit, such as a meal out or time off.

Stand Up and Cheer

When a player came out of the game, those on the bench had to stand up and cheer for him. Yes, sometimes this action felt coerced and contrived (take it from someone who had to do it practically his entire sophomore year!), but Coach Smith believed good little habits develop into good big habits. He also wanted us to be in the game just in case he called upon us to play. So we did what he told us to do. Plus, it didn't hurt to know that as he watched game films he would always notice if someone didn't stand up. And if we didn't stand up, the entire team would run the next day.

But I think he was trying to accomplish something greater. I believe he was creating synergy, the power of encouragement, within a team.

I do something similar occasionally with my staff. I'll gather all of us together and then put a chair in the middle of the room. Each person on the staff must sit in the chair for two minutes. They cannot say a thing. Then everyone else fills in the blank about the person sitting in the middle of the room. "I like you because... "

Yes, the person in the chair can be a bit embarrassed. But they really feel good about themselves! Everyone develops an attitude of encouragement. It's like, well, like applauding when someone comes off the court. It creates team spirit, and staff people love it.

Give Them a Chance to Rest

If someone became tired during the game, he stuck his fist in the air and asked to come out. If a player took himself out of a game, he could then put himself back in when he was rested. Coach Smith adamantly believed that a rested reserve would perform better than a tired superstar. The team must be considered first!

Many Carolina fans gasped during the 1993 NCAA championship game against Michigan, when Coach Smith inserted seldom-used point guard Scott Cherry into a closely contested game after the starting point guard, Derrick Phelps, had given the tired signal with a little more than six minutes left. Cherry only played a minute, but he played admirably without making a mistake. Phelps got his rest, re-entered the game for the stretch drive, and finished the game brilliantly.

Yes, Carolina won the game. Coach Smith simply knows that fatigue makes cowards of us all. He would not let fatigue be a factor in whether a game is won or lost. He let us make the decision to come out of the game when tired. Otherwise, the only reason he would ever take us out of a game was for lack of effort, not fatigue.

I don't hesitate to tell workers who seem tired to leave and go get some rest or do something fun. The job still gets done, most often better than if I had forced them to work continuously in their fatigue. That's why I carefully monitor if my staff is taking their weekly day off. It's partly to help them build their own families on a firm foundation. And it's a lot cheaper than paying a huge family-counseling bill! But it's also the realization that rested reserves play better than tired superstars. Proper rest determines job performance.

Let Innovation Flow from the Vision

When I asked Coach Smith if he had carefully planned out all these innovations, he laughed. "Not a one." He noticed my surprise and said, "David, I really didn't plan these things. They all just kind of happened. I was simply living by my conviction of the team being above the individual player. Then, as I lived by this principle, these innovations simply occurred."

Isn't his answer interesting? He did not spend hours trying to think about the innovations for which he is famous. He was simply living by his life principles — in this case, the principle that the team is what's most important — and the innovations simply fell into place.

Too often, I think, leaders do just the opposite. We spend countless hours trying to be creative. Yet with Coach Smith, the creativity flowed spontaneously out of a commitment to live by certain principles and core values.

As corporate structures and cultures have been downsized and work forces slashed, as lackluster performance in revenue growth occurs, some leaders have built a culture of cynicism and despair. As a result, they have lost their most important resource: human capital. Perhaps the answer is not pushing our people to work harder, but to ask the question, "Is the team our highest priority? Does this guide everything we do?"

If we emphasized this, perhaps the creativity and innovation that are necessary for any organization to succeed would flow more easily from our work associates.

Thought for the Day

Develop a philosophy, not a system.

Game Plan

- Teach the fundamentals
- Innovate as necessary
- Understand that change is constant
- Let innovation flow from the vision

Team Practice

- To what degree do you seek new solutions to problems?
- How do you prepare for change?
- How do you encourage others to innovate?
- What can your organization do to encourage innovation?

LEADERSHIP PRINCIPLE 6

AS INDIVIDUALS IMPROVE, THE TEAM IMPROVES

"If you want to make the team better, become a better individual player."

Between my sophomore and junior years at UNC, I made the decision not to transfer. I wanted to see if I could play in the ACC and particularly at North Carolina. But my personal aspirations had melted away; I primarily wanted to help the team be the best it could be. So I called Coach Smith and told him I was committed to staying at North Carolina.

"How can I best help the team?" I asked him.

"If you want to help the team," he said, "become a better individual player." He then reemphasized my weaknesses and strengths. He told me to work on both, become a better player, and the team would be better.

At first glance, you might think Coach Smith's statement contradicts his vision of the team being above the individual. On the contrary, it only enhances it. A team is made up of individual parts. It is the leader's job to take the unique giftedness of different individuals and mold them together as a team with a common vision and goal. The stronger, the more gifted those individual parts are, the stronger the team's potential.

I worked hard that summer to become a better player. Often in the hot sun of Orlando, Florida, as I ran sprints and lifted weights, I asked myself, "Why am I doing this?" I would always pant the answer, "Because this is making the team better."

Dave Hanners posed an interesting question when I interviewed him for this book. "Can you name one North Carolina player who didn't get better between his freshman and senior seasons?" he asked. He couldn't think of one, and either could I. Coach Smith had to deal with all our egos, trying not to bruise them, yet getting the best out of us for the sake of the team. "Most coaches can't do that," Hanners said. "They usually fail somewhere."

Coach Smith also mused with me about how much better some players became during their careers, even to his amazement. "Darrell Elston came here because John Lotz knew his high school coach," he told me. "Darrell had a basketball scholarship from Ball State and a football scholarship from Purdue. He was the fourteenth man on the squad in 1972. In the Final Four, he couldn't even dress for the game because the rules stated that only twelve players could dress. I told Darrell that perhaps he should go some place else where he could play. But he worked hard over the years and became an all-ACC performer. He worked very hard, and the team became better."

A great leader can motivate others toward self-discipline and personal responsibility. No matter how gifted the player may be, or how much playing time he may receive, Coach Smith believed that the individual — whether the manager, a bench player, a regular, or a superstar — can have tremendous impact on the team when he personally improves.

Teach Personal Responsibility and Self-Discipline

A jar rests on the corner of Coach Guthridge's desk. It's an "excuse" jar. When you come in to see him, the first thing you're expected to do is file your excuses in the jar. He simply won't listen to them. Every player on the team is constantly challenged to assume personal responsibility for becoming a better player. He knows it will make the team better. I'm certain that he learned this from Coach Smith.

I am one of the three chaplains to the NBA's Charlotte Hornets. Before the games I lead a 15-minute chapel service to remind the six or so players who attend about the true source of all their gifts. It's a time of reflection, a time to remember what's really important and who is really in control of all things.

The first time I led the service, I wanted to capture their attention. So I opened with a question. "Who is the toughest player you've ever tried to guard?"

George Zidek immediately said, "Hakeem Olajuwon."

Dell Curry didn't hesitate. "Number 23." (For you non-basketball enthusiasts, that is Michael Jordan's number.)

Anthony Mason just smiled. He wouldn't give an answer. I kept pressing him to give me a name. Finally, he said, "David, there's no one I can't stop!" Everyone laughed, for that's what Mason really believes!

I then told them about trying to guard Julius Erving in the NIT finals my senior year, and how he was unquestionably the most difficult opponent I had ever faced.

"But you know who is the toughest opponent you'll ever have to overcome in your life?" I then asked. "Yourself."

In the lives of all great people, the first victory they ever have to win is over themselves. If we could kick the person in the backside who is most responsible for our problems, we would not be able to sit down for a week.

Winston Churchill once said, "The price of greatness is responsibility."

William Faulkner said, "Don't bother just to be better than your contemporaries or predecessors. Try to be better than yourself."

Coach Smith taught this principle of personal responsibility in several ways. How? First, he demanded self-discipline. He truly believed that the self-disciplined person is a free person.

At every opportunity, he emphasized personal responsibility and self-discipline. I vividly remember a practice on Thanksgiving Day my sophomore year. We were a very good team, ranked number-two in the country during the preseason. Our best player was a very gifted junior named Charlie Scott. He could out-run, out-jump, and out-play anyone else on the team. His athleticism was wondrous.

However, in practice that particular day, Scott was not working very hard. Coach Smith stopped practice. As was his custom, he put us all on the end line. He used one of his famous lines on us: "When one of you doesn't hustle, the whole team suffers. We're going to run for Charles's laziness."

So we ran. Scott, however, refused to run very hard. Everyone knew that in a pure sprint Scott would beat the rest of us by a good 10 feet. But he simply coasted in the middle of the pack.

"We're going to keep running," Coach Smith said, "until Charles runs one sprint as fast as he can."

He blew the whistle and we started to run again ... and again ... and again. Scott refused to run one hard sprint, and Coach Smith refused to budge from his command. The immovable object had met the irresistible force! So we kept on running.

We must have run for an hour or more, over and over and over again. Finally, Rusty Clark, our 250-pound center, walked over to Scott and said, "If you don't run one sprint real hard, we're all going to kill you."

That seemed to be sufficient motivation, and Scott finally ran one sprint as fast as he could. Coach Smith blew his whistle and sent us to the showers with a final instruction, "Be back at three this afternoon so we can cover what we missed this morning."

Another way Coach Smith taught self-discipline was by insisting on punctuality. He knew that simple things like punctuality can turn out to be extremely important. So we had an iron-clad rule: if you're one minute late for the bus, it leaves without you. It didn't matter if you were a sub or superstar, the bus would leave you. If you were late for a pregame meal, you wouldn't start.

To this day, Bill Chamberlain worries that he may have lost the 1972 national championship for UNC. He was scheduled to be a starter, but was late for the pre-game meal before the Florida State game in the national semifinals. Florida State jumped off to a huge lead and UNC never recovered. We lost by four. Chamberlain wonders if his lack of punctuality disrupted team unity and caused a very important loss.

During my senior year, I had my own narrow escape with Coach Smith's insistence on punctuality. I had finally landed a date with a particular girl and decided to impress her by taking her to the Duke–

Carolina game. Both teams were nationally ranked and it promised to be a good match. Although I wasn't a starter, I was the sixth man and knew I would receive significant playing time.

We were supposed to be at Carmichael Auditorium by 6:30 for an 8:00 televised game. I planned to pick my date up at 6:00, to be sure I'd be on time.

I arrived at her sorority house at the appointed hour and let her know I was downstairs. Five, 10, 15 minutes passed. I began to panic. She finally came downstairs, strutting into the parlor as if every clock worldwide had ceased ticking.

I rushed her to the car and sped over to Carmichael, arriving 15 minutes late. I gave my date a ticket and sprinted to what we called "the cage" to pick up my uniform. Just as I headed toward the door, Coach Smith entered.

"Are you just now arriving?" he asked, studying my face intently.

"N-no," I stammered, "I was just sitting down, reflecting on the game."

He waited a moment and then nodded me toward the locker room.

I quickly dressed and sat breathlessly waiting for his arrival for the pre-game talk. I was certain I had just gone from sixth to tenth man on the team.

Coach Smith always commenced the pre-game meeting by writing the opposing team's starting five players on the board with their numbers next to them. Then he would write our starting five next to the player we would be guarding.

He walked to the board and listed the guards, then the forwards. Next to Duke's all-ACC center he listed my name! Our starting center, unbeknownst to me, had been late to practice the previous day. If you are late to practice, you don't start the next game.

I was so unnerved by my tardy escapade and my run-in with Coach Smith, it did not immediately sink in that I was slated to start against Duke in Carmichael Auditorium — and that I would be guarding Duke's all-conference 6'11" center.

That was probably the best thing that could have happened to me. I didn't have time to think about it, and I went out and hit the first three shots of the game. In fact, I ended up playing one of the best games of my career, with 19 points, seven rebounds, and five assists. We won 79–74.

Did Coach Smith know I really had been late? I never asked. Hopefully, he has a blessed case of amnesia to this day. Or, perhaps, knowing our center was not going to start, he couldn't dare bench me too.

Regardless, I was never late again. To this day I remember how fortunate I was, and what the consequences of tardiness could be.

Use an Inside-Out Approach

The individual is key for total quality to occur on a team. The leader must have this perspective. But Coach Smith saw this truth as an inside-out approach to management, so different from the way many organizations operate. They think that a new system or organization is the answer to productivity.

Management guru Stephen Covey wrote, "There must be individual growth, change, and development to make organizational development and change viable. And yet, as I see it, that basic fact is largely ignored. Too many executives think of change in terms of some outside force acting on internal people and conditions. But fundamentally, change that results in productivity requires an inside-out approach, not an outside-in approach."

Coach Smith used this inside-out approach to teach personal responsibility and self-discipline, and he did it with a very minimum of rules and regulations. That may seem strange. Too many of us tend to think that the more rules and regulations, the more disciplined someone will be. Coach Smith did not adopt this perspective.

Previously, I noted how the seniors annually made the rules for the following season. This action not only allowed tremendous buy-in by the players, but it also allowed those who most closely knew the individual personality of the team to make the rules.

When I visited with Coach Smith, he reminded me that he really only had one rule: don't ever embarrass me, yourself, or the team. Of course, he was the one who judged if that rule were ever broken. But, evidently, it is the one major rule he always had.

I vividly remember when I ran up against the "never embarrass me or the team" rule. It was my sophomore year, when I didn't get to play much. You can therefore imagine my surprise and excitement when Coach Smith touched me on the shoulder in the middle of a significant game and told me to enter. I tore off my sweats and ran to the scorer's bench. Play stopped and I entered the game. Here was my chance to make a positive impression. Here was my long-awaited opportunity to prove I could play at this level.

The ball came to me at the top of the key. No one guarded me. I glanced at the basket and let the ball fly. *Clank!* It bounced off the rim.

Before I knew it, the horn sounded and someone entered the game for me. I went to the bench, furious with myself. I had blown it! Coach Smith was not concerned with someone who could score points. I knew that. Everyone at this level could score. He wanted to see me do the little things: defense, box out, and rebound. I was so mad with myself that I took the towel the manager handed me and swung it to the ground in disgust — in the presence 10,000 onlookers in Carmichael Auditorium.

Coach Smith had witnessed this little fiasco. Very quickly and quietly, he walked down the bench and knelt in front of me. He simply said, "David, don't ever embarrass me, and I won't embarrass you." Then he walked back to his seat on the bench without saying another word.

I knew the one rule, and I had clearly broken it.

But I never did again. From that moment on, I disciplined myself to control my responses and never embarrass him or the team again. I knew I had to be governed from the inside out.

Develop Trust

Teaching personal responsibility and self-discipline through this inside-out approach requires the kind of meaningful and respectful relationship between leader and followers that will develop trust. We all respected Coach Smith. We truly did not want to embarrass him. The crucial dimension in all communication is the relationship. When the relationship is right, we can almost communicate without words. Coach Smith could give us a look in practice that sometimes communicated more than words.

And the key to all relationships is time. Someone once said that the way kids spell love is T-I-M-E.

Employees need time too. A leader should examine whether he is spending quality and quantity time with work associates in order to develop trust.

Is your door always open? Ged Doughton, a former player in the 1970s and now a successful Charlotte businessman, remembers being in Coach Smith's office one time when the intercom buzzed. The secretary announced, "Senator So-and-So is on the phone for you." Coach Smith said, "Tell him I'm with a player and I'll call him back." Ged felt as important as the president of the United States, and Coach Smith's action fostered a deep sense of trust and loyalty.

How then should you spend time developing trust? It is best accomplished with the private visit in your office or the work associate's office, the relaxed lunch, the private chat over coffee — in other words, a time when you are focused solely and specifically on that person, his fears, concerns, needs, hopes, and interests.

Do you as a leader spend time like this with your employees? Do they think you intimately care about their lives? Would employees feel they could come to you and share their concerns, or do they see you locked in your corner office with the view, unreachable and unapproachable?

The second way Coach Smith helped develop relational trust was by refusing to let us compare ourselves with one another. He constantly urged us to know our limitations as well as our strengths. He felt each individual was an important cog in the entire machinery. If he felt any envy among us, he would immediately confront us and remind us of the uniqueness of our own personal giftedness. Over and over again he would say, "Improve your strengths and weaknesses, and the team will become better."

At the beginning of every season, he developed team goals. At the end of the season, every individual would have personal goals for becoming a better player. Coach Smith was always brutally honest during this interview. If he did not think you would play, even with hard work, he would tell you. If he thought transferring was your best option in order to play, he would help you find the right school. But your name would still be on his letterman's list, and he would always consider you a part of the Carolina family.

In this way, Coach Smith taught us that as the individual improves, it allows the whole team to improve.

Nelson Mandela stated this principle eloquently. He said, "We ask ourselves, 'Who am I to be brilliant, gorgeous, talented, and fabulous?' Actually, who are you not to be? You are a child of God. Your playing small doesn't serve the world. There's nothing enlightened about shrinking so that other people won't feel insecure around you. We were born to manifest the glory of God within us...And as we let our own light shine, we unconsciously give other people permission to do the same. As we are liberated from our own fear, our presence automatically liberates others."

Mandela was simply stating the obvious: when the individual unleashes the enormous, unique potential he has, the team becomes better. He was also confronting the damage that occurs when a person starts comparing himself with someone else. It can only be destructive.

Coach Smith was brilliant when he refused to let us compare ourselves with one another. He knew this kind of comparison was deadly to a team. It destroyed the uniqueness of the individual and could abort the need for claiming personal responsibility. The snare of comparison keeps our inexhaustible godly qualities locked inside us.

Work Hard in the Off-season

Coach Smith also taught us to work hard in the off-season in order to become the best individual players we could. He placed that kind of motivation within us. We took responsibility for our lives. And we were willing to pay to price in self-discipline to make the team better.

William Oncken, president of the Oncken Corporation in Dallas, Texas, said, "Successful coaches bring many skills to the table. They provide their people the opportunity to become the best they can possibly be. The coaches set up an environment wherein people feel good about themselves, believe in themselves, care about each other, and feel empowered to make a meaningful contribution." That's another way of saying, "As the individual improves, so does the team."

In our annual performance evaluations in the church I serve, I ask each staff person what conferences they plan to attend the next year or what courses they are going to take for professional development. We're willing to pay for it. We know that as they become better leaders, the organization is greatly enhanced.

Moreover, we borrowed something from the world of academia. After the first seven years, each staff leader takes a two-month sabbatical. They have to submit to the Personnel Committee a description of where they are going, what they plan to do, and what they are trying to learn. We then try to pay for most of it.

These two simple requirements, annual leadership development and a sabbatical after seven years of faithful service (repeated after five more years on the staff), are our version of working hard during the off-season. And they have done wonders to develop personal responsibility.

Collins and Porras in *Built to Last* state that the extraordinary success of visionary companies is not so much because of superior intellect or supposed success secrets, but most often because the workers in the companies demand so much of themselves. "Becoming and remaining a visionary company requires oodles of plain old-fashioned discipline, hard work and a visceral revulsion to any tendency toward smug self-satisfaction."

Coach Smith's teams became better and better largely because individual players took personal responsibility and became better players.

It's a simple secret to success for all corporations and teams.

Thought for the Day

If you want to make the team better, become better yourself.

Game Plan

- Teach personal responsibility

- Teach self-discipline

- Use an inside-out approach

- Develop trust

- Work hard in the off-season

Team Practice

- To what extent do you take personal responsibility for what happens to you?

- How do you demonstrate personal responsibility?

- How do you reinforce personal responsibility in others?

- What can your organization do to build a sense of trust?

THE POWER OF POSITIVE WORDS

"By how many points do you think we'll win?"

A few years ago, Carolina was playing Duke in Durham. It has always been a very difficult place to play because of the incredibly vocal fans. I played in Cameron Indoor Stadium 25 years ago, and we called them the Cameron Crazies then, too.

Before this particular game, the Tar Heels were huddled in the locker room. The "crazies" were yelling, jumping, and screaming. The band was blaring the Duke fight song. Even in the locker room, the noise was almost deafening.

As the time came to run onto the floor, everyone knew they would be resoundingly booed. The Carolina players mentally readied themselves for every possible indignity.

Coach Smith calmly walked into the huddle and looked his players in the eye. He said two things: "First," he said, "Isn't it amazing at this moment that a billion people in China don't care one bit who wins this game." Then he paused. Then he continued, "Isn't it going to be fun to shut them up?!?"

Carolina won the game.

In explaining how Coach Smith motivated his teams, I would be remiss if I did not talk about his extraordinary ability to be a positive encourager in tough game situations. Carolina comebacks and victories under Coach Smith are now legendary. However, few people know what really went on in the huddles when strategic decisions were made that led to those victories. Often it was Coach Smith's ability to encourage through positive words that inspired incredible performances.

In one particular game, Carolina was down by several points with a little more than a minute to go. During a time-out everyone came to the bench with concerned looks on their faces. Coach Smith just smiled.

He turned to Ademola Okulaja and asked, "By how many points do you think we'll win?" Okulaja responded, "I think we'll win by five."

Then Coach Smith asked the same question of Antawn Jamison, who answered, "I think we'll win by three."

They won by five.

No one completely understands the power of encouraging words on another person. We know discouraging words spread negativism and a defeatist attitude among sports teams, families, and companies like a spark to wood after a 60-day drought.

One of my favorite illustrations is about a man who wanted revenge against someone who had severely hurt him, so he went to the devil to buy an instrument of pain he could use against his enemy. He looked at one weapon and asked what it was.

The devil said, "That's slander, and it's very effective. It's worth a million dollars."

The man then pointed to another instrument and asked what it was.

"That is a furious temper," the devil said. "I use it often to break apart relationships and hurt people. It is also worth a million dollars."

The man finally pointed to one instrument on the far end of the table. "What is that and how much will it cost?"

"Oh, no," replied the devil. "That's not for sale. It's called discouragement, and it is my most valuable weapon."

Discouragement is a powerful negative force. "Sticks and stones may break my bones, but words will never hurt me." Ever heard that one? It's a lie. Words do hurt. They divide and discourage us as nothing else.

Yet, on the other hand, how powerful positive words can be! They can inspire like nothing else.

This principle even works in the animal kingdom. Geese, for example, can fly 72 percent farther in formation than alone. Do you know why they honk as they fly? Because the goose at the point of the V cannot turn his neck to see if the other geese are still following him. The force of the headwind blowing against him is so furious that if he turned his neck, it would instantly snap in two. So the other geese honk to tell the leader not to quit, to let him know they are still in formation behind him, still supporting him. They honk their encouragement.

Become a Positive Encourager

You cannot give out encouraging words, however, if positive thoughts don't fill your own heart. It is my belief that Coach Smith thought positively, therefore he easily became a positive encourager.

In 1968 George Karl was a very highly recruited point guard from Penn Hills, Pennsylvania. He had narrowed his choices to Duke or Maryland. Coach Smith entered the recruiting scene late with George, but decided he really wanted him.

George was not very encouraging when Coach Smith visited.

"What are our chances?" Coach Smith asked Karl.

"About one in ten," he answered.

"I like those odds," Smith said. He convinced Karl to visit Carolina. George loved the campus, the program, the players, and, especially, Coach Smith. He signed a scholarship with UNC soon after his visit.

A leader can't give positive, encouraging words if he's not a positive, encouraging person himself. It all starts here!

How important are positive words? They can mean the difference between quitting and staying in the game long enough to win.

In his early years in baseball, Jackie Robinson, the first black player in the major leagues, was ready to quit. He could not stomach the continual racist slurs thrown at him. One day, when he was particularly ready to give it up, he brazenly decided to steal home in a very important game. Like a wild man, he rushed from third, sliding under the catcher's tag. As he ran to the dugout, a little boy right behind the dugout kept yelling at him, "Way to go, Jackie! Way to go! Keep it up!"

The boy's words kept ringing in his ears. "Keep it up!" And at that moment, Jackie Robinson decided not to quit.

Amazing, isn't it? Several simple sentences from an unknown little boy allowed baseball and the entire sports world to keep one of its greatest players. A few positive words of encouragement outweighed all the discouraging words of the critics.

One time during my ministry I wanted to give up, too. Life's pressures had become too great for me to bear, and I wanted to quit. I remember one night when my wife, Marilynn, and I were on vacation. I was sitting on the edge of the bed at two in the morning, staring out the window at the water.

Marilynn awakened and noted my odd behavior. "What's wrong?" she asked.

"I want to quit," I said. "Ministry is too difficult."

She leaned over to me, took my hand, and quietly said, "I believe in you, David."

That's all I needed to hear. I persevered.

The tough time did pass. Ministry became meaningful to me again. The church started to surge forward. How glad I am now that I didn't quit. How glad I am that someone spoke encouraging words to me.

Coach Smith placed such an emphasis on positive words that he never allowed one player to criticize another player. In fact, he even became angry with me once for criticizing a *football* player.

During my freshman year, Carolina had just lost a tough football game. The team had two talented quarterbacks. One was a gifted option quarterback and fine runner. The other was a fine passer who later played in the NFL. For this game, the coach had decided to play the option quarterback, relegating the passer to the bench.

It just so happened that the passing quarterback was a high school friend of my older brother, Howard. In the locker room after a practice that followed the football game, I mentioned to a teammate that I questioned the football coach's wisdom in not playing the passer, proudly pointing out that he was my brother's friend.

Coach Smith overheard my comments. He approached me with fire flashing from his eyes. He told me in no uncertain terms that I had no right to question the football coach's judgment, reminding me that we were not only a basketball family, but also a university family. "Don't ever do that again publicly," he told me as he walked away.

I was embarrassed, but I knew Coach Smith was right. To this day I watch my words when I say something publicly about another person. I understand that my silence carefully guards his reputation. It also helps guarantee unity.

There's an old maxim that says, "If you can't say something good, don't say anything at all."

That's dead wrong. Say something good! Say a lot of good, encouraging words to people. They can make a tremendous difference in their lives. Positive words can change a life. They can spark a team to victory.

See Victory in Your Mind

One of Carolina's most famous comeback victories occurred against Duke in 1973. The Tar Heels came from eight down with 17 seconds to go to tie the game at the buzzer, go into overtime, and eventually win. A key player in this victory was Bobby Jones. He told me that when Coach Smith called timeout with 17 seconds on the clock, the team came to the bench fairly dejected.

With a calm voice and a wry smile, Coach said, "Let's have some fun here. Let's decide we're going to win this game."

"Then he turned to me," Jones remembered, "and said, 'Bobby, you're going to make these two free throws. Then we're going to put on the trap and we're going to steal the ball. And if we don't get the steal, we'll foul them immediately. Then we'll talk some more at the next timeout."

"So I made the free throws and we put the trap on. Someone deflected the ball and we got possession. We scored a lay-up and immediately fouled again. We called timeout and went to the huddle. The crowd was tense and loud. Coach just sat down, all calm and relaxed, even smiling.

'Okay, here's what we need to do,' he said. 'They'll miss the free throws and we'll go down and score. Then call timeout again.'"

That's exactly what happened. "We're now down by two with a few seconds left," Jones continued. "In the huddle, he told us to throw a half-court pass to Walter Davis, for Walter to take no more than two dribbles, shoot the ball, score — and we would win in overtime.

"It was amazing. It all happened exactly as he said. And when we went into overtime, no one was really celebrating. We just knew that if we did what he said, we'd win. It was as if he had scripted it. But what was so amazing was how calm and positive he was in the huddle. And because he was so positive and encouraging, so were we!"

Coach Smith could see the victory in his mind, and that's what he transmitted to the players. Over and over he stimulated them to win by planting in their minds an image of how a big win could be achieved. Then he reinforced that image with positive words. As Jones said, it was almost as if he scripted the victory. It was that clear to him.

On the first day of practice one year, Coach Smith had each player climb a ladder and cut down a part of the net. This team was not predicted to do very well, so he wanted to plant in their minds from day one what it would feel like to cut down a net after winning a championship.

After that first practice, they went into the locker room and had a huge celebration. They draped the newly cut nets over the 1993 championship trophy and took a team picture around it. Later each player put a copy of that picture in his locker, to help visualize the championship.

Another season, the team members opened their lockers after the first practice and found a picture of the basketball arena in Charlotte. They knew it had been designated as the location for the Final Four that year. The scoreboard in the picture showed the Tar Heels winning the national championship. Coach Smith wanted them to see the victory in their minds.

Believe in Others

Roy Williams, one of Coach Smith's former assistants and presently head coach at Kansas University, shared a similar experience from the national championship game against Georgetown in 1982.

"David," he told me, "it was the greatest single experience I've ever had in my life about how positive encouragement can change people's attitudes in a tense situation. We were down by one and when the guys came to the timeout with about forty seconds to play, I really thought we might lose the game. I had believed we were the best team and were destined to win. But at that moment, I began to doubt."

Roy carefully studied the looks on the players' faces, and he believed they also thought they were going to lose the game.

"We coaches were kneeling down in front of the players," Williams continued, "and we knew the coaches were going to determine the outcome of this game. Coach Smith then proceeded to tell the players what we were going to do. He said to penetrate and look for the best shot possible. But what was probably going to happen, he said, would be a penetration that would allow us to kick it to the backside. We'd then get a shot and knock it in. He said not to worry if we missed the shot, because we would have the other side covered with rebounding. And if we missed and they got the rebound, not to worry because we'd foul them and they'd miss the free throw under that kind of pressure.

"I can't explain it. Suddenly their spirits lifted. I checked the scoreboard again to see if somehow we'd gotten ahead in the game. And then, as the players left the huddle, he patted Michael Jordan on the back and said, 'Knock it in, Michael.' He knew the shot was going to come to him.

"Needless to say, the rest is history," Williams concluded. "It happened exactly as he designed it."

Many fans have heard this story. However, what they may not know is what Coach Smith said to Matt Doherty in that same huddle. Doherty added the following account.

"Right before that timeout, I had missed a crucial shot, one that could have put us up by three with 1:19 to go. Instead, they went down and Sleepy Floyd scored to put Georgetown up by one. That's when we called timeout. When I went to that huddle, I felt awful. I had let all my teammates and coaches down. Coach Smith outlined the next play, like everyone has heard.

"As we broke from the huddle," Doherty continued, "he told Michael to knock it down. But what people don't know is that as I left the huddle, he said the same thing to me. Can you imagine? He was anticipating that

I was feeling down from missing the previous shot. He wanted me to be confident in case I was forced to take the final shot. His constant encouragement gave all of us confidence."

Coach Smith believed in his players, and he encouraged them to believe in themselves, even when the odds were against them.

Matt Doherty also shared an interesting way Coach Smith developed confidence through encouragement in practice. "He knew I was a smart player who competed, and I could pass the ball and do little things like that," Doherty said. "And I knew that if I did the little things I would play.

"So I really began to work on my screens. I wanted to be the best screener on the team. I remember him pulling me aside one day and saying I was the best screener in the country. It made me feel so good, I started working even harder on my screens. At clinics during the summer I told the kids that Coach Smith said I was the best screener in the country. I'd go downtown and meet a pretty girl, and I'd tell her that Coach Smith said I was the best screener in the country. It filled my black book with phone numbers! Anyway, his encouragement motivated me to do the little things better than ever."

Sometimes, of course, it is necessary to show disapproval. But Coach Smith always managed to do it in a positive way.

Lee Dedmon, a 1967–71 letterman and co-most valuable player of the 1971 ACC Tournament, said, "Oh, he can get angry. But he gets angry at the action, not the person. He often expresses his anger to groups, not individuals. He won't hesitate to bounce some chalk off your head if you're going to sleep while watching game film."

Mitch Kupchak said, "He can throw chairs with his eyes. I always felt that when he simply said, 'Change jerseys,' and moved someone in practice from the first to the second team. You knew his disapproval. But it was always done in such a way that you never felt belittled. In fact, you always felt it was best for the team, and somehow for you too!"

Ronald Reagan received his highest ratings ever right after he was shot in 1981. One year later, he received his lowest ratings ever, a 32 percent approval rating. His underlings were terribly discouraged. Sensing this, he gathered them all together and said, "Don't worry. Every thing will be fine. I'll just go out and get shot again!" His ability to put a positive slant on a discouraging situation helped his staff get through a difficult time.

A great leader has the ability to impart to his followers a positive attitude that can overcome anything. Ken Blanchard, author of the enormously successful book, *The One Minute Manager*, said, "Of all the concepts that I have taught over the years, the most important is about 'catching people doing things right.' There is little doubt in my mind that the key to developing people is to catch them doing something right and praising their performance. The minute you begin talking about catching someone doing things right, praising that person, and letting him or her know you noticed their good performance, that person's attention perks up."

No leader should ever underestimate the power of positive words. When you're managing by walking around, a hand on the shoulder and a statement like "I really appreciate how much you mean to this corporation" go a long way. Everyone likes to be praised. Look in the eyes of your child when you offer praise. Remember, an adult is often just a grown-up child. We need encouragement just as much as they do.

A good question for all leaders to ask themselves would be, "Do the people who work with and under me feel positive encouragement coming from me, no matter what the odds?" People feel cheated if all they ever receive from a leader is information. All workers in every organization need information, but they need even more huge doses of inspiration and congratulation. They need positive encouragement.

Walter Bennis, in a speech delivered on C-Span entitled "Managing People Is Like Herding Cats," said, "All leaders expect positive outcomes. The glass is not half-empty or half-full, but always full." That expresses the necessity of a positive outlook.

Preparation Fosters a Positive Outlook

While positive encouragement is a necessary principle for any successful leader, an important part of Coach Smith's ability to be positive, to believe when everything seemed impossible, was his absolutely thorough preparation.

Every day Coach Smith would post a thought for the day on the practice schedule. Each player had to read it and recite it if called on during the practice. If he couldn't do it, the individual and/or the team would have to run.

One of Coach Smith's favorite thoughts for the day was, "Luck is when preparation meets opportunity." John Lotz told me that in the 35 plus years he has known Coach Smith, he has never heard him say, "Good luck." Not once. "He simply doesn't believe in luck," Lotz said. "You win by being prepared, not by being lucky."

It's fascinating to study how Coach Smith prepared for an opponent in light of his commitment to the team above the individual. First, he insisted that his teams be the best-conditioned in America. He vowed that we would never lose because our opposition was in better shape than we were.

Moreover, we prepared for every situation. In our two-hour practices, each one timed to the minute, we spent time going over every possible game situation. What would we do if there's a minute left and we're down by two? Ahead by two? There are 10 seconds left, we're down by one, and we have the ball? We were prepared for those situations before the game ever started.

"During the 1983 season," Buzz Peterson told me, "we were playing Tulane. We were in triple overtime. Down by three. Coach Smith drew up a play on his paper. He said, 'Buzz, you're here. Matt, you're here. Michael, you're here.' I remember thinking there sure were a lot of lines going all over the place, but I remembered where I was supposed to go. Something in practice reminded me.

"I came out of the huddle and looked at Matt and asked, 'Do you know what you're supposed to do?' He said, 'Yeah.' Then he asked me, 'Do you know what you're supposed to do?' And I said, 'Yeah.' Then he said, 'Well, let's do what we're supposed to do!'

"The only thing I remembered was to go to a certain area. I saw the ball go over my head, then Michael had it in his hands and was shooting a three. We went into another overtime and won the game. We were a better team, but we didn't play that well. But we won, I think, because we were really prepared and in better shape!"

Coach Smith was so thorough in his simulation of game situations that he once had the team practice the same drill for almost four straight months. Every day in practice he set up the same situation: Pearce Landry guarded Jerry Stackhouse with 10 seconds left on the clock, down by one, and the opposing team had possession of the ball. Landry's assignment: prevent Stackhouse from catching the ball for five seconds, and force a violation and a turnover.

Understandably, Landry wearied of repeating this simulation, often wondering why he had to do this hackneyed drill over and over again.

Then Carolina played Wake Forest in Winston-Salem. For most of the game UNC was down by 15 points — which is where the Tar Heels were at the 12:00 minute timeout in the second half. Smith called the team over and said, "At the 8:00 minute timeout, we'll be down by ten. Then at 4:00 we'll be down by five. Then it's anyone's game."

That is exactly what happened. They kept whittling the lead down until, with 10 seconds left, UNC was down by one and Wake Forest had the ball. Smith called a timeout and summoned Pearce Landry to enter the game. "Pearce, it's your job to keep Randolph Childress (Wake's superstar guard)from catching the ball."

The ball was handed to the Wake player inbounding the pass. Carolina applied pressure. Wake tried to get the ball to Childress, their best free-throw shooter. But after guarding Stackhouse in exactly the same situation every day for four months, guarding Childress was a piece of cake for Landry. Childress never touched the ball.

The five-second call came and the ball was awarded to Carolina. Donald Williams got the ball, drove the right side of the lane, and hit a running one-hander as time expired to win the game.

When your preparation is that precise, you can see the victory in your mind and you can achieve it on the court.

Woody Durham, the Tar Heels' radio announcer, shared another story regarding Coach Smith's legendary preparation. "I have always believed that his preparation is the key to his success. I will never forget 1990. Carolina was not considered to be one of the stronger teams going into the NCAA tournament. It may have been the lowest seed Carolina had ever had. They were the eighth seed and got shipped out to the Midwest regional in Austin, Texas. We won the first-round game and then had to be matched up against the number-one team in the nation in Oklahoma.

"At that time we were doing Coach Smith's pre-game interview during the pre-game meal. While the team and the assistant coaches were down in the dining room, I would go to his hotel suite to do the pre-game interview. I remember knocking on the door of his hotel room. He came to the door and let me in. He was still watching some Oklahoma tape. It was Oklahoma versus Kansas. He knew Kansas did a lot of things like us, and he was looking for any advantage. I watched him run the tapes back and forth, over and over again. He studied them intently. Finally, he sat back in the chair and said, 'I think I know them pretty well. Now, if I can just translate it to the players.'

"About six hours later, Rick Fox made a lay-up in the last second. Carolina upset the number-one team in the country and moved ahead in the tournament. I'm convinced he knew Oklahoma's tendency to over-play on defense and he was prepared to run that play, in that situation, if necessary, before the game ever began."

Durham told another story that illustrates the same principle. "It was North Carolina versus Virginia in the late 1980s. Virginia had the ball with a few seconds left. If they make the shot, they win. During the time-out huddle, Coach Smith reached for the clipboard to diagram something. He diagrammed the play Virginia was going to run. He turned to Scott Williams and told him they were going to inbound the ball to Richard Morgan. Morgan would then come left of the foul circle and take the jump shot from that point. He told Scott to release from his man when Morgan moved left from the jump circle. 'When you release,' he said, 'I want you to leap in the air, and I believe you can get a hand on his shot.' Then he smiled and said, 'And after you block the shot, just run into the locker room to the cheers of our fans.'

"So Virginia threw the ball to Richard Morgan. He dribbled to the left of the circle and went up in the air; Scott Williams ran toward him, tipped the ball with two fingers, and then ran into the dressing room. Carolina won the game. It happened just as Coach Smith diagrammed it. You should have seen Scott Williams's face as he described this to me. He wondered if Coach Smith was some kind of soothsayer or psychic!

"But he's simply very well prepared. Coach had looked at so many tapes of Virginia that he had spotted a pattern for a last-second play. He had seen them run this same play in two games, so he believed they would do it again. There was no luck involved. He was simply prepared."

Vision Fosters Preparation

I believe Coach Smith's best preparation, however, did not consist of simulating game situations or studying the opposition but in tenaciously believing in his philosophy. Yes, he was ready for Virginia's final play. But the defensive commitment to have his big men expose themselves on a pick is what allowed Scott Williams to switch and block the shot.

Day in and day out we spent more time in practice going over his offensive and defensive schemes than we did memorizing the plays of our opponents. We did become familiar with them. However, we spent most of our practice time going over our philosophy. We repeatedly ran through our preparation until we were ready to play. Coach Smith concentrated on teamwork rather than on the opposition. He felt that this would win games — and 80 percent of the time he was right.

What a leadership insight! Too many leaders spend most of their time studying their opposition instead of perfecting their own teams. That's not to say we should never study others. We can glean some important insights from analyzing competitors. However, our greatest productivity comes in performing our vision well. If that vision does not consistently win, perhaps the vision is inadequate. A good vision motivating a high-performing team that places the team above the individual should win in spite of what the opposition is doing.

Practice prepared our team to face the opposition. Coach Smith stayed centered on what was most important for us to perform. I believe this preparation allowed him to focus on the things that were important, not urgent.

When talking about urgent tasks that leaders too often respond to but then later regret, Charles Hummel said, "The appeal of these tasks seems irresistible, and they devour our energy. But in perspective, their deceptive prominence fades; and with a sense of loss, we recall the vital tasks we pushed aside. We realize that we have become slaves to the tyranny of the urgent."

The city of Charlotte recently commissioned a study regarding how the city can continually be on the cutting edge of growth in the twenty-first century. The study's emphasis was not on attracting industries from outside Charlotte to move here. Instead, the emphasis was on Charlotte's major, already-established, successful industries to continue to do what they do well. This, the study concluded, would better foster expanded growth plus naturally attract new industries thereafter. I think Coach Smith as a leader would enthusiastically endorse this conclusion.

Coach Smith concentrated on his vision and specifically how he thought a team should play together. He spent hours each day carefully teaching this vision. We were aware of the other team and what they did. But what drove us was our philosophy. We performed this vision at peak performance. And we won 80 percent of our games!

Positive words, plus positive envisioning, plus a positive vision equals success...to the tune of 879 successes for Coach Smith!

Thought for the Day

Positive words can change a life and spark a team.

Game Plan

- Be a positive encourager
- See victory in your mind
- Believe in others
- Preparation fosters a positive outlook
- Vision fosters preparation

Team Practice

- How do you encourage others?
- How do you demonstrate that you believe in others?
- How do you show disapproval in a positive way?
- What can your organization do to foster positive encouragement?

PASSING ON
WHAT YOU KNOW

"If they learned anything from me, I'm grateful."

O n April 16, 1994, Coach Smith received the Apple Award for Distinguished Achievement from Kansas University. In presenting the award, given annually to a School of Education alumnus, Chancellor Gene A. Budig said, "Dean Smith is a world-class teacher. His players always reflect the skills and values he acquired as a student-athlete at the University of Kansas."

Every great leader is also a teacher and mentor. His concern is not simply for himself, but to teach what he has learned to those who share his passion. Coach Smith's basketball family tree has produced many coaches who have taken his vision of team before the individual to every level imaginable — from junior high leagues to the professional ranks.

I believe his passion in life is to teach young people how to play basketball and that he would be content coaching at a small Division III school. If he had no media attention, no ability for television cameras to reach him in a high school gym, he would easily adjust. I think he would like to announce that basketball try-outs will be on such and such a day, have kids come out who really love the game and simply want to play it for no other reason, and then start teaching. The only trouble is, he would be such a successful coach that within a year the press would be swarming all over him.

Coach Smith's passion for teaching started out as a passion for learning. "Whenever you talk about Dean Smith being a teacher of the game of basketball," Coach Bob Knight said, "you must first acknowledge that he was a student of the game of basketball. He spent countless hours talking the game of basketball with experts from his earliest years. And, in being a very good student, he put himself in a very good position to be an excellent teacher. He has taught basketball the way it is meant to be played. He gets the kids to work together unselfishly and to play in such a way that they receive recognition through team accomplishments. That's his underlying philosophy."

Michael Quigley, dean of the graduate school at St. Rivier College in Nashua, New Hampshire, wrote an article titled, "The Leader as Learner." In it he suggests that leaders must constantly be developing personal intellectual habits as well as the ability to analyze and interpret information for the purpose of strategic decision-making. In other words, the leader who is a teacher or mentor must also be a student. That's why Bob Knight suggested that being a great student of basketball was Coach Smith's greatest asset as a teacher.

This principle has been discovered by the corporate world as well as academia. For example, Richard C. Bartlett, vice chairman of Mary Kay Holding Corporation, says one of that corporation's key accomplishments has been to develop a culture of success that stresses continuous learning as a corporate "given." The leader who is teacher must first be a learner.

Coach Smith's learning and teaching genes run deep in his family. With both parents being schoolteachers, it was natural for him to become a teacher. Alfred Smith, his father, won the state basketball championship in 1934 at Emporia High School. He taught a dogged commitment to team play.

"I practically grew up in a gym," Coach Smith told me, "and I went to a couple of basketball clinics with my dad. When I was in college, though, Dr. Phog Allen wanted me to go into medicine. I guess I enrolled in one pre-med course, but my real interest was always in coaching."

His mother also made an impact upon Smith as an educator. In 1988 he gave $50,000 to Kansas University to establish the Vesta Marie Edwards Smith Scholarship in Education. It's named in honor of Smith's mother and is given to students in the elementary education program. The scholarship is awarded on the basis of monetary need and academic promise to kids from Allen, Lyon, and Shaver counties in Kansas — places where Coach Smith's mother taught for 40 years.

Coach Smith was on the 1952 national championship team at Kansas University. After this successful season, Phog Allen wrote all the members of the team:

> It's been great fun. But twenty-five to thirty years from now you boys will radiate and multiply your recollections of your struggles and successes and your defeats. All these will be rolled into a fine philosophy of life, which will give you durable satisfactions down through the years. It has been wonderful for me to be so closely associated with such a fine group of outstanding Kansas men as you.
> Sincerely,
> Dr. Forrest C. Allen, 'Doc'

So, Coach Smith was a student of the game from his father and Phog Allen. In a way, they both mentored him. He learned the vision of the team before the individual from both of them. Basketball was a vehicle to teach his vision of team over the individual but also to teach young men a philosophy of life. Now coaches who played under him and shared coaching responsibilities with him are doing the same.

How did Coach Smith not only teach his players, but particularly his players and assistants who have now become coaches? How intentional was he? Was there a program or philosophy that guided him as a teacher and mentor?

Intentional and Imitational Mentoring

I interviewed a number of men who coached with Dean Smith about how he mentored them. Was there a program he set up to teach them? Did he intentionally mentor them as future coaches? From the different answers, I discovered two different approaches to mentoring, both of which Coach Smith modeled.

The first approach is intentional mentoring. Many of those presently in the basketball coaching profession — Larry Brown, Phil Ford, George Karl, John Kuester, Eddie Fogler, Buzz Peterson, and King Rice, for example — were all point guards for Coach Smith's teams. During the preseason and the regular season, these basketball "quarterbacks" regularly met with Coach Smith about his overall basketball philosophy and his game-by-game personal strategy. These sessions were intentional mentoring classes that laid the foundation for the next generation of coaches. Even after they became head coaches, these men would meet with Coach Smith for several days each summer, in a kind of continuing education program.

While these were intentional sessions on the principles of coaching, most of Coach Smith's mentoring flowed out of his peripatetic teaching style. The word *peripatetic* means to walk up and down and refers to the kind of teaching that takes place while moving or traveling from one location to another.

This is the style Jesus used in teaching his disciples how to do ministry after his departure. He first built a close, meaningful relationship with them. They spent three years with him, observing what he did and how he did it. As he went about doing his ministry, he simply told his disciples to pay attention, to ask questions if they didn't understand anything, and then he told them to go and do likewise.

Similarly, Coach Smith had students who loved basketball work with him. He found teachable moments during the everyday routine of practice and training. He permitted interaction. He allowed questions and asked for input. As the students drew closer and closer to him, they never stopped observing and asking questions. Later, they adapted what they had learned to their own head coaching experiences.

For example, Eddie Fogler, head of the University of South Carolina's basketball program, told me that Coach Smith never actually taught him to coach. "I simply had the experience and the exposure of working with him," he said. "I was in all those meetings and closed practices. I saw how he handled the players' meetings. I saw how he organized the travel plans. I saw first hand the ups and downs. There was no formula he took us through. Now I draw from those experiences and try to apply them as best as I can here at South Carolina."

One time Coach Fogler was on the bench next to Coach Smith in a tight game. Coach Smith turned to him and asked what he thought they should do in this situation. "I thought for a few moments, then gave him my opinion," Fogler recalled. "He didn't do what I suggested, but he did turn to me and say, 'I just wanted to see if you were paying attention.'"

George Karl, coach of the NBA's Milwaukee Bucks, told me that it's a privilege to be with Coach Smith every summer for four or five days. "We talk a lot about basketball and a lot about life," Karl said. "He's never tried to impose his system on me. He's simply been available, and I do a lot of observing and asking questions. I guess that's how he mentored me as a coach."

The on-the-job training he learned from Coach Smith is what sticks in assistant coach Phil Ford's mind. "I learned largely how to do things by observing his philosophy. The hardest thing is to get that philosophy out of his head and into my heart, and that's the objective of coaching. But I learned how to do that by observing him and asking questions."

Coach Smith's intentional mentoring did not extend solely to his key players. For example, Roy Williams, Kansas University's very successful coach, never played on the varsity team at Carolina. "I had to start working for a living in college. So I worked in the intramural office and refereed basketball games, umpired softball games, or whatever needed to be done. I usually started at four in the afternoon, and I would go by and watch a little bit of practice beforehand. Practices were closed, but Coach Smith let me stay. He sensed I really wanted to coach. I still have those notes from the freshman and varsity practices I observed.

"When I was in graduate school, they asked me to work the summer camp because I was a good official. I refereed the scrimmages at night. After college I got a high school job and stayed there five years. But I continued to work the summer camps, and eventually Coach Smith asked me to be an assistant. But, you know, he has never had a set agenda for mentoring me. I simply observed, asked a lot of questions, saw how he did it, then adapted his style into my own. I think that every day I was with him he was preparing me to have my own program."

Bill Guthridge, Coach Smith's successor at Carolina, said he thought that Coach Smith "wanted all of us to become head coaches, or at least to have the opportunity. He encouraged us, both on and off the court, always to think like we were head coaches. He would constantly ask us, 'What would you do here if you were the head coach? Give me some suggestions.' Then he would digest our input. Sometimes he would use what we'd suggest, sometimes not. But we felt included. And I think this helped prepare us for that day when we would be head coaches ourselves. Of course, it's always easier to give suggestions than to live with decisions, but I think I was as prepared as I could have been to follow him."

In talking with many of those who have become coaches after sitting under Coach Smith's tutelage, it is obvious that he had no formula for mentoring them. The similar thread woven through all their testimonies is the "teaching on the go" experience that he offered those who wanted to learn.

Stephen Covey described this type of teaching as "modeling and mentoring." He said, "You can only become a mentor to someone if you are first a model, an example, and then build a relationship. Many people, including entertainers and athletes, are models, but they have no meaningful relationship with their fans. If you are a model and have a relationship, you can be a true mentor ... and in a mature mentoring relationship, when you make mistakes, you do not destroy the faith of students because their faith is not based on you — it is based on the same set of principles."

The most significant learning occurs within the context of a relationship. Coach Smith gathered gifted people around him and allowed their friendship to grow. Then he allowed them to observe his genius, often asking for their input. He gave them every opportunity to learn from him as he performed his daily coaching responsibilities. They could ask any questions they wanted. Any question was a good question, he told them, if they didn't know the answer. Then, when the time came for them to become head coaches, they went and adapted his style to their own unique personality and setting. Their success speaks for itself.

To a larger group — all of his players, not just those who wanted to become coaches — Dean Smith engaged in what I call imitational mentoring. This is what some people would simply say is being an exemplar, or role model. For his other lettermen, and for many associates, his involvement with us as a friend was a model for how life should be lived and how leaders should lead. Many people joke with me and say I lead the church I serve like Coach Smith did the Carolina basketball program, I haven't spent much time with him personally since I graduated. However, I have constantly observed his leadership. I learned by observing then imitating. It wasn't intentional mentoring to train us as coaches, but imitational mentoring to teach us how to live and lead others.

Yet both approaches involve mentoring, influencing through leadership and example to be the best players and people possible.

This imitational mentoring is so effective that no one will ever know just how many people Coach Smith has affected. He is admired by many and copied by multitudes because of who he is. Indeed, because of his imitational mentoring in my own life, I'm now writing this book — which hopefully will extend the influence of Coach Smith to even more people.

Mentoring Future Generations

Therefore, Coach Smith's mentoring of his players, both intentionally and through imitation, will affect many generations to come.

For example, Bobby Jones is now the head basketball coach of Charlotte Christian High School. One of his former players is Luke Boythe, now a forward for the University of North Carolina at Greensboro. Here is how Boythe described what Jones has meant to him as a person first, and then as a player. "Coach Jones was genuinely concerned for us as individuals more than as athletes," he said. Boythe recalled Jones developing the team as young men, not just basketball players, and that he led by example.

It's no coincidence that the way Luke Boythe describes Bobby Jones is exactly the way former players talk about Coach Smith. That's what true mentoring is: taking your life and pouring it into another person, who then takes the same principles and pours them into another person, who then...You get the picture.

In fact, you almost get the picture that Luke Boythe is who he is because Coach Smith's father and Phog Allen were who they were in Coach Smith's life. Coach Smith passed that truth on to Jones, who gave it to Boythe, who, hopefully, in one way or another, will pass it on to the next generation.

All effective leaders lead with an eye to future generations. Max DePree, in his very popular book *Leadership Is an Art*, said, "Leaders are also responsible for future leadership. They need to identify, develop, and nurture future leaders." No one can lead exactly like you, but there are basic principles that are applicable for all generations. How I apply them for my generation may be different for those mentoring under me, but the principles themselves remain constant.

An outstanding example of how Coach Smith's mentoring has affected following generations of players and coaches can be found in the Chicago Bulls' six world championships. Now, I know Coach Smith never coached for Chicago. So let me explain what I mean.

The reason the Bulls have won six world championships is because of defense. That has been their imprimatur. "You don't know how lucky you are," Don Nelson, coach of the NBA's Dallas Mavericks, once told Bulls coach Phil Jackson, "when your two best offensive players are your two best defensive players." He was referring, of course, to Michael Jordan and Scottie Pippen. When Dennis Rodman, another great defensive player who loved to rebound, was added to the equation, the team was solidified.

Michael Jordan willed himself to become a great defensive player. But he also had a wonderful teacher and mentor, Dean Smith, who sensed Jordan's amazing athletic ability and saw his limitless professional career. Smith therefore pushed him early on to become a great defensive player. He constantly told Michael Jordan what he had told us: "Anyone can score on this level. Few really want to be great defensive players. But if you want to be a great player at the next level, you will have to play defense."

Jordan listened to his mentor. He became a great offensive and defensive player in college. This was most unusual for a young player. Most simply want to score and have little to do with the grinding, exhausting, in-the-trenches work of defense. But Jordan had learned from Smith that defense wins games, and winning was his highest priority. He ultimately hungered for championships, not MVP trophies. In fact, early in his career he mentioned to reporters how he yearned one day to be named the NBA's defensive player of the year as well as the league MVP.

Most people snickered that it couldn't be done. NBA pundits thought that it would require too much energy on both ends of the court for a player to accomplish such a feat. In fact, Jan Hubbard, then with the Dallas *Morning News,* said as much in one of his articles. Evidently Jordan read it, for when he did win both awards in the 1987–88 season, he reminded Hubbard of his mistake. That's how intensely competitive Michael Jordan is.

Then Scottie Pippen joined the NBA and the Chicago Bulls with tremendous raw skills and natural talent. He possessed quickness, jumping ability, and extraordinarily long arms — with an even wider span than Jordan's. It became evident early on that Pippen would offer the unique ability to guard every one on the floor, from a point guard to the center. He could cause major disruptions to another team if his defensive skills could be honed.

Enter Michael Jordan. Nothing in those early years helped Pippen more than playing against Michael Jordan every day in practice. Jordan made a commitment to teach Pippen how to play defense. He killed him every day in practice. Michael had a reputation for making or breaking his teammates, and Scottie offered a special project with potentially exceptional rewards. In essence, Jordan became Pippen's mentor.

Pippen responded in kind. Where other players might have been driven from the league because of Jordan's relentless pressure in practice, the young, gifted, voracious Pippen fought him at every corner. Michael Jordan knew this simple reality: if Pippen could guard Jordan every day in practice, he could guard anyone in the league. And he did. What's more, the Jordan–Pippen combination on the court became Chicago's lethal weapon. So powerful did the two become together that Jordan once said it was like having his twin on the court with him.

No one can predict what impact mentoring one gifted person can have on the future. Why has Chicago won six national championships? It is at least partly attributable to Dean Smith. When he taught Michael Jordan to play defense, he was teaching Scottie Pippen and all the other Bulls on those championship teams how to play defense. The results rest in the annals of NBA folklore and history.

Coach Smith believed the team to be more important than the individual. He doggedly taught that defense wins games. He believed he was preparing people for life, not just to be better basketball players. Those who played for him or coached with him observed him and learned these principles. They are now practicing the same things. And those working under Coach Smith's former assistants will one day pass these same truths on to the teams they coach.

No one could ultimately guess the numbers of people worldwide who, over the next decades, will be positively affected by Coach Smith because he mentored a few. That, in essence, is what teaching and mentoring is all about. An effective leader understands this truth and passes it on to those who work with him, those who will be leading long after he retires.

The leader who influences others to lead others is a leader without limitation. The more people you develop, the longer your legacy.

Leading Generation X

As I told different people about working on this project, many of them wanted me to ask Coach Smith for advice on how to lead Generation X. It appears members of this generation are different from previous generations and may need an altered leadership style.

I not only asked Coach Smith, I asked many other successful coaches how they dealt with Generation X. Their answers, which follow, were helpful and insightful.

"On this subject," Bob Knight said, "I feel like I'm on an island with sharks swimming all around. Leadership was so much easier when you weren't trying to do it all by yourself. You simply don't have the assistance you had fifteen years ago. Somewhere along the way parents have let kids get away with a whole lot more than mine did.

"So I think leadership today is much more difficult. You don't have the authority support from their parents. I always felt that demands placed on kids to improve behavior and performance were essential for their development. Even the school system has lessened those demands. There is a struggle in our society for what is right and wrong, acceptable and unacceptable. Kids now have a harder time figuring that out.

"Therefore, with this generation, I still keep the demands high. Maybe I'm even tougher today than I was fifteen years ago. Certainly a lot of people think so. But I'm trying to prepare kids for life, not a career in professional basketball. I can't let up. I keep pounding away, knowing I won't reach everyone. So my demands are the same for any team of any generation. That's the only way, in my opinion, you can coach this generation today. Demand the best from them. Discipline is still the key, although you will be lonelier and more isolated in this position than you have ever been before."

Phil Ford has a similar viewpoint. "You're talking about the difference between young men worrying about being drafted in the Vietnam War and guys today consumed with listening to LL Cool J. Yet I would say that you must deal with these guys the same way you dealt with previous generations. You make demands. You tell them what you want. Then you discipline them if they don't do it. You ultimately work with the kids who want to work. That's still the beginning point for success."

"You've got to recruit character," according to Kansas head coach Roy Williams. "Then you mold them into a team with clear expectations. You help them learn how to enjoy a teammate's success. But I simply won't recruit a kid from this generation who won't play team basketball or who has a bad attitude. I think that's the same for all generations."

I remember a particular player Roy Williams once recruited. He was a spectacular high school player, but during the recruiting season he publicly questioned "Roy's substitution pattern." Can you imagine? To this day I still call Coach Smith "Coach." Even now I can't bring myself to call him by his first name because of my deep respect for him. After this teenager's diatribe, which clearly questioned whether he would receive enough playing time to adequately prepare his professional career, Williams abruptly announced he was no longer recruiting this individual. Williams's way of leading Generation

X? Recruit young men who understand the nuances of team basketball!

Jerry West said that working with Generation X "has been the most difficult and challenging part of being a general manager in the NBA. They need to know the rules, just like our generation, and the rules need to be uniformly enforced. I think they are willing to respond as long as they know the expectations."

"I think you have to clearly let them know that the inmates are not going to be allowed to run the asylum," Matt Doherty said. "You have to tell them from day one to be on time. If not, the bus will roll without them. Otherwise, they won't ever believe you again and you'll lose the respect of the other guys. They're different than fifteen years ago, but that's still the way you must lead them."

George Karl offered an interesting insight into the origin of some of the difficulties in leading Generation X. "Part of the problem with the Generation X athlete today in the NBA is caused by marketing the wrong stuff," he said. "For example, the Seattle Supersonics never play the Los Angeles Lakers. It was always Payton versus O'Neal. Very seldom do you hear people talk about team assists and fundamentals." Karl remembered how Coach Smith hated stat sheets. "He didn't like them in the locker room because they emphasized the individual over the team," he continued.

"Today, in the NBA, you not only have to communicate something to the player, but also to his agent, his parents, sometimes his wife. Now his personal problems are not only team problems, but also national news. To deal with this generation, you simply have to communicate. You must demand your principles in games and practice. You have to have a degree of discipline and commitment. And when the players see the team winning and that they are getting better every year, most buy in. Those who don't probably need to go."

There is a similar approach to the way all of these coaches are dealing with Generation X, and it's echoed by Coach Smith. The bottom line is that people may be different, but the basic principles remain the same.

"When I accepted the job at Carolina," Coach Smith said, "the school demanded we recruit good people who were serious students. That certainly helps the leader accomplish the vision of the team above the individual. To help insure they are good people, we would talk to their high school coaches. We asked their teammates what they thought of the players we were recruiting. We talked to their high school teachers. As coaches, all of us tend to inflate our players. I know I have done that with players and the NBA. But teachers are generally good people who are good judges.

"In recruiting, you don't always take the greatest player, but the one who is a good player and also a serious student with good work habits. If you do this, with any generation, and then let them know what you expect, I think you can get any generation to perform. It's more difficult today, so you have to be more intentional when you recruit or hire. But good people properly motivated with clear expectations and lines of authority can still perform — even Generation X."

In talking with these successful coaches about Generation X, a common theme ran through their comments. They all affirmed it is a more difficult generation to lead and manage. But they all also said that people are people, and what motivated previous generations still motivates today.

That makes sense to me, especially after studying the leadership techniques of Coach Smith and other successful leaders. It seems they all support a principle-centered leadership style. Their principles, not the players' whims and fancies, guide their coaching. Therefore, they treat all people from all generations the same, because *the principles* are the same. They are inviolable laws in the relational realm, as real as gravity is in the physical realm.

When practiced, these principles work for all leaders.

Thought for the Day

Mentoring requires a relationship, not a formula.

Game Plan

- Be an intentional mentor
- Find teachable moments
- Value questions and input
- Be an imitational mentor
- Build relationships
- Set an example

Team Practice

- What steps do you take to pass on what you know?
- How do you demonstrate to others that you value their input?
- To what extent do you look for positive qualities in others?
- Do you consistently live in a way that reflects your values?

A COMMITMENT
TO CHARACTER

"Your reputation is what other people think of you. Character is what you think of yourself."

Jim Smithwick, now a physician, played for Coach Smith from 1962 to 1966. He was a member of the team that experienced perhaps the most traumatic, potentially debilitating moment in Coach Smith's career.

Carolina had just lost a heartbreaker to Wake Forest. The trip back to Chapel Hill was somewhat somber, even depressing. When the team bus pulled up to the gym, an eerie sight greeted the players: a dummy of Coach Smith swinging from a tree. Some angry students had hung him in effigy.

The team sat in stunned silence. Everyone waited for Coach Smith's response. Smithwick, who was a sophomore on that team, gave this account: "He looked at the dummy, then turned to us. He was not angry. He just said, 'Your reputation is what other people think of you. Character is what you think of yourself.' Then Coach got off the bus and left."

"Billy Cunningham ran off the bus and angrily tore down the dummy. But I'll never forget Coach Smith's words as long as I live. I've tried to follow this principle all my life and even pass it on to my children."

Coach Smith understood something about character: it's who you are when no one else is looking. Therefore, character is not determined by what others think of you, but by what you think of yourself.

I personally think Coach Smith is a person of outstanding character. This quality is fundamental for a great leader. Yes, Coach Smith has warts and human failures. There are certainly things in his life that, if he could do them over again differently, he would. Yet he is a man of tremendous integrity. A man of principle. A man of character.

Antoine de Saint-Exupery once said, "It is only with the heart one sees rightly. What is essential is invisible to the eye."

Coach Smith's invisible principles are what have helped bring him visible success. He always understood that there are no shortcuts to character, and he believed that if he lost his character, he would lose his credibility. We players instinctively followed him because we knew his words matched his life. We knew he was a person of high moral character. We sensed his humility, his compassion, and his care for us.

He never chose what was fashionable or easy over his character. He was always guided by doing what he felt was right, even when the critics decried him loudly and said the game had passed him by.

Leadership expert Stephen Covey wrote, "What is often missed in leadership is the character side. Without character, you can't have wisdom, in spite of competence. And without wisdom, you simply can't build and maintain an enduring institution, whether it be a marriage, a family, a team, or a company."

I believe there is a character crisis among leaders today. So many seem to be falling prey to the temptations of personal success and pleasure as their ultimate reasons for being in leadership. But before we can *do*, we must *be*. It's who we are when no one else is looking.

What are the character traits that have guided Coach Smith through the years? Let's look at some of them.

Humility

When I asked Dean Smith what 879 wins represent to him, he quietly responded, "That I'm old."

Immediately after he broke Coach Rupp's record, he was interviewed on national television. He began to praise all the lettermen who had ever played for him. He really doesn't want the spotlight.

In fact, he hates interviews. He once told me, "I don't go out and talk on television after the games, except in the NCAA's. They make me do it or they kick you out of the NCAA. I prefer to send players out. I want them to be up front to the public."

John Lotz said that if you go to Coach Smith's home today you will not find any basketball memorabilia. That's very unusual for a successful leader in any field. "Oh, he is very aware of what he has accomplished and who he is," John said. "Yet he is also aware of all the people necessary for him to achieve all this. Therefore, personal exaltation seems inappropriate to him."

How many leaders would do this? Would they take the awards and commemorative photos off the walls to give evidence of all those who have helped them succeed?

In 1998 ESPN wanted to bestow upon Coach Smith the Arthur Ashe Award for courage, because of the many things he has done to promote racial equality in Chapel Hill and around the country. Smith did not want the award. He truly did not think he deserved it. Ashe's wife had to call him and ask him to receive the award on behalf of her husband and others who appreciated everything Coach Smith had done. He finally relented.

When he received the *Sports Illustrated* Sportsman of the Year Award for 1997, he demonstrated his customary humility. He named others he thought to be more deserving. Then, surprisingly, upon receiving the award he referred to Roland Thornqvist, a player on UNC's tennis team who did something amazing when he was about to win an important match. Smith said, "The referee made a bad call and gave him a point to win the nationals. He had it won, but he said, 'My shot was out.' He wouldn't accept it. He went onto win, but those kinds of guys are Sportsmen of the Year."

Dean Smith's humility illustrates something Stephen Covey wrote. "One of the characteristics of authentic leaders," Covey said, "is their humility, evident in their ability to take off their glasses and examine the lens objectively, analyzing how well their values, perceptions, beliefs, and behaviors align with 'true north' principles" (a term Covey uses to describe unchangeable principles that should shape every leader's life).

Covey went on to say that "as people become increasingly principle-centered, they love to share recognition and power." That aptly describes Coach Smith. He believed that if the team won, there should be enough recognition for the team. He hated the personal adulation, yet he would patiently sign autographs for anyone who wanted one. He simply believed that the more he refused to seek praise, the more that was left for the players. Remember what he said? "Players win games. I lose them."

Roy Williams, a former assistant and now coach of the very successful Kansas program, said, "Every time you talk to him, he starts trying to deflect his success to his team, his players, his assistants — the janitors." Talking about the phenomenal record of 879 wins, Williams said, "This record is a situation where the attention has to be focused on him...I think every player who's ever played at Carolina wanted it for him at least a thousand times more than the man wanted it himself."

When Smith announced his retirement, many of his former players gathered to support him. The championship trophies were all lined up behind him. Everything around him should have reminded him of his extraordinary success. Yet how did he respond? I think he did something very courageous. He shrugged his shoulders at his success and then gently chided the many reporters and the thousands of television viewers. He scolded them about total obsession with sports and winning.

As he reflected on the human condition worldwide, he could not reconcile it with the adulation being poured on him for simply winning basketball games. He said that if a Nobel prize-winning professor had just retired from UNC, hardly anyone would have noticed. It would not have begun to approach the fanfare of his retirement.

Any intelligent person knows Dean Smith is right. He simply has the courage, the principles, and the humility to state it.

Then, he started thanking all those with whom he had been associated through the years, especially his former players, for his success. Upon mentioning the former players, he began to cry.

A penetrating question for all leaders to ask is this: do I desire to receive the praise personally, or do I sincerely desire my employees to receive it? Someone once said that anything is attainable if we don't care who receives the credit. In a corporate climate of downsizing, where CEOs are jumping out of corporations with their golden parachutes and workers are left in anxiety wondering if they even have a job, humility would seem to be an important personal virtue for every leader.

Indira Gandhi summed up this perspective well. "My grandfather once told me," she said, "that there are two kinds of people: those who do the work and those who take the credit. He told me to try to be in the first group; there was less competition there."

I believe Coach Smith is in the first group. Most effective leaders are.

The church I oversee has grown and recently faced a multi-million-dollar building expansion. I inwardly struggled about spending so much on a building while there are so many needs in the world. So, naturally, I sought Coach Smith's counsel. After all, the University of North Carolina had built a 34-million-dollar basketball facility in 1986 and put Coach Smith's name on it. I wanted to know how he dealt with this.

When I asked him about it, a sheepish look crossed his face. He quickly responded, "I didn't like it one bit. I didn't want it and objected to it in every way. But they were determined. Frankly, it embarrasses me." It doesn't embarrass me or any other athlete who played for him. We think it's richly deserved and needed to be done in his lifetime to honor him. But he was genuinely embarrassed by how much money was spent. He said, "I wish all the players who played here for me could have their names on the building. That would be more fitting."

John Kilgo, editor of the UNC sports publication named *Carolina Blue*, shared with me how he witnessed the struggle Coach Smith felt internally during fundraising for the construction of the Smith Center. "He went with Skipper Bowles, a well-known UNC alumnus, when they were asking people for money. The plan was to double-team potential donors. Skipper knew how to raise money. Dean was the name.

"They went into the office of this multi-millionaire and started talking about the new building. The guy turned to Dean and said, 'Well, Coach, how much money do you need from me?' Dean became very uncomfortable. He wondered if the man thought he was giving the money to him personally, or giving just because Dean was asking.

"Dean asked tentatively, 'Would ten thousand dollars be okay? If you could give that, well, that would be sensational.'

"Skipper excused himself and took Dean into the hall. 'Next time,' he said, 'do everything you just did, but when the guy asks how much he can give, you be quiet and give it back to me. I'll take over.'

"So they went back into the office and Skipper asked the guy to please ask the question again about how much money he should give. The guy did and Skipper then asked for one and a half million dollars. The guy gave one million, but Dean still felt like ten thousand would have been more than enough. At that point, I think Skipper committed to leave Dean at home when asking others for contributions to the construction of the Smith Center. It simply made him too uncomfortable to ask for it."

Receiving Dean Smith's permission to have his name placed on the building was an equally daunting task. Several influential people kept pressing him for approval. He steadfastly refused. Finally, someone was smart enough to get some of the former players to approach him. They knew that only members of "the family" could ever convince him to change his mind. So several players went to him and asked him to accept this acknowledgment on behalf of every player who had ever played for him. That was the trump card. He finally agreed, for our sake, not his.

Hard Work

A successful mega-church pastor once told me about a young, aggressive seminarian who asked him the secret to his success.

The pastor quietly asked, "You really want to know the reason for my success?"

The seminarian enthusiastically nodded yes.

The pastor went over to his window, looked outside, and closed the shades. Then he went to the door, opened it and looked outside to see if anyone was looking. He called the seminarian to his side. In a hushed whisper, he said, "You want to know the reason for my success? Here it is: hard work."

Will Rogers once said, "Even if you're on the right track, you'll soon get run over if you just sit there."

Much of the reason for Coach Smith's success is that he simply out-worked and out-hustled his opponents. Yes, he was a great teacher and coach. Yes, he recruited well and had superb talent. Yes, he could moti-vate. But he also worked very hard.

For example, right after winning the national championship in 1993, he was in Rasheed Wallace's home the next day, enthusiastically — and successfully — recruiting him to play at North Carolina. Coach Smith was able to function on a few hours' sleep per night. He spent countless hours watching game films. He never lost a recruit because someone else worked harder. He always modeled a strong work ethic.

Personal Appearance and Conduct

John Ashcroft, senator from Missouri, was a guest on my weekly radio program on WBT here in Charlotte. He had recently written a book about lessons he had learned from his father. He said, "Concerning my appearance, dad always taught me daily to dress as if I were dressing for my next job."

Coach Smith demanded the same from us. When on the road, he demanded we dress nicely. In my days at UNC, it was in uniform, with a Carolina blue blazer and similar pants. He thought our outward appear-ance was extremely important, that it communicated something about what we thought of ourselves.

Woody Durham, the veteran voice of the Tar Heels, once did a tele-vision interview with Bob McAdoo, former UNC All-American in the early 1970s, outside of Carmichael Auditorium. "He had on one of those knit berets that was the rage," Durham said. "Coach Smith was pulling out of Carmichael to go some place. He suddenly stopped, interrupted the interview, and whispered something into McAdoo's ear. I quickly figured out what he said to McAdoo: take off the beret for the interview. McAdoo immediately obeyed."

When I interviewed Matt Doherty, now head coach at Notre Dame, he did not know I was doing an ancillary video piece. When he saw the camera as we started the interview, the first thing he did was apologize to Coach Smith for not wearing a tie and not using a good razor to get a close shave for the video. Coach Smith's message that personal appearance says something important for us publicly was a message that Doherty clearly understood!

In addition to teaching us to present a good image by dressing appropriately, Coach Smith insisted that our words reflect our character. He had a very strict rule about not cursing.

Was this a silly personal principle of integrity to emphasize? After all, cursing has become terribly common in our society. I played under Coach Smith for four years. In all that time I cannot remember one time I ever heard profanity from him.

Michael Jordan said, "No cursing. Yeah, I still remember that. You got to run the steps if you cursed. I had to run the steps a couple of times."

Phil Ford told me, "I never heard him curse at me, but sometimes I wish he had!" I knew what he meant. Sometimes his glare of disapproval was worse than a tongue-lashing.

I believe a couple of principles guided his thinking about bad language. It wasn't necessarily because of his rather strict Baptist upbringing, although I'm certain that did influence this area of his life. Nor is he prudish, self-righteous, or judgmental. To the contrary, he is one of the most accepting, gracious men I know.

I believe he did not curse nor allow us to curse because he wanted the best for us and himself. Dean Smith is an extremely bright man. When he entered the University of Kansas, he scored in the ninety-seventh percentile in math. In fact, Coach Guthridge says this may need to be the first thing people address when looking at Coach Smith's life. He is extremely intelligent, perhaps bordering on brilliant. Therefore, cursing for him represented an inadequate vocabulary — he told me he scored in the lower percentile in the verbal test! I think he strives to be the best he can be in anything he tackles, including his speech. For him, cursing represents a denigration of speech, an inadequacy of vocabulary he refuses to tolerate.